GIFTED TO THE WOLF

Chase Meadows

ALSO BY CHASE MEADOWS

Rejected by the Wolf

Dragon's Captive

Mortal Shift (Darkveil Academy Book 1)

CHAPTER ONE

"I don't want to be mated!"

I threw the dishcloth in the sink and stared at my father. How could he just walk in here and dump a bombshell like that on me?

"Tough." He folded his arms across his chest and glared at me. "This pack has raised and sheltered you since you were a pup. Now you're going to repay the debt, whether you like it or not."

I snorted. Raised and sheltered? That was rich. Sheltered me from what? Not the daily beatings I got from the alpha kids, that was for sure.

"Do you think you can defy me?" he demanded, his voice dangerously low as he loomed into my personal space. Inside me, my wolf whimpered, backing down from his wolf's dominance. I swallowed. And then I met his eye.

"I won't do it."

"You will do what you are told!" He slammed his palm down on the worktop beside me and towered over me. "Alpha Devlin of the Broken Ridge pack has accepted you as a bonded mate for one of his sons. Bonding with him will strengthen the alliance between our packs. You should be thanking me for arranging this. Mating an alpha's son is more than any omega could hope for."

"Well, excuse me if I hoped for more than being forced to bond with a stranger, ready to be thrown aside the moment he meets his true mate!"

"You ungrateful little bitch!"

I ducked past him, putting some space between us.

"Maybe you'd rather meet *your* true mate," he said, his lips curving in derision. "And see what happens when they learn you're an omega."

I flinched and averted my eyes from his.

"I am the Beta of this pack," he continued, "and you will obey me. You've been a thorn in my paw for eighteen years."

"Well, maybe you should have thought about that before screwing a human!"

I knew I'd gone too far the second the words left my mouth. Time to get out of here before he could think of a punishment for my lack of respect. I darted past him, ducking under his outstretched arm, barged through the door, and sprinted for the woods. As soon as I made it into the cover of the trees, I stripped off my clothes, tossing them into an untidy heap, and reached for the wolf inside me.

Yes, she whispered. *Run, run, run.*

That seemed like a good idea to me. The heat of the transformation rushed over me, leaving me in my wolf form—pure black except for the splash of white across my right shoulder. I took off at a sprint, letting the trees and dirt blur around me, and allowing my senses to take control of my mind. Everything was simpler in this form.

I wasn't sure how long I'd been running aimlessly through the woods before I pulled up with a snort of derision. I felt my beast's curiosity inside me, but I ignored her. As if I could outrun my problems. Outrun my status. What I was. Omega.

My wolf flinched from the word as I thought it. Half shifter, half human. An outcast. Not for the first time, I wondered what would have happened if my mother hadn't died giving birth to me. My father would never have known I existed, and I'd have been raised in the human world. My wolf snarled in response to that thought—she didn't like the idea of being without a pack. Honestly, it didn't sound so bad to me. Better than being at the mercy of my father, the alpha kids, and anyone else who wanted to take a lump out of me—not least my stepmother.

I could understand why she hated me, of course. I was a constant reminder that my father had been unfaithful to her. I just didn't see why she had to take it out on me instead of him.

A twig snapped behind me and I spun round, hackles raised and teeth bared. A gray wolf walked towards me, and I heaved a sigh of relief. It was Jace—the youngest of my half-brothers. He, out of the three of them, treated me with the least disgust and hatred. Sometimes he even stood up for me against the other wolves in our pack. Never the alpha kids, of course, but no-one could stand up to them.

A backpack dangled from his mouth by one strap, and he dropped it on the floor. I could see some clothing sticking out of the top, and my tongue lolled from the side of my mouth in amusement. He'd always been sensitive about being naked, even though he was a year older than me. He shifted back to his human form, and quickly pulled on his clothes.

"Would you shift back, Jess?" he said. I eyeballed him, and he nudged the bag towards me. "I grabbed your clothes, too."

When he realized I wasn't going to, he shook his head and leaned against the tree behind him.

"Maybe it won't be so bad," he said, and scuffed his feet in the leaf litter. "I mean, it can't be any worse than what you deal with here, can it?"

Part of me knew he was right: being mated to an alpha's son would spare me the torment I went through every day as part of the Winter Moon pack. Assuming the alpha's son wasn't as bad as the alpha kids of this pack, of course—and I had no reason to assume that.

"And if he never meets his true mate, you'll be together for life."

And if he did meet her…well, I didn't want to think about that. There weren't many things that could make my life worse, but there were some. I was glad I was in my wolf form, so Jace couldn't read my face.

3

But he seemed to know what I was thinking, anyway. He'd always been good at reading me.

"I know you're not happy here. Maybe this will be a chance at a fresh start."

Yeah. Because being traded like a horse to some stranger was *exactly* the sort of fresh start I was looking for.

"Look," Jace said after a moment. "There's something else. Alpha Devlin…Dad didn't tell him about you being an omega."

My breath caught in my throat and I gave a startled cough. Was he insane?

"Don't you get it?" Jace said, his voice low and urgent. "You can leave it behind. All of it. All Alpha Devlin knows is that you've got beta blood."

I backed away, a whine slipping from between my lips. How could Jace think this was a good thing? Not only was I being traded to a total stranger, that stranger didn't know that I was an omega. He thought I was a pure-blooded beta, and if he found out what I really was, who knew what he would do? Kill me, at the very least.

"I've got to get back," Jace said. "I've got patrol training. You should say your goodbyes—Alpha Devlin will be coming tomorrow."

Tomorrow? That soon? Jace started to move away, leaving me reeling with the abruptness of the changes being forced on me. He paused for a second, glancing back over his shoulder at me.

"Whatever you do," he said, "don't let anyone at Broken Ridge find out you're an omega."

That wouldn't be difficult, I thought to myself as I stared out into the trees. Because tonight, I was escaping.

CHAPTER TWO

The air was still as I slipped out of my back door. It was that time of night when most normal people were tucked up in their beds, sleeping— for all I knew of normal. Deep inside me, my wolf whined. She didn't like my plan. She wanted to stay with her pack.

"Stupid wolf," I muttered to her as we crept away from the house. "They're not going to be our pack for long, anyway. Do you *want* to be traded away like a Pokémon?"

Want to obey the alpha, she replied. Right, of course. Obey the alpha. Accept our lot in life. No. Freaking. Way.

I kept low to the ground as I cut across the packlands. Our house was close to the woods, and once I got there, I could move more freely. Not in my wolf form, though. She felt too strongly about this, and if I shifted, I didn't think I'd be able to stop her from going back. She was whining and writhing inside my chest. Seriously. Why didn't she get it? It was like she *wanted* to be traded. I curled my lip in disgust. She'd been an omega too long. But I was through being an omega, and I wasn't about to swap it for the role of someone's pet. I was better off on my own.

My wolf howled inside me and I clenched my jaw before the sound could burst out into the night, shattering our plans.

I managed to make it to the tree line without her giving us away, but I couldn't afford to relax yet. The pack ran patrols through here sometimes, though usually only under the full moon. But it meant I hadn't been able to risk bringing anything with me—just the clothes I was wearing, and a pocketful of all the cash I'd saved up over the last two years. It wasn't completely out of character for me to take a night-time stroll through the woods, though admittedly usually as my wolf. Carrying a backpack of supplies would have given me right away. At least this way, no-one who saw me would know what I was planning. I'd still get a

5

beating if they caught me out here on my own—because why pass up the opportunity, right?—but I'd be spared anything worse.

Once I got clear of the packlands, I'd hitch a ride. It didn't matter where. The further away I got, the harder it would be for them to track me, and that was all that mattered.

I moved easily through the dense trees, following narrow game tracks that had only the barest scent of wolf on them. I knew every inch of these woods. It was the one thing that have saved my hide when the alpha kids' blood had been up.

Maybe it was that which made me complacent.

Careless.

I was way too close when I caught their scent on the breeze. My wolf, who'd been restless for the last ten minutes, had become near frantic again, and I hadn't even noticed.

Dammit. I should have been paying closer attention. But I was paying attention now. I froze, with my back pressed against the wide trunk of one of the old oak trees, heart hammering.

It wasn't just that I could smell wolf on the breeze. I could smell *strange* wolves. Outsiders. The pack patrols might give me a hard time, but they'd always stop short of actually killing me. I couldn't say the same about intruders.

What should I do? I was so close to the edge of the pack's territory now. If I turned back, I wouldn't get another chance to escape. But I wouldn't get much of a chance to escape if I was dead, either.

Go back, my wolf urged, but I knew I couldn't listen to her. She'd been telling me the same thing since I left my house. Her reasons for going back were very different from mine. She wanted to obey the will of the alpha. I just wanted to survive. And survive on my own terms. Freedom was so close I could almost taste it.

That decided it for me. I wasn't going back. Not ever.

I took a deep breath, steeled myself, and sprinted from behind the tree. If I could get clear of the woods, out into the road, the intruders wouldn't dare follow me. Not in their wolf forms—too much danger of running into non-shifters. A shifter could heal from most things, but a head shot from a hunting rifle wasn't one of them. They wouldn't risk that to hunt down a resident pack's stray.

I made it a dozen steps before I heard someone moving behind me. I bit back a yelp and pushed my legs to move faster, pounding through the trees, no longer caring about making noise. I didn't have to be faster than a wolf. I just had to reach the road before it reached me.

A snarl ripped through the air from somewhere behind me. I threw a glance back over my shoulder in time to see a flash of mottled gray between the trees. It was close, and getting closer.

I wrenched my head forwards again in time to narrowly miss taking myself out on a low-hanging branch. I ducked aside and found myself staring straight at a cream-white wolf. It stalked towards me, hackles raised and lips peeled back in a snarl.

I skidded to a halt and backed up, almost crashing into the gray wolf behind me. It snarled and started to circle me as the other continued to advance. Panic flooded through me, and my wolf screamed to be let out and fight the two intruders in *our* packlands. For a moment I almost let her...but we were outmatched. These were huge, powerful, male wolves, beta blood at least, maybe even alpha, and they were both bigger than me.

The cream wolf reached me, and the gray darted at my legs, snapping his teeth at my heel. His bulk took my legs from under me and I crashed to the ground, hitting the solid ground hard. Pain lanced through me and the air left my lungs in a sharp burst. I gasped and tried to get back up, but a foot landed on my chest and pinned me to the ground.

My eyes tracked the human foot to its owner; tall and well built, with close cropped dark hair. His expression was shadowed in the moonlight, but something in his eyes made me want to shrink away. There was no mistaking it. The trespasser was of alpha blood.

The two wolves fell in at his sides, snarling down at me.

This was it. I was dead.

But dammit, I wasn't going down meekly.

I grabbed his foot and rolled, trying to throw him aside. He dropped down to straddle me with a snarl, and I threw a punch at his face. He blocked it, then caught my wrists and pinned them to the ground above my head. I growled at my own pathetic resistance. Eighteen years of being an omega should have left me with better fighting skills than this.

"Get off me," I snapped, taking my anger out on the stranger, writhing under him with absolutely no effect, other than to make amusement flash across his irritatingly handsome features. He couldn't have been much older than me, but he was strong. Too strong for me. I curled my lip. "You're trespassing."

"And you were trying to escape the pack's boundaries. I'm here by invite."

I stilled under him, my blood running cold.

"I am Kade, son of Alpha Devlin."

CHAPTER THREE

My head spun. The son of Alpha Devlin. I wasn't sure how many sons Devlin had, but I was willing to bet there was only one reason any of them would be in our packlands.

"Let me guess," I snarled. "You've come to pick up your bride?"

"I have. What do you know about her?"

What the hell. He was going to find out sooner or later. Better to just face whatever was coming.

"You're sitting on her, jackass."

He blinked down at me.

"What?"

"I said, you're sitting on me. So get off!"

I tried to shove him off me again and got no further than my first attempt. Behind him, one of the wolves' heads bobbed up and down, open-mouthed, and if I didn't know better, I'd have said he was laughing. Kade seemed to think so, too, because he shot a glare in the wolf's direction, then turned back to stare down at me through narrowed eyes.

"Why were you trying to escape?"

"Why do you think?" I scowled. "I don't like being sold."

"Sold?"

"Yes, sold! What, did you think it was some love match without us ever laying eyes on each other? My father sold me to your father to strengthen the alliance between our packs. Hell, he didn't even sell me. He *gave* me."

Kade's eyes widened a little.

"But…surely you agreed to it? You must want this as much as our packs do?"

I rolled my eyes with as much sass as it was possible to do when pinned to the leaf litter lined floor of a damp forest at night.

9

GIFTED TO THE WOLF

"Does it *look* like I want this?"

His mouth opened and then closed again, and I squirmed under him, using my hips to try to flip him off me.

"Would you get off me already?" I snapped, and his face hardened again. I stilled under him.

"Pack is more important than anything," he said. "Why would you not want to honor your alpha's wishes?"

"Uh, did you miss the part where he freaking *sold* me to your father?"

"And did you miss the part where it will strengthen the alliance between our packs?"

He leaned forward over me, glaring down.

"Trust me," he said, "Being bound to someone who clearly has no respect for hierarchy is hardly top of my wish list, either, but unlike you, I know what my duty is."

No respect for hierarchy? As if I hadn't had my ass kicked because of hierarchy every damn day of my life thanks to being an omega—not that I could tell him that.

"You don't know the first thing about me."

"I know you're the sort of wolf who tries to betray her pack and run away in the middle of the night."

"They betrayed me first!" I spat, before my brain caught up with my mouth. Shit. Hopefully he just thought I meant about the whole being sold thing—which was one hell of a betrayal as far as I was concerned. Just not the first. "Maybe if you actually knew anything about betrayal, you wouldn't be sitting on a total stranger in the woods in the middle of the night, crushing her half to death."

Uncertainty flickered across his face.

"If I let you up, will you try to escape again?"

"It's not like I can outrun your two little friends there, is it?"

10

It was true, and it annoyed the hell out of me. That had been my best chance of escape, and I'd blown it. Why the hell hadn't I been paying more attention to what was going on around me? Now this moron was going to drag me back to my pack, and tomorrow I'd be hauled off to be bonded to him, and there wasn't a damn thing I could do about it.

The fight went out of me, and my shoulders slumped in defeat, not all of it faked.

Kade searched my face and nodded.

"Hey," he said, smoothing a lock of hair from my face, his voice unexpectedly gentle. "Maybe it won't be as bad as you think. I'm not all bad. If you give it a chance, you might like your new life."

I twisted my head to one side, jerking away from his touch. I felt him sigh, and then he released my wrists, and climbed off me, watching me cautiously the whole time.

I sat up and shuffled back, putting some space between us, and then got to my feet. The cream wolf started forward and I turned my glare on him.

"Take it easy, Balto. I'm not going anywhere."

The wolf peeled his lips back in a snarl. Kade chuckled and turned to him.

"It's fine, Dean," he said, and then to me, "Okay, I let you up. Now you can do something for me."

I eyed him meaningfully. "I'm not that sort of girl."

He laughed, the sound completely out of place in the dark woods, and it made his face appear softer, less threatening, somehow.

"You're funny. No, nothing like that. I just want the truth. Why are you really running away?"

"I told you. Because I don't want to be s—"

"Sold. Yeah, you already spun me that line." He closed the gap between us, lifting one hand to my face but stopping short of touching it,

11

instead tracing its outline from an inch away. "But we both know that's not the whole story. Talk to me, Jessica."

I stared into his eyes, and my voice caught in my throat. It was like he could see straight into my soul, like he would find my darkest secrets hiding behind my eyes. My shameful secret. I tried to look away but couldn't.

"I…can't," I whispered.

"Yes. You can. I promise."

People had made promises to me before. I managed to jerk my eyes away then, staring over his shoulder at the two wolves, both watching us closely. Kade caught the direction of my attention.

"I'll send them away," he said. "Whatever you want to tell me, it's between us."

I forced the next words out, resisting his honey-silk tones.

"I've got nothing to say to you."

It took a second for him to process the words, and then his face hardened and closed from me.

"Fine," he snapped, grabbing hold of my arm. "Then we're going."

"Where?"

"Back to your pack. You can say your goodbyes. We're leaving first thing in the morning, and we won't be coming back."

CHAPTER FOUR

When the sun rose, it found me in a room in the town's only motel, under guard. I hadn't tried to escape again last night—if only because Kade's pet wolf buddies had taken it in turns to watch me from inside the room itself. It was the same reason I hadn't gotten a whole lot of sleep.

I dragged myself out of bed, glaring at Dean where he sat on a chair, watching me in silence. In his human form, his hair was cropped short, and almost as pale as his wolf's. His expression was just as belligerent. It wasn't a big room, and I had to squeeze past him into the bathroom.

He rose from his seat, and as I went to shut the bathroom door, he caught it in one hand and held it open.

"What the hell are you doing?" I snapped, rounding on him.

"Kade said to watch you," Dean grunted. I gaped at him.

"While I take a shower? I don't think so." I tried to yank the door free from his grip, but he was stronger than me and it didn't budge. I growled in frustration. "Look around!" I flung an arm at the tiny room. "There's only one door, and you're standing in it. There's no window. And last time I checked, I couldn't dig through concrete."

He stared back impassively, not saying a word. I swallowed a scream of frustration, and forced my voice to come out calm.

"What's Kade going to say if I tell him you've been perving over his future mate?"

A flicker of uncertainty shadowed his face. I took advantage of it to yank the door from his hand and slam it shut, shoving the lock across.

I could still hear his breathing, so I knew he hadn't gone anywhere, but at least he wasn't trying to bust the door down, so I was calling that a win. Still, best not to push my luck too far. I took a quick shower and

13

cleaned my teeth with the motel toiletries before getting dressed, tying my hair back, and unlocking the door again.

I stepped out into the room, and froze.

"Good morning, Jessica," Kade said. He was leaning back against a wall with his arms folded over his chest, and a smug expression on his face. As ever, his two buddies were flanking him like a pair of all-weather shadows—except these shadows were capable of overpowering me.

I glowered at the three of them and stooped to grab my sneakers from the floor.

"Come to drag me back to your cave by my hair?" I snipped. He raised an eyebrow.

"Well, I *had* come to see if you wanted breakfast, but I guess we'll just get going."

My stomach rumbled loudly in response, and my wolf whined. Shifting burned a lot of calories, and I was starving. The idea of spending the day traveling without a decent meal inside me did not appeal. And somehow, I didn't think Kade was going to be making a food stop anywhere I might run off.

"I'm hungry," I admitted in a small voice. Kade snapped his head round to the dark-haired guy on his right.

"Ryder, bring her something. Dean, you can wait outside."

The pair of them left without a word, sealing me in the room with Kade, alone. He pushed himself off the wall and closed the gap between us.

"Listen to me, Jessica. I know you're reluctant about this union, but you're going to have a good life in Broken Ridge. I'm not a monster–"

"Could've fooled me," I muttered.

"–and I'll make sure you have everything you need. I'm second heir to my father's pack, and that's a step up in status for the daughter of a beta. You just need to give it a chance. That's all I'm asking. Get to know me before you judge me."

"My name's Jess," I said.

"What?"

"It's Jess. Not Jessica." I took a deep breath. "If we're going to get to know each other, you should at least get my name right."

He smiled.

"Jess. Got it. What else should I know about you?"

His eyes probed mine, and I was sure he meant the secret I'd refused to tell him in the woods last night. I ducked his gaze.

"That I wasn't joking about being hungry."

"Ryder won't be long."

"Can't we just go down and get something?"

He shook his head. "I'm sorry, we can't."

"Why not?" I demanded with a scowl. "If you want to convince me you're not a monster, you could start by not treating me like a prisoner."

"It's not that," he said, and before I could accuse him of being a liar, he added, "You've got a visitor. He wants to see you before we leave."

"Who?"

"Your brother, Jace. Do you want to see him?"

"Of course I want to see him!"

He stepped back with a nod and opened the door. Outside, I saw Dean move aside, and then I caught a glimpse of Jace. He stepped into the room and inclined his head respectfully to Kade. He had shadows under his eyes and his hair was in disarray. I guess he hadn't had much more sleep than me.

"Thank you for allowing me to see her, alpha-son," he said to my captor, his voice stiff with a formality that didn't suit him.

Kade didn't leave the room, denying us any sort of privacy for our final goodbye. I don't claim to have had a happy childhood, but it was

15

made more tolerable because of Jace, and he'd put his neck on the line for me more than once. I was going to miss him.

My eyes burned hot and I dashed the tears away with the back of my hand before they could fall. Jace crossed the room quickly and wrapped his arms around me.

"You'll be fine," he murmured in my ear. "Better than fine."

I swallowed, and leaned into the hug. There was a tap at the door, and Kade moved away to open it.

"What the hell were you playing at last night?" he hissed in my ear.

"Saving myself," I hissed back. Jace tossed a glance in Kade's direction; he was taking a plate of food from Ryder.

"You can't give them reason to doubt you're a beta blood," he said, his voice so low I could barely hear it right next to him.

"I *am* a beta blood," I answered.

"You know what I mean. If you keep behaving like this, he's going to ask questions."

Jace was right, of course. Kade was already asking questions, ones that I couldn't afford to answer. I nodded against his shoulder. I didn't like what was happening, but things would get a whole lot worse for me if Kade and his father worked out that I was an omega.

Kade cleared his throat, and Jace broke away from me.

"Goodbye, Jess," he said. "Take care of yourself."

His eyes held mine, making sure I didn't miss his true meaning, and I tried to conjure a smile for him. And then he left, and I knew I'd never see him again.

From here on out, my life was in Kade's hands.

CHAPTER FIVE

I ate what turned out to be a tasteless breakfast—though that probably was less to do with the quality of the food, and more to do with my realization I'd seen my family for the last time. They weren't perfect—hell, my father had made a gift of me to strengthen our pack's alliance with Broken Ridge—but they were still my family, and they'd been there my entire life. Shitty life it might have been, but they'd been there.

"It's time to go," Kade said, when I pushed the tray aside, mostly untouched. I rose without an objection, Jace's warning still ringing in my ears. Besides, where would be the point in fighting him? Anyone inside this town would just hand me right back over to him, probably with a few new bruises to remember them by. And that was assuming I could get past his two hulking bodyguards, which seemed like a stretch. No, it was better to go along with it.

Then when I did run, they'd never see it coming.

He led me out to his car, with Dean and Ryder following in our wake, no doubt ready to grab me if I bolted. Kade opened the rear door for me, and I started to get in. A thought struck me and I paused, half in, half out.

"Wait," I said. "What about my stuff? From my house?"

I didn't have many possessions, but I valued the ones I did own. Plus I'd be needing a change of clothes sooner rather than later—mine were covered in mud and dust from last night in the woods.

"Already in the trunk," he said.

I ground my teeth together and snapped my head round to glare at him.

"You went to my home without me, and went through my stuff?"

It rubbed me the wrong way that he was already treating me as though I had no will of my own. What the hell gave him the right? He

17

broke eye contact and let his gaze slide off to one side. His voice, when he spoke, was low, just for my ears.

"Your, uh, mom had it bagged up and left outside."

Of course she did. I bet she couldn't wait to see the back of me, and every reminder I'd ever been there. A hollowness filled my stomach and I just nodded and slipped silently inside the car. It wasn't like it mattered, anyway. It was just stuff. And I'd have to leave it behind when I made a break for it. Stuff wasn't important.

Dean slid into the driver's seat, which surprised me because I'd assumed as the son of an alpha, Kade would drive. Alpha bloods weren't too good at handing over control. Ever. Until I realized it left him free to sit in the back seat beside me, no doubt watching in case I tried to make a break for it. I ignored him as I clipped on my seatbelt, casually brushing my thumb over my pocket as I did, and reassuring myself the wad of cash was still there.

Ryder climbed into the passenger seat, and Dean thumbed a button, locking us all in. I rolled my eyes.

"Really?"

No-one answered, which didn't surprise me. I hadn't been doing as good a job of convincing them as I thought.

"Rest," Kade said, as the car rumbled to life. "We have a long journey ahead of us."

Right. Like that was going to happen. I was sitting in the back of a car being driven to some strange new place where I was going to spend the rest of my life as the pet of some alpha brat.

…Except there wasn't much I could do about it while we were driving. And I hadn't slept much last night. My eyelids grew heavy within minutes of being on the smooth asphalt road out of town, and I drifted off into an uneasy sleep, filled with dreams about wolves and cavemen.

When I woke, my mouth was parched and the sun's light was dimming. I frowned.

"How long was I asleep?" I asked no-one in particular.

"About five hours," Kade said. "We're almost there. We crossed the border into my pack's territory a couple of minutes ago."

Five hours. I was a long way from home. And I had one hell of a crick in my neck. I rolled it out, stifling a yawn, which cut off midway through when I realized what that meant.

We were almost there. We weren't stopping anywhere. There would be no escaping on the journey. We had crossed into the pack's territory, which meant anyone who saw me sneaking around would know who I was, and who I belonged to.

Escaping just got a whole lot harder.

I buried the thought, but apparently not before it could show on my face.

"What's wrong?" Kade asked, scrutinizing me. I shook my head.

"Nothing. It's just…well, I've never been this far from home before."

His face softened.

"Don't worry about that. This is your home now, and you'll never have to leave it again."

We'll just see about that, I thought, but made myself nod along with his words. My wolf, who had been strangely quiet ever since we'd been taken to the motel, started to stir, and I could feel her unease thrumming through me. She didn't like being in another pack's territory, not even if we were about to become part of that pack. I hoped she'd hold on to that feeling, and use it to help us get the hell out of here when the time came. Maybe not tonight—they'd be watching us too closely for that. But soon. She whined in agreement with me, even as I felt her wariness about going rogue.

Better to be rogue than a prisoner, I reminded her, but she wasn't convinced by my words. She wanted to be part of a pack, and in theory I had no objection to that. I just didn't want to be part of this one—or any other pack who thought I was a prize to be traded and passed around.

There would come a time when I determined my own fate, and I wasn't prepared to wait forever.

Dean slowed the car to a halt and I looked out of the window, then directed a curious glance at Kade. The house we'd stopped outside was practically a mansion, surrounded by high walls and metal gates. It was aged and imposing, and at one end was an honest-to-God spire. A freaking tower. The whole thing was elaborate and gothic, and far too much for any twenty-year-old to own, even the son of an alpha.

"We're visiting my father," he said. "Any new shifter in our territory needs his approval to stay and become a pack member."

Then there was hope. I quickly suppressed it and turned to face the building, running my gaze over its expanse as I hid my feelings. His father had agreed to this union, but Kade hadn't known I didn't want anything to do with it, so his father probably hadn't either. Maybe if I told him how I felt about it, he'd take pity on me and send me back. Or let me leave under my own steam. And if that didn't work, I'd have to find some way to convince him I wasn't worthy of his son—without revealing my omega status, because I wanted to be free, not dead.

Kade opened the car door and stepped out onto the graveled driveway, and I shuffled out behind him. A trio of people emerged from the mansion, and I figured they had to be the alpha and two of his bodyguards. As we got a little closer, I realized I was wrong—the family resemblance was unmistakable. It had to be Alpha Devlin, and his other son, and the stoic man behind him his beta.

Kade looped his arm through mine and half-ushered, half-towed me forward. The lean alpha turned his gaze on me, locking eyes across the courtyard.

And everything changed.

It was like no-one else existed in the world. I couldn't drag my gaze from his gray eyes, set into an ageless face that could have been anywhere from forty to sixty, or even older—shifters didn't age in the same way humans did.

And none of that mattered.

It was all I could do not to wrench my arm from Kade's and race towards the tall, silent alpha.

Alpha Devlin. My true mate.

CHAPTER SIX

Kade's grip tightened on my arm. Could he feel every muscle in my body tense? My wolf howled and screamed inside me, fighting to be let free, to throw herself at our mate. *Our mate.*

My head reeled, and the whole world spun until I no longer knew if I wanted to run forward, back, or collapse to the floor in a dizzy heap. My mate. How was it even possible?

"Father," Kade said, bowing his head in respect. "It is my honor to present Jess Whitlock of the Winter Moon Pack. I formally request leave for her to remain in this pack, as my bonded mate."

The alpha's eyes flickered over my face with casual disdain, and my heart hammered frantically in my chest. Didn't he recognize me? Surely, he must see what I was. See that we were promised to each other by fate, that we were meant to be together, and that nothing could ever come between us? My wolf whined her confusion and a lance of pain shot through my chest.

"Kade." His voice was gravelly and carried the slightest hint of a growl to it. My wolf shivered in anticipation at the sound. I'd misread his expression, of course I had. Now he would tell Kade that he could not grant his request, because he and I were fated.

"I hear your request, and I shall consider it. According to pack law, the newcomer shall be kept under guard while she is in order borders, until such a time as I determine whether she might prove worthy of this pack, and be permitted to remain here."

"What?" The word burst from my lips before I could stop it. Kade squeezed my arm a little tighter—hard enough to bruise, but shifter healing meant the marks would be gone by morning. Not that it mattered—my mate would claim me before then. He *had* to claim me.

"Silence," the alpha said, rounding on me with a fierce glare. "Speak when spoken to, wolf."

I shrank back.

"Forgive her, Father," Kade said. "I'm sure she's just overcome from the long journey. She has never left her packlands before."

Devlin inclined his head in a curt nod, and Kade twisted his lips to my ear.

"What the hell are you playing at?" he hissed in a whisper too quiet for the others to hear, even with shifter hearing. "You might not want to be here, but you *will* show respect to my father. Understand?"

"Remove her from my sight," the alpha commanded. "Take her back to your home, and present her to me when she knows her place."

A shiver ran through me, and I wrapped my arms around myself, as best I could with Kade still clamping my upper arm in his vise-like grip.

My mate didn't recognize me. Something was wrong. Something was very wrong. I'd never heard of true mates not recognizing each other the moment they first met. And I'd known him the second I'd laid eyes on him. I knew that man was my home. My wolf howled, long and low, inside my chest, and the pain was so intense it felt like my heart would burst. He was my home, but I was not his.

As he turned and walked back inside his house, it was all I could do not to collapse to the floor in a heap. I offered no resistance as Kade dragged me back towards the car and ushered me inside. The moment the doors were closed, he rounded on me in fury.

"My father is the most powerful alpha in two hundred miles. You had no right to speak to him. You will never address him again without permission, is that clear?"

I stared at him, unable to arrange my expression into anything that could be considered repentant. I could barely process his words—they were little more than a buzzing in my ears, nearly drowned out by my wolf's grief and my own agony. He didn't want us. He'd banished us into the home of another wolf. A wolf he intended to let mate me. My wolf howled anew, and I clamped my jaw shut, trapping the sound of our torment inside.

Kade ran a hand through his hair.

"I don't know how they did things in your pack, but you're in Broken Ridge territory now. You're going to need to learn our rules. Don't expect me to cover for you like that again."

He nodded to his friends through the car window and they got inside. Dean turned the key in the ignition.

"Take us to my house," Kade said. "I'm going to have to teach my new mate some manners before she gets herself killed." He fixed me with cold eyes. "Or worse, shows me up again."

One of the wolves in the front chuckled darkly. I couldn't quite tear my eyes from the home of my true mate to see which of them it was, nor convince myself to care.

"You need any help with punishing her?"

Kade bared his teeth. "I think I can handle one stupid little girl."

If they thought that was going to scare me, they were mistaken. I'd spent my whole life being 'punished' for imagined misdemeanors, and I'd survived. But as Dean eased his foot on the gas and the car slowly rolled away from the alpha's mansion, my wolf howled again, and I knew there was one thing I might not be able to survive. Knew no way to survive.

Being rejected by my true mate.

CHAPTER SEVEN

When we reached Kade's home—modest, compared to his father's, but large by any other standard, and far bigger than any twenty-year-old should have—Dean and Ryder slipped away, leaving the two of us alone together, but not before Ryder gave me an amused look. Right. My 'punishment'. That was going to be a barrel of laughs.

Kade dumped my bags in the hall as we stepped inside, then closed the door behind me and locked it. He tucked the key carefully into his pocket.

"In case you get any ideas about going wandering," he said. "While we're under alpha's orders to keep you under guard."

I shrugged like being a prisoner didn't bother me and turned my stony expression on him.

"Just get it over with."

He looked puzzled for a moment. "Get what over with?"

I rolled my eyes and tried not to look like I was worried about whatever pain he was about to mete out, which probably wasn't convincing because, despite being beaten up by the alpha brats in my pack on a near-daily basis, I still wasn't much a fan of my blood being on my outside.

"My punishment. Just beat the hell out of me and get it over with."

"Oh. I'm not going to hurt you, Jess."

"You're giving me whiplash," I said, folding my arms over my chest. "One minute you're the big bad alpha blood. The next you want to be my best friend. Then you're a dominant asshole again. Can you make your mind up already?"

"Can't I be both?" He glanced at the bags by my feet. "Do you want a hand to get those up to your room?"

"No, you can't be both," I snapped. "I'm not friends with assholes." Which, now that I thought about it, probably explained why I hadn't had a whole lot of friends in my own pack. I followed the direction of his gaze, and his words finally caught up with me. "My...my room?"

"What, you didn't think I was going to chain you to my bed, did you?"

I said nothing, because that was *exactly* what I'd thought. Kade exhaled heavily.

"I know we got off on the wrong foot, Jess. But despite what you think, I'm *not* a monster, and I really do just want to make this as easy as possible. For both of us. You didn't want this. I get that."

I jerked my gaze up to meet his, and he continued.

"I didn't ask for this myself. You know how it works. The alpha commands, and the pack obeys. But that doesn't mean this can't work out well for the both of us. You're here, and neither of us has a choice about that." He stooped to grab a couple of my bags. "But we have a choice about how we handle it. The pack has expectations of us, there's no getting away from that. But that doesn't mean we can't take things slow. Come on, this way."

I blinked at his retreating back a few times, then grabbed my remaining bag and hurried after him.

"So," I said, as we climbed the stairs, "You're a dominant asshole who wants to be my best friend. What else should I know about you?"

"That I won't tolerate being disrespected in public," he said, without turning to look at me. "I'm an alpha blood, and I can never appear weak. But inside these four walls, you have a little more freedom."

I snorted. "That's ironic, since that key being in your pocket has literally deprived me of my freedom."

"You've got a mouth on you, don't you?" he said, as he pushed open a door.

I looked inside, and the sassy response I'd been about to deliver died on my lips. The room was three or four times the size of the one I'd had in my old home, bright and beautifully decorated and furnished. The bed was large and the mattress looked deep and soft. My bag slipped from my hand.

Kade turned and saw me standing in the doorway. He set my bags down and gave me a half smile.

"I know it's not much," he said. "It's just for now. It's the only guest room I've bothered to have decorated. But my room—our room, when you're ready—is nicer."

"Are you kidding?" My lips spread into a slow smile. "This room is gorgeous. And so big."

I stepped inside the brightly lit room and held my arms out to my sides, spinning in a slow circle.

"It's incredible."

Kade chuckled.

"Maybe I should have put you in a broom closet. How am I supposed to lure you to my bed if not with the promise of luxury?"

"This is more luxury than I've seen." I cleared my throat. "You know, for a jail cell. Are you going to lock me in here, too?"

His jaw clenched and he glared at me.

"Your attitude is starting to test my patience."

"Yeah, there he is. The big bad alpha blood. What now? Are you going to hit me?"

"What the hell is your problem, Jess?"

My wolf howled loud inside me in answer to his question, and I swallowed the sound, because what was I supposed to tell him? I'm your father's true mate, and he doesn't even see me? There was no way that was going to go down well. He probably wouldn't even believe me. He'd think it was some ploy to escape, but there was nowhere for me to run, not anymore. Even being this far from my asshole mate was torture for my wolf. Leaving the town? Unthinkable.

"You know what?" he said, taking a deep breath. "It's been a long twenty-four hours. I think we could both use some rest. Take some time, get your head around what's happening—because it *is* happening, and you acting like a brat is just going to make it harder for us both."

"Fine," I snapped.

He brushed past me and then threw a glance back at me over his shoulder.

"Don't try to leave the house—or my patience will run out."

CHAPTER EIGHT

With Kade's warning ringing in my ears, I pulled the door shut and sank onto the bed. This was such a mess. I was stuck in a strange house in a strange town with a literal stranger. I was trapped here. I would never see my family again. Well, okay, that last part wasn't such a bad thing, for the most part. I'd miss Jace, and I'd miss the familiarity of home, but not even through my nostalgia could I bring myself to miss most of the people I'd shared it with.

They certainly wouldn't miss me. My stepmother had made that clear enough when she'd tossed all my worldly possessions—such as they were—into a couple of trash bags and left them on the front step.

With a sigh, I set about sorting through them. It was amazing how little I'd accumulated in eighteen years, and how little most of it meant to me. Some clothes, a few old photos and childhood memories, though not many—most of them I'd wanted to forget. Trinkets. Useless trinkets. Nothing that could help me now. My cell charger, but no cell—one of Kade's pet bodyguards probably still had that. I barked a dark laugh. Like it would have mattered. Who would I have called? No-one from my pack would come for me, not even Jace, the one person who gave a damn about me. And not the cops. My family had gone to lengths to make sure I knew outsiders weren't safe. Humans couldn't be trusted. Better to be locked in this gilded cage than chained up in some human laboratory being used as an oversized lab rat.

Better not to be locked in a cage at all.

My hand fluttered down to my pocket and touched on the wad of cash there. I sucked in a deep breath and cast a glance at the door. Still shut, and no sign of Kade coming back. I pulled the money from my pocket and looked around the room. After a moment, I lifted the mattress and slipped it underneath. I'd find a better hiding place later.

Maybe under a loose floorboard or taped to the bottom of a drawer. This wasn't the first time I'd had to hide something. But it didn't look like Kade had anyone come in to clean, so it should be safe where it was for now. Ready for when I—

My wolf whined in my chest.

Find mate.

I flumped back on the bed and growled in frustration. "We can't do that," I told her. "It's not safe."

Mate will keep us safe.

"Dammit, he doesn't even want us. He doesn't feel the same way."

He is mate, she said simply, as though that answered everything. As though she hadn't just seen him turn his back on us not an hour ago.

"Just shut up."

I rolled onto my side, pulling one of the pillows down and cuddling it. Today. I would allow myself today to be weak. Today to feel sorry for myself. Because tomorrow, I had to start working out how to get myself out of this situation.

Mate will get us out—

"Don't say it," I snarled under my breath. "He'd rather see us dead."

The truth of my words slammed into me the moment they left my lips and I gasped at the realization. I'd been so wrapped up in my pain, in my wolf's pain, that the full implications of finding my mate had been lost on me.

I'd better hope he never recognized me for what I was. If I was lucky, he'd just go about his day, thinking the new wolf was just some impudent pup who needed to learn her place, and then forget all about me. Forever.

My wolf whined at my fervent desire, and part of my soul itself twisted and keened.

"Please let him forget me," I whispered into the pillow. "Please don't let him know. Let him forget me…"

Being half human made me an outcast. An omega. Undesirable. That's why my father had lied to Alpha Devlin about my blood status. I was no good to him as a bargaining chip if the alpha knew what I was. It was a dangerous ploy, but going along with it meant I had half a chance at a tolerable future.

Or it would have done.

Because an alpha blood would never accept being paired with an omega. If he learned my secret, he'd reject me, and probably start a war with my pack for my father's actions.

But that wasn't the worst thing that might happen now.

Because there was one thing worse than being paired with an omega—and that was having one for a true mate. It was shameful, an embarrassment, for any full-blooded shifter, regardless of their rank. But for an alpha? And the alpha of one of the most powerful packs in the country? Unspeakable.

It would make him look weak, and the one thing an alpha could never be was weak. It invited attacks, both from beyond their borders, and within their own pack. No alpha—no shifter, of any rank—would ever take such a chance, or accept such an insult. For a wolf in that situation, there was only one course of action, and it was set in stone. For an alpha, it was set in law.

If Alpha Devlin discovered his true mate was an omega, I would be killed.

CHAPTER NINE

I couldn't stay here. That much was clear. Maybe Devlin recognized me as his true mate, and maybe he didn't. Either way, it was too dangerous for me here now. I couldn't avoid the alpha forever—my wolf whined at the mere thought—and I couldn't trust myself not to do something stupid next time I saw him.

We should sniff his butt.

Yeah. Something like that. I rolled my eyes, and sat up, tossing the pillow aside. It was clear my wolf was going to be no help in this escape.

Not escaping, she said stubbornly. *Obey the alpha. Win our mate. Prove ourselves worthy.*

"Yeah. I'm not doing any of that stuff. Have you seen the mess trying that has gotten us into? Anyway, we *are* worthy, idiot. It's *him* who isn't."

Can't know that. Didn't stay long enough to find out.

I could practically hear the pout in her voice. I exhaled slowly. Sometimes, I was dealing with an apex predator. Other times, it was like dealing with a little kid.

"We didn't have a choice," I said softly. "Don't you miss having choices?"

Miss our mate.

There was no reasoning with her when she was like this. I just hoped she wasn't going to try to blow this whole escape. Again.

I hopped off the bed and grabbed a backpack from my pile of stuff and started ramming it with anything I might need. Then I shook my head and yanked it all out again. No way was I getting out of here with a backpack without drawing the attention of the whole pack down on me. And that would be bad. Very bad. I was pretty sure if I got caught escaping, the first thing they'd do was haul me in front of the alpha.

Mate? My wolf raised a hopeful eyebrow.

And then he'll kill us, I thought back at her forcefully. She huffed her disagreement and I went back to ignoring her.

The backpack was out. Carrying much of anything was out. I lifted the mattress and pulled out my wad of cash, thumbed it carefully, and then thrust it back into my pocket. I could shift and hunt for food once I got outside of the pack's borders. I could sleep in my wolf form if I needed. The money should be enough to buy anything else I needed. It would keep me going for a couple of weeks, and that would be enough. It would have to be.

I eased the door open and cocked one ear to the crack. No sound of movement. Escaping in the middle of the afternoon, while it was still light out and Kade was awake, was hardly ideal, but I had no clue if he planned to take me back to see his father this evening, and I couldn't chance that. It had to be now. At least Kade probably wouldn't expect me to be dumb enough to bust out so soon. I clicked the door closed again.

I had no hope of getting the key, so the front door was out, but this room had a big window and I muttered a silent prayer of thanks to whichever architect had designed the house to be so bright and airy. Kade had been expecting to return here with a willing bride, not a prisoner, so with any luck—and I was sorely due some luck right about now—he wouldn't have thought to lock it.

I crossed to it and gave the latch a gentle tug. A slow grin spread over my face as it budged a fraction. It was stiff, but not locked. All things considered, I was calling that a win.

I wiggled the latch some more until it gave way, and shoved the window open, letting a wave of fresh air rush in. The window opened onto Kade's front garden, and I could see the forest a little distance away. A half-mile, at most, and then I'd be under the tree cover, and away from prying eyes. And not long after, far away from here.

My room was one floor up—close enough to the ground that, thanks to my wolf's strength, I could jump down without doing myself too much damage. And any injuries I did get should be mild enough that they'd heal in a minute or two.

If everything went to plan, I'd be well away from Broken Ridge territory by nightfall. I ducked back inside and, as quietly as I could, I dragged the chest of drawers in front of the door. If Kade tried to come in, he'd assume I was sulking. Hopefully for long enough for me to get clear before he could raise the alarm.

I looked my handy work over with a satisfied nod, then hurried back to the window. There was no more time to waste. Without hesitating, I climbed through, sucked in a deep breath, and launched myself through the air.

I landed on the ground with a soft thud, dropping down into a crouch as my knees bent to absorb the impact. A slow grin spread over my face…and then I felt the shadow fall across me.

Rising to my feet, I found myself staring into the face I least wanted to see.

Alpha Devlin's cold eyes fixed on me.

"Hello, Jessica."

CHAPTER TEN

"Uh…hi. I was just…" I remembered the whole 'don't address the alpha without permission' thing and trailed off. Well, that, and I didn't really have a good way to finish that sentence.

"Going for a stroll?" Devlin suggested with a raised eyebrow.

I ducked my head and averted my eyes from his. I was officially screwed.

Our mate, my wolf sang inside me. Great. Just what I needed. The apex predator was fangirling. Over the man who didn't want us.

He came for us.

"Cat got your tongue?" he said. His voice was deep and sent ice through my spine—and fire through other parts.

"Wolf." I blushed and stole a look at him, then quickly wrenched my eyes away to one side before I landed myself in any more hot water. "Uh, I mean…I, uh, was talking to her. My wolf."

Oh, my God. Was I really babbling while I stared at his freaking earlobe? Get it together, Jess. Complete sentences are a bare minimum.

Bare flesh would be better.

I caught my hand reaching unconsciously for the top button of my shirt and thrust it into my pocket. Dammit, wolf, I'm not undressing for him in the middle of Kade's front lawn! Or at all.

Devlin stared at me through flat eyes until I squirmed on the spot.

"I'm sure my son will be interested to know about your…exercise."

"Please don't tell him," I squeaked. I swallowed, and then tried to make my voice more dignified. "I mean, I wasn't doing anything wrong."

"Is that so, little wolf? Because I know you heard me say you were to remain under guard, and I know you cannot be naïve enough to think breaking rules comes without punishment."

35

"Exactly," I said quickly, and my breath definitely did not catch in my throat at the way his lips rolled around the word 'punishment'. "Why would I be foolish enough to go against your rules?"

"Why, indeed."

"I might just be a dumb—" I broke off quickly. I'd been about to say 'omega'. Shit. I needed to be more careful. "—girl, but I'm not that stupid."

Amusement crinkled around his eyes and relief flooded me. He hadn't noticed my slip. That had been close.

"What, then, shall we tell my son?"

My heart thudded painfully at the way he said 'we' and I turned an inward scowl on my wolf. She needed to knock that crap off before— Well, she just needed to stop. Besides, it wasn't like he even recognized the mate bond. Which was a good thing, because I didn't much fancy being killed because fate had a warped sense of humor.

"Or perhaps," Devlin said, his voice hardening again, "you've changed your mind about me not telling him."

I started to shake my head, and then stopped. I was exhausted. After everything that had happened today, I was too tired to keep playing these games. I didn't know what Devlin wanted from me, and right now, I didn't care. I just wanted to curl up somewhere—preferably somewhere far from Broken Ridge territory—and sleep for a week. I jerked my eyes up to meet his.

"You know what? Tell him whatever you want. You're going to, anyway."

He stared at me, first with shock and then with something that passed over his face too quickly for me to identify, and then his lips pressed into a hard line. He grabbed hold of my upper arm, and pounded on the door with his free hand.

I could feel his calloused fingers digging into my arm hard enough that it would have bruised a human.

He's touching us! My wolf was almost beside herself with delight, stupid animal.

He's holding us prisoner, I reminded her. He's doing it to stop us running away.

Why would we run away? She seemed genuinely perplexed, like we hadn't been over this a dozen times, and like he wasn't currently leaving finger marks on my flesh.

His skin touching ours…

I could reach up with my free hand, and trail my fingers across the rugged planes of his face…

Enough of this! I shook the image from my mind. They were driving me crazy, the pair of them. I yanked my arm back against his grip, and Devlin turned a stare on me that froze my blood and immediately quelled any thoughts of getting loose and running. He was an alpha. Not just any alpha, but the most powerful alpha in over two hundred miles. Pissing him off would be a very bad idea. And he wanted me to know it.

His grip tightened, and now I knew he was leaving bruises.

"Do not try that again," he commanded, and my chin dipped of its own accord in a nod. I kept my gaze on the floor, my heart hammering, and I could feel his stare boring into me.

Obey the alpha. Please our mate.

Yeah, all of that stuff. But mostly, try not to give him any reason to kill me before I escaped.

I heard a key scraping in the lock, and then the door swung inwards. My breath caught in my throat. Despite appearances, I wasn't an idiot. Kade had made it pretty clear that I wasn't to leave the house. He'd also made it clear that he had to keep up appearances when he was around the rest of the pack. Devlin was his father, but he was his alpha first, and there was no way Kade would risk losing face in front of him.

Kade nodded to Devlin, and then he caught sight of me. Confusion passed over his face, and then his gaze caught on Devlin's hand locked around my upper arm.

Submit, submit, submit, my wolf chanted, and for a moment I thought about doing that—apologizing and throwing myself on his mercy.

Then I caught a glimpse of the fury in his eyes, and I knew it was much too late.

CHAPTER ELEVEN

"Father," Kade said, his head inclined respectfully. And then he turned his eyes on me and his voice dropped several degrees. "And Jess."

"I gave you strict instructions she was to be kept under guard at all times," Devlin snapped. "Not left to roam the territory unsupervised."

"I'm sorry, Father. It won't happen again."

"See that it doesn't," Devlin snapped, and thrust me bodily to his son. Kade's rough grip took the place of Devlin's, and he dragged me inside.

"I'll see that she's punished for her disobedience," Kade said, and this time I didn't think he was bluffing. A shiver ran through me—and not in the way it had when Devlin had talked about punishing me. No, this time my body had a sane reaction—like wanting to get the hell out of there, unscathed. Unfortunately, it was too little, too late, and I didn't like my chances of getting out of this one. Especially not with Kade's father here.

Any hope I had that he would say whatever he'd come to say to Kade and then leave wilted and died as he crossed the threshold, and shut the door behind him, sealing the three of us inside the house. My wolf rejoiced at his proximity, and I cursed the fates for their cruelty.

"I'm sorry," I said, bowing my head to Kade and hating myself for it. But I needed to be in one piece—and to win his trust back—if I was going to escape later. Beaten and bloodied was going to slow me down. And also hurt. A lot. I really wasn't keen on that part. "I will leave you and the alpha, and await my punishment in my room."

Devlin snorted, and my eyes flicked to his face and then quickly to his feet. Even that glimpse was enough to set my heart racing.

"The same room you just tried to escape from? I don't think so."

"I won't try to escape again. I'm sorry. It was stupid."

"Yes, it was." I felt the pressure of the alpha's stare leave me and move to Kade. "Learn to control your future mate—or I will banish her from pack territory."

My wolf howled in anguish at the thought of being sent from our mate, even as a spark of hope settled in my stomach. Could it be that easy? Just break a few rules and they'd let me go? Maybe my hope showed on my face, because Devlin curled a lip and continued.

"I can just as easily trade her to one of the other packs if it will spare me any further inconvenience."

Inconvenience. This was my life—my whole life which happened to be falling apart in front of my eyes, and he was worried about the inconvenience? Worse, being traded to another pack put me no closer to my freedom, and there was nothing to say whoever they gave me to would be any better than Kade.

"I'm sure that won't be necessary, Father," Kade said quickly. "She's still adjusting to life here."

"I will decide what's necessary."

"Yes, of course, Father," Kade immediately deferred.

Great. If Devlin decided to sell me on, I clearly couldn't count on Kade to stand up for me. What a surprise.

"I will follow the rules," I said quietly, keeping my eyes averted like a good little she-wolf. "I won't disobey Kade again."

I was watching Devlin through my lashes, so I caught the odd look that passed through his eyes before he narrowed them. It seemed almost...possessive. Then he reached out a hand and gripped my chin, leaving traces of fire and need on my flesh. It was all I could do to keep from moaning at his touch. Shit. If I didn't get a better grip on myself, they were both going to know something was up, and then I really would be screwed.

"You will obey pack law," he commanded, his eyes boring into mine so that I couldn't have looked away if I'd wanted to—and I really didn't want to. It felt like it was only his grip on me that was keeping me from melting into a pile of pathetic at his feet...and I couldn't quite bring myself to care.

Our mate is touching us, my wolf rejoiced, and maybe that was what snapped me back to my senses.

"Yes," I whispered.

"And you will pay the price for your disobedience." He broke eye contact, snapping his gaze to Kade. "Take her to your room. I will witness her punishment."

"I would prefer to punish her downstairs," Kade said. My heart hammered in my throat. What sort of punishment were they talking about?

"Oh?" Devlin raised an eyebrow, and I almost missed it, and what it meant. Kade was questioning an order. For me. I went very still. "And where did you have in mind?"

"The kitchen," Kade said. "She hasn't earned the privilege of being in my room."

"Very well."

I didn't resist as Kade took my arm and marched me into the kitchen. I hadn't been in here before, having been taken straight to my room when I arrived, but like the rest of the house, it was bright and airy, and more modern than I would have expected in the heart of one of the country's oldest and most powerful packs.

The center of it was dominated by a large, wooden table, and that was where he led me.

"Bend over it," he ordered me, and I glanced back over my shoulder, my eyes wide with terror. I thought I saw a flash of pity in his eyes, and

GIFTED TO THE WOLF

he added gruffly, "Don't act like you've never been spanked before. Obedience clearly isn't a habit for you."

A spanking. Humiliating. And painful. But not as bad as I'd feared for a horrible moment. I gave him a small, grateful nod, hidden from Devlin by Kade's broad shoulders. He was the dominant asshole who wanted to be my friend. Right now, I'd take it.

Of course, he'd also warned me that his patience would run out if I tried to leave the house, so it shouldn't have surprised me when, instead of using his hand, he pulled his belt from his waistband. I looked at it and blanched.

"Eyes forward."

I pivoted my head back forward. Best to get it over with, and better not to see it coming, anyway. I leaned my weight on my forearms—because one thing I'd learned about punishments was fighting back would make it a hundred times worse. And I wasn't dealing with the alpha kids back at Winter Moon now. This wasn't something I could outrun, or hide from until they got bored. But at least I knew they'd stop short of doing any serious damage, not like that time I was eight and got my arm broken.

At least this time I—

A whistle split the air and something slapped my butt, and a split second later, the pain followed. I howled as much from surprise as from the pain—I'd had worse. Never from someone who claimed to be a friend, though.

I glanced back over my shoulder and saw Devlin grind his teeth together. What the hell was his problem—wasn't it hurting enough for his satisfaction? Maybe I should howl louder next time. Or maybe I should tell the pair of them to bite me.

I yelped as the leather stung my flesh again, even through my clothing. And the next time, and the time after. Ten lashes in all, by which time I didn't have enough breath left to tell them to bite me—or anything else. Probably for the best. The rest of today would be uncomfortable enough as it was. But I would heal by tonight. Kade had gone easy on me, for some reason. Not that I was complaining. Just confused.

I rose and turned around in time to see him tugging his belt back on, and behind him, Devlin scowling deeply. He stared at me past his son, and a shiver ran the length of my spine.

Mate will keep us safe.

Our mate ordered the beating, you dumb wolf, I grumbled at her.

He will protect us.

I exhaled heavily, and leaned back against the table, then yelped as fire raced across my ass, and shuffled forward again. He'd gone easy on me, but not *that* easy.

Devlin nodded solemnly.

"It would seem your future mate has begun learning her lessons. I will give you one week to convince me she is tamed—or I'll find a new pack for her."

CHAPTER TWELVE

"Are you hungry?"

I glanced over at Kade and shrugged. The truth was I was starving, having not eaten anything since breakfast at the motel that morning, since I hadn't much fancied eating after Devlin's little visit.

It was hard to believe this time yesterday my life had been normal, or at least what passed for normal for an omega in the Winter Moon pack. I'd been plodding along like always, keeping my head down and doing my chores, without a single thought of what was looming, of the bargain my father had already struck. How much twenty-four hours could change.

One thing that hadn't changed was my appetite. Healing burned almost as many calories as shifting, and I was hungry enough to eat a horse. Heck, I was hungry enough to eat pineapple on a pizza.

Well, okay, maybe not *that* hungry. But I was still plenty ravenous.

"Really, Jess? You're going to keep giving me the silent treatment? I thought you were eighteen, not eight."

"Fine. Yes, I'm hungry."

"Great. I'll make us something to eat." He got up from the armchair across the room from me and I blinked in surprise.

"You can cook?" I asked, curiosity getting the better of me. He laughed and I scowled.

"Yes, I can cook. There aren't a whole lot of other options aside from starvation when you're living on your own." The amusement dropped from his face. "You, uh, want to come help?"

So that he could keep an eye on me. It wasn't really a question, so I didn't bother to give him an answer, just got to my feet and followed him from the room. He hadn't let me out of his sight since his father's visit. Apparently, I wasn't the only one who didn't want Devlin to follow through on his threat to send me away. I didn't know why Kade gave a damn, though. One she-wolf was much the same as another to him. Maybe he just didn't fancy having to drive across state lines again.

I paused at the threshold of the kitchen. It was about my least favorite room in the house right now, given the events of this afternoon. But that wasn't why I paused. Devlin's scent lingered in this room, spicy and exotic, and my beast stirred in reaction to it. I reminded her stiffly that everything that had happened here was his fault, and then stalked into the room.

Kade, oblivious to my hesitation and probably to the fact I actually had emotions, rummaged through the fridge. I caught the scent of fresh meat as my feet carried me over the threshold. He piled a couple of steaks on the counter and tossed a few potatoes my way. I snatched them out of the air.

"Peeler's in there," he said, nodding to a drawer on my right.

I made a start on the potatoes while he seasoned the steaks, both of us working in silence. It wasn't until the potatoes were boiling and the steaks were in the pan that he spoke again, glancing at me in between watching the meat fry.

"How are you feeling?"

"What, you mean from the beating, or from being dragged away from my home?"

"Both."

"Like shit, actually." I took a slow breath and shook my head. It wasn't his fault. At least, not all of it. Even if he was a dominant asshole. "Forget it. I've had worse days."

"Life's tough for the daughter of a beta?" He cocked a disbelieving eyebrow and I opened my mouth to tell him he didn't have the first idea, then snapped it shut again. I could hardly tell him that I got pretty much daily beatings worse than the one I'd had earlier because the alpha bloods didn't like me. Not without having to explain why. I settled for giving a sharp shake of my head.

"You don't know the first thing about me."

"Right back at you, Jess. But at least I'm trying."

"Yeah? Well, I'm trying, too. This hasn't exactly been a walk in the park for me, you know."

He laughed again, but this time the sound was bitter.

"You think you're the only one having a hard time with this? I spent two years trying to find my true mate. *Two years.* Then my father gives me the order to bond through marriage instead. Tells me it's time to do my part for the pack. Raise some heirs. Says that he's found a match from another pack. Someone in the same situation as me."

He shook his head and a flash of raw pain passed over his face.

"I didn't want this, Jess. But when he said that, for one moment, just one moment, I dared to hope that I might find someone I could make a connection with. Someone who understood, who'd stand by my side and help make the best of the hand we've been dealt. Instead, I got you."

"Well, I'm sorry I'm such a disappointment. But it's not the first time I've been told that, so forgive me if I don't keel over with grief." And still, pain lanced through me, and his words echoed in my ears. *Instead, I got you.* No-one wanted me. Not my family, not my true mate, not even the man who was settling. Jess Whitlock, universal reject, that was me.

"Dammit, Jess! Would you grow up for one minute and stop feeling sorry for yourself? If you could see further than the end of your own nose for just one moment, you might realize that this isn't the worst thing in the world."

"Not the worst thing in the world?" I couldn't keep the incredulity from my voice, nor did I bother to try. "That's easy for you to say. You're not a prisoner in a strange pack, surrounded by strange people who treat you like a damned commodity. I have a mind of my own!"

"Yeah, I had noticed that." A smile played over his lips. "And I don't want us to be strangers, Jess. Like it or not, we're in this together, and I really do want us to make the best of it. Can't we at least try not to be enemies?"

I opened my mouth to tell him where he could shove his 'in this together' bullshit, but an acrid scent caught at the back of my throat at the same time and I saw a wisp of smoke coming from the pan behind him.

"The steaks are burning."

"Shit." He spun round and yanked the pan off the heat, then dumped the smoldering steaks onto a pair of waiting plates and prodded at them mournfully. "So much for wooing you with food."

I met his eye, and a chuckle bubbled up in my throat. His lips twitched, and before I knew it, the giggle spilled out of my mouth, and we were both laughing.

"Wooing me with food?" I said in between laughter. He lifted one shoulder in a half shrug, and I rescued the potatoes and tossed them next to the blackened steaks.

"It works in the movies."

"Fess up," I said, eyeing the dubious looking meal. "You're not a great cook, are you?"

"Are you kidding? I practically survive on takeout."

I set the plates on the table—because, burned or not, that was decent steak and I wasn't about to waste it—and chewed my lip thoughtfully as we settled into our seats. Much as I didn't want to think about what happened at this very table earlier, it was kind of hard to keep my mind from going there.

"Why here?" I asked. "My punishment. Devlin said your room, but you insisted on it being here. Why?"

I didn't buy what he'd said about privilege, and I didn't think Devlin had, either. Kade set down his knife and met my eye across the table.

"When you come into my room, it will be of your own free will. I will never let anything bad happen to you there, and I will never force you to go in there."

"Thank you."

He looked surprised. "For what?"

"For not being a total dominant asshole."

One corner of his lip lifted in a smile.

"Any time. But you should probably have higher standards than that."

"Well, you did cook me dinner. Kinda."

I prodded the steak with my knife and grinned.

"We could shift and go for a run, if you want," he offered. "There's plenty of prey in the packlands."

My wolf stirred inside me and I pushed her down, rising from the table quickly and turning away before Kade could read my expression. If I let my wolf out now, she'd drag me straight to Devlin, and get us both killed. I couldn't risk it.

"Maybe another time," I said, grabbing a glass and heading for the sink without looking back at him.

His chair scraped back and I caught the scents swirling through the air as he moved across the room, his footsteps barely making a sound. I felt his body heat behind me and set the glass aside, then turned round. Only inches separated us. I stared up at him, and he stared down at me.

And then he lowered his head and touched his lips to mine.

CHAPTER THIRTEEN

The heat of his mouth covered mine, and his hand slid round to the small of my back, drawing me close. His lips pressed against mine, slowly and softly, with a tenderness I hadn't expected. For a moment I leaned into his touch, allowing my lips to move against his, allowing myself to enjoy the closeness to another person.

And then my wolf howled in anguish.

Not. Our. Mate.

I stepped back, breaking the kiss and pulling myself free from Kade's embrace. My wolf's fury almost deafened me, so that it took me a moment to process the look of hurt that passed over Kade's face, and then it was gone.

"Jess? What's wrong?"

"I…" I could hardly tell him to truth, that my wolf was screaming for me to run straight to his father and report the trespass against our mate bond. The mate bond that he didn't even seem to feel. I turned my back on him quickly. "I'm sorry. I can't. Not now. Not yet."

I waited for him to flip out at me. That was why I'd been traded to this pack, after all. I wasn't naïve. I knew what was expected of me. I knew I was here to bear him an heir.

"I understand. You need time to adjust to everything. I'm…sorry."

I got the sense he didn't apologize very often; the word sounded stiff and alien, but still sincere. Or maybe it was that I wasn't used to people apologizing to me. The word was as foreign to me as his promise earlier.

I heard him move away, and turned around to watch him retreat to the other side of the kitchen.

"I'm the one who's sorry," I said, looking down at my feet. "I know I'm not what you expected. Not what you wanted."

"Jess, what are you talking about? You're perfect. You're gorgeous, and smart, and funny, and yeah, kind of a brat, but I'm giving you the benefit of the doubt on that one."

A smile flickered over his lips, and my own smile in return was tinged with sadness.

"You think I'm...gorgeous?" I couldn't keep the incredulity from my voice.

"Of course you're gorgeous. Haven't you ever looked in the mirror? You must have had half the pack chasing after you."

I barked a bitter laugh. "Not in the way you mean."

"I...don't follow."

I shook my head. It wasn't like I could explain they all wanted to kick the crap out of me for being an omega. "It doesn't matter. That was, uh, that was my first kiss."

"Your first kiss?" He ran his hand over his face. "Aw, shit. Your father told mine you were 'pure', but I thought that was just some archaic bullshit."

"Sorry to disappoint," I snapped. "I'm sure you'd prefer someone with more experience."

"You do that a lot, you know."

"Do what?"

"Get defensive when you're feeling vulnerable."

I rubbed my hands over my upper arms, and swallowed the desire to hit him with a cutting retort, or, preferably, a saucepan. Because getting snarky in the face of all the shit that had been thrown at me had been the only thing that had dragged me through the last eighteen years in one piece...but that belonged in my old life.

Not that that meant I was staying here, or anything. But I didn't need to make my life any harder before I found my way out of Broken Ridge territory.

My wolf howled inside me, at the thought of leaving Devlin, or the thought of going rogue, I couldn't tell which.

Kade crossed partway across the room to me, and then stopped.

"You don't need to feel vulnerable here, Jess. I will protect you from anyone who would hurt you."

"And who's going to protect me from you?" The words were out before I could stop them.

"Dammit, Jess, I'm trying here. Can you at least meet me halfway?" He spun around and stalked away, his hands bunching into fists at his side, then his shoulders shuddered with a deep breath, and his hands smoothed out again. I stared at his broad shoulders in silence. A week ago, I'd have found him attractive.

He ran one hand through his short hair as he turned back to me.

"You infuriate me, Jess. You push every single one of my buttons…and I'm pretty sure I've never wanted anything—any*one*—as much as I want you."

He wanted me. The words stunned me and I leaned back on the counter behind me, bracing myself against it. No-one had ever wanted me before. Not even Jace. He'd been my closest friend at Winter Moon, and he'd handed me over to a total stranger with barely a goodbye. Kade wanted me.

And it could never be enough.

"I know I'm not what you were expecting," he said, "but isn't there any part of this that you don't hate? Any part that maybe you could even come to love…in time?"

I knew what he was asking, and I couldn't give him an answer. At least, not the one he wanted. My wolf would never accept him, never return his…affection, or whatever this was. So I gave him a grin and the only answer I could.

"Well, I don't totally hate my room."

He looked shocked, then he laughed as my words caught up with him.

"Oh, well, if I'd known it was that easy to woo you, I wouldn't have bothered with the cooking."

"Probably for the best." I shrugged and glanced at the ruined meat. "I don't think that was really helping."

"Right. I better show you my hunting prowess, then."

I raised one eyebrow as he sucked a deep breath into his lungs, making his chest swell, and rolled out his shoulders. He stalked forward, more beast than man, exuding power and danger…and yanked open a drawer. He pulled three flyers from inside and dropped them on the counter next to me.

"Chinese, Indian, or some good old fashioned comfort food?"

*

We tossed the steaks, and ate a decent meal of noodles and chicken and spicy beef, gorging ourselves until we were too stuffed to eat another bite. We even talked, a little. But it was hard, watching every word I said, and I knew I could never live a lifetime like this. Maybe it would be better not to get too close to Kade. It would only make it harder on him when I ran. And I had less than a week to make my move.

I helped Kade clear away the cartons, and glanced out of the kitchen window. Looming in the distance I could see the forest, the trees almost glowing beneath the just-past-full moon.

"We could go for that run, if you like?" Kade offered. "Shifting might help you feel more at home."

Shifting would not make me feel more at home. Every part of my body yearned to change, to swap two legs for four…but I knew where those four legs would carry me. Straight to a certain mansion occupied by a man who was just looking for an excuse to trade me to another pack, where I'd have no chance of ever escaping. At least my imprisonment here was only temporary. But I couldn't explain that to Kade, and sooner or later he was going to want to know why I never shifted. Maybe he'd think I couldn't, and go right ahead with Devlin's plans to send me away.

But that was a problem for another day. I had enough to deal with right now. And if I got much more comfortable around Kade, I was going to slip up and say something that I shouldn't.

I stretched my arms over my head and yawned loudly.

"Maybe another night, if you don't mind?" I asked. He hid his disappointment quickly.

"Of course. You've had a long day. You must be tired."

I nodded. Tired was the last thing I was, but at least in the privacy of my room I could think clearly, and work out what the hell I was going to do.

He walked with me upstairs, and I buried a stab of annoyance that he insisted on escorting me to my door, because at least he was keeping his word and not locking me in his room with him.

"Well, this is you," he said, stopping outside my door. "I'll see you in the morning. Goodnight, Jess."

He ducked his head and his lips brushed against my cheek in a chaste kiss, and then he straightened again.

"Uh, yeah. Night."

I shoved open my door and tumbled inside, then slammed the door shut behind me and slumped back against it, trying to understand the emotions battling inside my chest.

My wolf was raging that he'd dared to kiss us again, but my heart was fluttering from his gentle touch, and my brain was screaming that I was his literal prisoner and I shouldn't trust a single thing he said or did…which did nothing to stop the butterflies stirring up a whirlwind in my stomach.

Would it really be so bad? Staying here, with Kade? Someone who cared about me, who desired me? Someone who wanted me to be a part of his life?

Someone who beat me, part of my mind snapped back. With a belt.

Yeah. There was that. But he'd been under orders, and who knew what worse things Devlin would have done to us both if he'd refused?

Our mate would never harm us.

Yeah? Then why did it feel like my heart was being torn in half by his rejection?

I crammed my fist in my mouth, stifling my whimper, and closed my eyes for a long moment. When they opened, I was staring at the window, and the moon hanging in the clear sky. I rose to my feet, and crossed to it, staring out at the forest in the distance.

I couldn't do this. I couldn't let myself be torn in half. The longer I stayed, the more confused I'd get.

I had to leave. Tonight.

CHAPTER FOURTEEN

I wasn't a complete idiot—though to be fair the jury was probably still out on that. Still, I knew I couldn't risk running off half-cocked again. I had to be careful.

At least this time it was pretty unlikely that Devlin would be about to pop round for a visit. Which was great, because if he caught me trying to run a second time, he'd have me bundled into the back of a car and crossing state lines before I could say 'oops'.

I waited two hours, until I was sure Kade must be asleep, and changed my mind fifteen times by then. It was reckless to run again so soon…but if I didn't, I might not get another chance. If I waited, I might not want to run…and maybe that wouldn't be such a bad thing. Gah! The fact that I could even entertain the idea meant I'd already stuck around too long. Who knew what I'd think in a week? No. I had to go now, before I talked myself out of it.

I wasn't sure where I'd go yet, but that didn't matter. I just had to get out of town and keep moving until I wound up some place where I couldn't smell wolves. Lose myself in the human world.

I shivered. I knew nothing about them. I'd never left Winter Moon territory before, and ordinary humans never came into the packlands. I didn't know how to be around them. But I knew most ordinary humans didn't sell their daughters to strengthen alliances. I knew most ordinary humans wouldn't hate me for having a human mother.

But they're human, my wolf whined. *We're not like them.*

Well, we're not like the idiots round here, either.

Our mate isn't an idiot.

Really? I rolled my eyes. Because last time I checked, he was too dumb to even notice we were mates. And my ass still ached.

My wolf rumbled her discontent but made no further argument. Not because she agreed, I was sure—probably just because she'd grown tired of the same argument.

Will never grow tired of defending our mate.

Right. Or not.

Go to mate.

I rolled my eyes again as I lifted the mattress and grabbed my stash of bills. That was the last place I was going. Ever.

Go to mate.

Great. She was back in stroppy toddler mode. Guess I was getting out of here on two legs, not four. She'd take the first chance to go running straight to him. It was probably for the best, anyway—a wolf carrying a pile of clothing was pretty conspicuous.

But it sure would be nice if just once, when I needed her, she was actually on my side.

She didn't want to leave our mate. She didn't want to go rogue. I didn't, either, at least, not the second part. I had no issue leaving the mate who didn't recognize us. But want it or not, there was no choice. Staying wasn't an option. Going home wasn't an option.

And hell, maybe one day we'd find a new pack. My wolf pricked her ears at that, and I let her have her consolation prize. Somewhere far away from here, far away from my pack, where no-one knew who I was. What I was.

I just had to get there first.

I eased the window open, and swung my legs over the sill.

You better be ready for this, wolf, I warned her. We weren't getting anywhere on a broken leg. I felt her stir under my skin and nodded to myself. She was ready. One deep breath and one shove later, I was free-falling through the air.

I dropped to the ground in a crouch, grateful this time not to find a pissed off alpha looming over me. My wolf rumbled in my chest. Apparently, I was the only one who felt that way. Shocker.

I cocked one ear, listening for any sounds coming from the house, but it was silent. Kade hadn't heard me jumping out of the window. Good. Time to get out of here.

I rose from my crouch and hurried across the lawn, staying low and keeping to the shadows as much as I could. The gates were just ahead, and my breath caught in my throat as I moved towards them, trying to keep myself from breaking into a run. My freedom was so close I could taste it.

I reached for the gates…and then a shadow moved behind them.

I jumped back, gasping, and kept backing away. The gates swung open, and I threw a glance back over my shoulder, then snapped my gaze forward again.

The figure stalked inside, and as the moon fell across his face, my breath caught in my throat. I knew him. It was Dean.

I backed up further, and crashed into someone. A pair of hands grabbed me from behind, pinning my arms behind my back, and I thrashed as Dean came towards me.

"Stop fighting," Ryder growled in my ear. "Or I'll hurt you."

A whimper slipped from my throat. They'd caught me. I was caught. My escape was blown, I was stuck here. The fight went out of me.

"We knew you'd try to run again," Ryder rumbled in my ear.

"A…again?"

"Don't play dumb," Dean said. "Kade told us about your little escape attempt earlier. Makes me wonder though…"

He eyed me in a way that made me want to curl up and hide.

"…Why are you so desperate to get away?"

57

"Because I don't like being sold," I snapped, putting as much venom as I could into my voice. Dean shook his head slowly from side to side, the corners of his mouth twisting in malice.

"No, I don't think that's it."

"I don't care what you think," I tried again, twisting in Ryder's grip. He yanked on my arms, sending a searing pain along my shoulders. I bit back another whimper, and my wolf snarled, urging me to fight back, but I knew that would be a very bad idea.

"Ow! Get your hands off me. If I get hurt, Kade will kill you."

Ryder chuckled and looked past me to Dean.

"She's got a pretty high opinion of herself, doesn't she?" His face twisted back to me. "We've been by his side since we were pups. He's known you less than twenty-four hours. He could replace you in a week."

A shiver ran through me.

"Come on, let's go." Ryder jerked on my arms and I glared at him over my shoulder.

"Go where?"

"Back to your beloved, of course. Do we have to drag you, or will you walk?"

"I'll walk," I muttered sullenly. Since running was out. Tonight, at least.

Ryder released me and I felt their stares prickling at my skin. I rubbed at my arms, studiously ignoring them both.

"Let's go," Ryder repeated, and made to shove me. I jerked away from his touch.

"All right, all right, I'm going. Keep your hands off me."

Dean smirked and I glared at them both before stalking back towards the house, both shifters shadowing my every step, as if I'd be stupid enough to try to run with them watching.

We reached the front door and I stopped and raised an eyebrow.

58

"Well? Now what? It's not like I have a key."

The door swung inwards, and Kade stood silhouetted in the frame, fully dressed in his day clothes.

"I tried to give you the benefit of the doubt, Jess. I won't make that mistake again."

CHAPTER FIFTEEN

"Benefit of the doubt?" I said with a snort. "Are you kidding me? Having these two creeps hiding in the bushes while you pretend to go to bed does *not* count as giving me the benefit of the doubt."

I made to push past him into the house and he caught my arm.

"And climbing out of the window in the middle of the night doesn't count as deserving the benefit of the doubt. What, did you think I would be dumb enough to leave you with the exact same way you tried to run off last time?"

I said nothing, because yeah, I kind of had. Guess he showed me. Bully for him. He lowered his voice and leaned in close.

"What happened, Jess? I thought we had a connection."

I twisted my head round to stare up into his eyes. It wasn't like I could tell him that was the problem.

"Yeah? Well think again. You're my jailor, not my friend."

I yanked my arm out of his grip and stalked past him into the house before I could blurt something I shouldn't. I heard two sets of feet cross the threshold, and whirled round to see Dean and Ryder standing inside. Kade shut and locked the door behind them, slipping the key into his pocket. I eyed the pair coldly.

"What are they doing here?"

"Staying the rest of the night," Kade said. "In case you get any more stupid ideas."

"Whatever." I made straight for the stairs.

"Where do you think you're going?" Kade demanded.

"My room. I'm tired."

"Maybe you should have thought about that before you climbed out of—"

"My window in the middle of the night. Yeah. I know."

I rubbed my hands over my upper arms and tried not to shiver. I really was tired. Kade moved quickly, so quickly he was between me and the stairs before I could do much more than blink. Shifter speed. He was fast, even for an alpha blood. Or maybe it was just that I was tired. I didn't much care either way. I just wanted to crawl into my bed and forget this whole sorry mess until the morning. I glared at the man standing between me and sleep.

"Unless you've changed your mind about forcing me to sleep in your room?"

He stepped again, closing the gap between us, and over his shoulder I saw Dean and Ryder slip away into the living room, giving us some measure of privacy. I was one hundred percent sure that was a bad thing.

"Listen to me, Jess, and listen carefully," he muttered, low enough that I was sure the other two couldn't hear, even with shifter senses. "I am doing everything I can to keep you from getting yourself killed, and I would appreciate a little help from you on that front."

"And I'd appreciate not being a prisoner, so I guess we're both out of luck."

"If you keep trying to run, you're going to find out exactly how out of luck you are."

I laughed, but there was no humor in the sound.

"Really? Am I supposed to be afraid? Is that meant to scare me? Because I'm sorry to burst your bubble, but you're not the first shifter to threaten me, and you're not the first shifter to hurt me."

He narrowed his eyes. "Yeah, why is that?"

Shit.

"Look, I really am tired. Can I just go to bed? Please?"

"No."

I crossed my arms and glared at him.

"No? What, you're going to make me stand here all night?"

61

"No. We're going to talk. I want some answers, Jess. There's something you're not telling me."

My heart hammered in my chest. If he found out the truth, I was finished. Why the hell hadn't I just kept my head down and played along until he was less suspicious? Dammit, I was so stupid. Jace had warned me not to risk anyone finding out, and that was exactly what I'd rushed off and done. So I did what I always did when I panicked. I went on the offensive.

"You're not being honest about who you are, either," I said, my voice sounding small and worse, hurt. "You said you wanted to be my friend, but that was a lie."

He exhaled heavily and ran one hand through his hair.

"I'm trying, Jess. I am. But you don't make it easy. I just...I don't understand why you don't want to be here. With me."

"You don't understand why I didn't want to be traded to a stranger? Seriously?"

He closed his eyes slowly, and then opened them again. "I get that. But you're not the only one who was put in that position, you see that, right? The difference is, I respect what my alpha wants."

"Yeah, well, my alpha can bite me."

His eyes widened with shock and I clamped a hand over my mouth. I couldn't believe I'd just said that to the son of an alpha. There really was no limit to my stupidity today.

"I'm sorry. I didn't mean that. I—"

He laughed, and my apology stuttered to a halt. I blinked at him quizzically.

"You've got spirit, I'll give you that. And one hell of a mouth on you. I don't meet many people like that." He cast a glance at the living room. "Let's go upstairs."

I looked at him like he'd lost his mind, because he obviously had. "I'm not about to climb into bed with you just because you tell me I've got a big mouth. I'm starting to understand why you're still single."

"I have had enough of your insolence," he snapped loudly, his voice hardening. "It's time for your punishment."

CHAPTER SIXTEEN

I blanched.

"I…What?"

How the hell had we gone from him laughing to him wanting to beat the crap out of me? I guess he didn't appreciate my 'spirit'. Or my big mouth.

He shook his head and pressed one finger to his lips, casting an exaggerated glance at the living room. Then, just in case tonight wasn't panning out weirdly enough, he winked at me.

"I will not tolerate your disobedience," he said loudly and then held my eye. "Do you understand me?"

"I…"

He winked at me again. Oh. Ooooh! I finally caught his meaning. I was definitely slow on the uptake this evening. I raised my voice so that it carried easily to the shifters in the living room.

"Yes, Kade. I'm sorry. I won't do it again, I swear."

He shot me a quick grin, and then his face went serious again, and his voice was stern. "That's not good enough, and we both know it. Actions have consequences."

"No, please…"

"I warned you not to leave the house. You've left me no choice. This is going to hurt."

"No, please don't, Kade, I'll behave, I promise."

It was all I could do to keep from bursting out laughing as I pictured Dean and Ryder lapping up every word, but I managed to keep my voice serious, and it rang with desperation as I pleaded.

"It's too late for that. Get up those stairs right now, or I'll drag you the whole way."

He took my hand in his, and I let him lead me up the stairs, not saying a word as he took me to my room. I waited until he shut the door before I spoke, keeping my voice low.

"What was all that about?"

He pressed his finger to his lips again, and quickly crossed the room to shut the window.

"Sorry. People have…expectations."

I walked to my bed and perched on the edge of it. "You're giving me whiplash, you know. I never know if you're happy or pissed off."

He shrugged. "Well, normally I'm both around you. You bring out the worst in me, Jess…and the best. I'm trying to be understanding. I just wish you'd trust me."

"I will. In time. I swear." I knew it was a lie as soon as the words left my lips, but some part of me wished it could be true. And that part of me needed to get a grip and remember that I was a prisoner here. Literally.

…But maybe I could afford to forget, just for a while.

Kade gave me a sad smile that called me on the lie.

"Well," he said, his voice upbeat, "It's time to put your acting skills to the test."

"Uh…excuse me?"

"You need to scream," he said. "Like I'm beating you. Preferably convincingly enough that Dean and Ryder don't think I'm going soft."

"Why…" I swallowed and stared down at the carpet between my feet. "Why are you lying to them for me?"

It occurred to me that I probably shouldn't give him any reason to actually take his belt to me again, and I bit down on my lip.

"Because," he said, hooking one finger under my chin and using it to lift my eyes to meet his, "I'm not planning on living with them for the rest of my life."

GIFTED TO THE WOLF

I wasn't sure what to say to that. Kade let go of my chin and stepped back.

"I'm not stupid, Jess. I know you're not planning on sticking around. I know that the moment I turn my back, you're going to run again. But you're not stupid, either. You have to know that doing that will probably get you killed. My father was willing to let me punish you this afternoon, and if word gets back to him that I punished you severely for trying it a second time, he'll probably trust me to handle it. But what do you think will happen when you're caught trying to escape a third time?"

I didn't answer. I didn't plan to get caught again, but so long as Kade was playing nice, I saw no reason to mention that—or do anything else that might convince him to make my fake beating a real one.

"I want you to make me a promise," he said. "And I want you to mean it. Promise me you're done trying to run. Give me a chance to show you what your life could be here, as the bonded mate of an alpha blood."

I opened my mouth and snapped it shut again. That wasn't a promise I could make. And yet...and yet it didn't seem that unreasonable. To stick around for a few weeks, to give him a chance. And when he was being like this, it seemed like maybe it wouldn't be so bad. But he wasn't always like this. And I wasn't sure I could stand being so close to my true mate...and so far away.

"I can't," I said, my voice small. I didn't want to lie to him. He really did seem like he was trying. So maybe I could, too. I sucked in a breath and met his eye. "I can't promise that. But I promise I'll try."

He held my eye for a long moment, and then nodded.

"Good enough. And I'll try, too, to give you a reason to stay." He smiled. "So, are your lungs warmed up enough for some screaming?"

I nodded, and unbuckled his belt. I blanched and leaned away from him, eyeing the strip of leather.

"Sound effects," he said, tugging it loose. "Ready?"

He drew his arm back and slapped the belt into the bedpost so loudly that the sound ricocheted around the room. My eyes widened. He'd definitely been going easy on me this afternoon. I made a mental note to never truly piss him off. Then I remembered I was supposed to be in pain, and wailed pitifully.

He raised a brow at my terrible acting skills, and I shrugged. He rolled his shoulders out and the belt whistled through the air again, slapping against the bedpost a second time. I screamed, long and loud, and he chuckled under his breath.

"Very convincing," he murmured. I stuck my tongue out at him and he grinned as he brought the belt down a third time. We repeated the act until we got to ten, and he nodded with satisfaction and pulled his belt back on.

"Well," he said with a grin, "I reckon that's about done it. Feel like you've learned to respect the man of the house?"

"Oh, I'm positively trembling in awe of you."

"Good." He glanced out of the window, where a sliver of moon was still visible. The playfulness left his voice. "Get some sleep. We've got a big day tomorrow."

"We do?"

"We do." He pulled open my door and shoved his head out. "Dean!"

The sound of his shout echoed in the hallway, and then I heard footsteps coming up the stairs.

"What are you calling him for?"

"How long are you going to keep underestimating me?" he said by way of answer. "I know you're still thinking about running. Dean's going to spend the night in here. And Jess?"

He paused until I stopped pouting and looked at him.

"If you try to leave again, next time I won't be pretending."

CHAPTER SEVENTEEN

It wasn't a restful night, and I would have stayed in bed long after the sun rose if it hadn't been for the shifter watching me from across the room, scoring a solid ten on the creep chart.

I rolled over and groaned with disgust.

"Are you just going to sit there staring at me?"

"Yup."

"Talk about déjà vu. Could you give me a break already?"

"Nope."

I growled in frustration and sat up, my blankets pooling around me. I'd slept fully clothed, because nothing about the idea of waking up half dressed in the same room as Dean appealed to me. In the same room as any of this trio, in fact.

Dean smirked at me.

"What the hell is your problem?" I demanded.

"I think that's my line," he said, folding his arms across his chest. "Why'd you run?"

"None of your business."

I got out of bed and snatched up my toiletries and a change of clothes.

"I'm going to find out, you know."

"Yeah, yeah, whatever," I muttered, and made for the bathroom, making sure to lock the door behind me—I didn't want any surprises.

I felt almost normal by the time I'd washed up and taken a shower, aside from the fact I was living inside a stranger's house, and that stranger oscillated between friendly and asshole so often I was getting dizzy.

I tied my hair back and headed down the stairs, wondering which version of him I'd find this morning.

He was sitting at the kitchen table with Dean and Ryder, holding a mug of coffee. He cut off halfway through whatever he was saying when I stepped into the room, and a smile played across his lips.

"Good morning," he said.

"No, it's not," I said, before I could stop myself. His expression darkened, and I heard Ryder catch his breath. Kade started to rise from his seat and I held up a hand—because it was too early in the day to get my ass kicked. "Sorry, sorry. I didn't sleep well. That was out of line."

I held my breath while he stared at me, his expression unreadable, then he dipped his chin.

"You've had a lot to take in. Make sure it doesn't happen again."

I nodded to the mugs. "Is there one of those for me?"

"No."

"O…kay?" It came out as a question. Seemed a bit harsh, especially when I was running on virtually no sleep thanks to Dean.

"We're going out for coffee and breakfast," Kade said, getting up and giving me another of those smiles that would have taken my breath away…before I'd met his father. "I want to show you off to everyone."

The look on Dean's face told me he didn't think that was a good idea—which was the deciding factor as far as I was concerned.

"Sounds great. I'll get my coat."

I was wrong. It wasn't great. In fact, it was a lot like being back in my own pack, or my old pack, or whatever it was to me now. People stared as we walked down the street. Whispers started up as we passed other shifters. But at least these whispers sounded excited, not hostile. Or at least, they weren't *all* hostile.

One of them definitely was. A blonde shifter in skinny jeans, boots, and a tank top, whose eyes narrowed when she saw us. The woman with her whispered something in her ear, but the blonde shook her head and sashayed over to us.

"Hi, Kade," she said, flipping her hair over her shoulder, and I didn't think I imagined the flirtatious note to her voice, or the less than flattering way her eyes ran over me—and dismissed me.

"Hi Camille," Kade said warily. He reached out and took my hand in his, and her eyes tightened.

"It's true, then," she said. "Your father found you a mate from another pack."

"Yes." He gave her a benign smile that didn't reach his eyes. I'd known him less than a day and I could see through it, so I had no doubt that Camille could, too. "This is Jess."

"Jess." Camille sniffed as she ran her eyes over me again, like she was assessing livestock. I'd seen that look before—but not on the face of anyone who didn't know what I was. But it was pretty clear Camille's issue with me wasn't what I was—it was who I was with. I supposed an alpha's son was quite a catch, if you cared about that sort of thing. I didn't, and as far as I was concerned, she could have him. I wisely kept that thought to myself.

"Hi Camille," I said. "It's nice to meet you."

"Yes," she said, her smile all teeth. "You, too. You must be quite the woman to be worthy of Kade. We should get to know each other sometime."

"Sure. I'd like that." About as much as I'd like pulling my own teeth out with a pair of rusty pliers.

"We're just going for breakfast," Kade said. "We'll see you later, no doubt."

"Oh, sure." Her smile brightened, and if she flashed any more teeth, she'd look like a piranha. "Wouldn't miss it for the world."

She turned and sashayed back to her friend, and I definitely wasn't imagining the way Dean checked out her ass as she went.

"Who is she?" I asked Kade as we carried on walking down the street. He gave me a puzzled look, like he wasn't quite sure if I was simple.

"Camille."

I rolled my eyes at him. "No, I mean, *who* is she?"

"Jealous?" he asked with a raised eyebrow, and Ryder snorted with amusement.

"Hardly," I said. "I'm just wondering if I need to worry about my back sprouting a knife."

Kade tensed.

"You're my mate," he said. "No-one would dare harm you."

"Right." Except for him, his father, and, presumably, both his buddies. But that was still a whole lot less people than I was used to, so on balance, I'd take it. I forced a smile. "You don't like your girls blonde and flirtatious, then?"

He grunted. "Nope. I prefer them dark-haired and a pain in my ass."

"Two for two. I'm on a roll."

That raised a smile from him—not that I cared. Obviously. He was still my jailor. Anyway, he only cared about me getting hurt because it would look bad on him.

We were pushing through the doors of a well-lit café when the rest of her words sank in.

"Wait, what did she mean?"

"What did who mean?" Kade asked, pausing in the door long enough for everyone to look at us, and then steering me towards a booth. Everyone we passed ducked their heads in acknowledgement—which I was sure was why he'd brought me here. But if he wanted to impress me, it was going to take more than power and status. Straight answers would be a good start.

"Camille."

"You're still thinking about her?" He smirked and rolled his shoulders, ushering me into the booth.

"Just answer me," I said, gritting my teeth, and immediately saw the warning flash through his eyes. He'd already told me that as an alpha blood, he could never appear weak. And me challenging him in public made him look exactly that. I relaxed my jaw into a smile before we could draw any attention. "Please."

I sank into my seat and he slid in beside me. Dean and Ryder sat opposite us, saying nothing, watching to see what Kade would do.

"You're going to be the death of me," he muttered, so low I was sure I was the only one who heard. I gave him a conspiratorial smile and answered in the same low voice.

"At least you won't die of boredom."

He barked a laugh that had half the heads in the whole café swiveling to stare at us. Again with the staring.

A middle aged waitress hurried over before he could answer me.

"Kade. It's good to see you again," she said with a smile that seemed genuine. Huh. Weird. I guess I hadn't figured him to be Mr. Popular, what with the whole dominant asshole vibe he had going on. "And this must be..."

She turned her gaze on me.

"Jess," I said. "It's nice to meet you."

"You, too. I'm Lori. You ever need anything, you ask for me, all right?"

"Uh, thanks."

"Right now we'll settle for some coffees," Kade said a little stiffly, but if his tone bothered her, it didn't show on her face.

"Coming right up, honey. I'll get you some menus." She turned her smile back to me. "You take care of him, he's a good one." She gave me a wink and then hurried off. I watched her go, not quite sure what to make of her.

"She's a character," Kade said, following the direction of my thoughts, or maybe just my gaze. "But you can trust her. Her family are low rankers in the pack, but she's loyal."

"So," I said, turning back to him. "Are you going to tell me what's happening tonight?"

"Pack tradition," he answered. "When a newcomer joins us, we all get together."

"Like a party?" I ventured. He shook his head.

"Like a hunt. Tonight, the whole pack will shift, including you."

74

Oh. Crap.

CHAPTER EIGHTEEN

The evening came round far too fast.

Dean and Ryder had parted ways with us when we left the café, but I'd caught sight of a shadow moving in the grounds later in the day. Apparently, Kade still wasn't taking any chances, which really sucked, because nothing appealed to me more than running right about now. I couldn't trust my wolf to be loose around Devlin.

Mate?

I shook my head and stared out of the window. She would run to him first chance she got, and then Kade would know something was up.

Kade isn't mate. Go to mate.

She didn't understand. It wasn't her fault—she *couldn't* understand. She was all instinct and impulsiveness.

And the moment I let her free, she was going to get us both killed.

Mate won't kill us.

She sounded utterly confident in that, which made precisely one of us. Given that Devlin wasn't even acknowledging me, at the very least he'd probably banish us. But more likely, he'd just kill us there and then for showing such blatant disrespect for his rank. I wasn't even a full member of his pack yet. Even so much as approaching him without permission counted as disrespecting his rank. And I was pretty sure my wolf wanted to do a whole lot more than that.

I exhaled heavily, and let my gaze wander through the night sky. In the distance, a wolf howled. This was it. There was no way to run from this now, not with the whole pack gathering.

Fine. I could control my wolf. I *would* control my wolf. I was a shifter, which meant I could take control. I'd done it a thousand times before.

…Just never when I was running near my true mate.

A hand rapped on my door.

"Jess? Are you ready?"

"Uh…yeah, just coming."

I turned away from the window and opened the door.

"So," I said, avoiding Kade's eye. "How does this work? Do we shift here and then go to meet them, or…?"

I trailed off, not really sure what the alternative was. Kade shook his head.

"No. The pack will gather in a clearing in the woods. We'll go down there human, and I'll formally present you to the pack for consideration. Then we'll shift and hunt, and the pack will 'appraise your hunting skill'."

Great. No pressure, then. I was completely screwed.

"Hey, don't worry," he said, taking my hand and squeezing it lightly. "No-one really cares about that stuff anymore. Just stick close to me and you'll be fine."

That was what I was worried about.

"Uh, thanks."

It didn't take us long to reach the woods, even human and on foot, and when we did, I saw two wolves sitting just inside the tree line, waiting. Dean and Ryder. Great. Just when I thought today couldn't suck any worse.

The pair of them escorted us through the trees, flanking us as we moved along a well-worn game trail. My nose twitched as we moved, and I felt my wolf stirring inside me. The scent of prey was all around us. Good. Maybe she'd be too distracted by the hunt to worry about Devlin. The fact that she didn't respond when I thought his name gave me some glimmer of hope, at least.

I stuck close to Kade because I didn't want Dean or Ryder to get it into their heads that I was trying to sneak off. I didn't need a whole pack of pissed off shifters on my tail right now.

We walked in silence, Kade seemingly completely at ease, and me just too anxious to speak, until I saw shadows in the trees ahead. Kade took my hand and gave it what I was sure was supposed to be a reassuring squeeze, but it just felt like his hand clamped around mine was stopping me from running. Which I really, really wanted to do right now.

"You'll be fine," he said, his voice barely louder than a breath. "You're strong."

I sucked in a deep breath and let it out again slowly. He was right. I could do this. It wasn't like being back with my old pack. They didn't want to hurt me, and as long as I kept my wolf under control and away from Devlin, nothing bad would happen.

Right. Easy.

Dean and Ryder trotted out onto the track in front of us, and led us through a break in the trees. The forest opened up around us, revealing a large, grassy clearing...and what had to be a couple of hundred wolves. Shit. It really was the whole pack...and it was a big pack.

The wolves were spread around in a large circle, several rows deep, and as we reached it, Dean and Ryder slipped away to fill two empty spaces. Every pair of eyes was trained on Kade...and me.

His pace never faltered as he led me right up to them, and the wolves parted, letting us step into the center of the circle.

One wolf, grizzled gray, scarred, and bigger than the wolves around him, stepped into the circle, and the wolves around us lowered their heads and averted their eyes. But even without their deference, there could be no mistaking who this was.

Power and dominance rolled off the alpha wolf in waves, and it was utterly intoxicating. His body was layered in thick slabs of muscle, covered by a sleek fur coat. His eyes locked onto me, and my heart hammered like it would smash straight through my chest in its bid to escape and get to him. My feet wanted much the same thing, because how could I bear to be this close to my breathtakingly stunning true mate, and yet not touching him, not holding him in my arms?

Kade's hand tugged on mine, and for a horrible moment I thought he'd sensed me trying to go to his father.

"Lower your eyes," he hissed in my ear.

Oh. Right. I was staring at the alpha wolf. I ducked my chin and stared at my feet, hoping no-one had seen my desperate, stupid, ridiculous desire. From the corner of my eye, I saw Kade's head bowed almost as deeply as my own.

"Alpha Devlin," he said, his voice a stoic rumble. "And the wolves of Broken Ridge. If it pleases you, I present Jess Whitlock of the Winter Moon pack. I ask that she be permitted to run with us, and should she prove worthy, make a home in our pack as my mate."

My wolf shrieked in fury and I clamped my jaw shut, fighting to keep her outrage trapped inside me. Dammit, wolf, knock it off. You're going to get us both killed!

Not our mate, she raged. *Never our mate. Not him. Not ever.*

Fine. I know. I know he's not our mate, I promised her. Not now. Not ever. But we have to keep our heads down and get through this. She said nothing, but I could feel her pacing restlessly inside me.

Across the circle, oblivious to my internal agony, Devlin inclined his head in a solemn nod. Even that single gesture sent shivers through me, pooling deep in my stomach.

Kade shed his clothing, tossing it to the ground, and I gaped at him in horror. Take my clothes off? In front of the whole pack? He had to be kidding.

He raised one hand to my cheek and gently turned my face until I was staring at his eyes.

Relax, he mouthed, and I frowned. He gave me a short smile, and mouthed silently again. *None of them are looking.*

79

I looked around, and saw he was right. Every single wolf had their eyes averted from me. Many of them had their eyes closed completely. Those had to be the lower ranking members of the pack. No wolf of alpha or beta blood would ever close their eyes when surrounded by other wolves, even their own pack. To do so would make them appear vulnerable. Weak. And there was no room for weakness here. I flicked a glance at Devlin and my eyes widened. He, and he alone, was watching.

And part of me thrummed with excitement.

I turned my back on Kade—no way was I willing to let *him* see me naked right now—and tugged my top over my head. Devlin watched me impassively, and it was all I could do not to march my half-naked self right over to him. I shook my head. That definitely would not be helpful.

I wriggled out of the rest of my clothes, and tossed a glance over my shoulder at Kade.

"You can shift whenever you're ready," he murmured, and I needed no further invite to swap my naked and overly horny human body for my strong, lupine one.

I allowed the heat to rush over me, and then I fell forward onto four legs, catching myself on powerful paws. My senses sharpened immediately, and I heard Kade hit the ground beside me.

I lifted my head, and everything else melted away. There was only one thing left in my world.

Alpha Devlin.

CHAPTER NINETEEN

Every cell in my body screamed to run straight to him, to rub my body against his, to cover him in my scent and mark him as my own for the whole pack to see. To stand proud beside my true mate and dare any other wolf in this pack to challenge me, to come between us.

A whine slipped from my lips and I locked my jaw, fighting a battle against myself.

Go to mate. Claim mate!

My wolf was frantic inside me and I shook my lupine head, trying to clear my thoughts.

Get a grip, I hissed at the beast. Everyone is staring at us.

Exactly. Claim mate for all to see.

If I could roll my eyes in this form, I would have. As if we'd make it two steps towards him before someone tried to take us down. Probably the beta standing on his right flank, or the slightly smaller gray wolf on his left flank—his eldest son, if I had to guess. Heir to the pack, right above Kade.

I tried to break through to my wolf. We can't approach him, I reasoned with her. *He* has to approach *us*.

She stopped fighting me at that, and I felt her interest turn inward.

Impress mate with our hunting prowess.

Sure thing, wolf. Whatever you gotta tell yourself. How about we start by proving we can follow, since you've managed to imprint on a damned hot—Uh, a damned *alpha* wolf.

Hot alpha wolf, she agreed, tongue lolling from the side of our mouth. *Impress mate. Bring him a big deer.*

Ugh. Whatever. Stop ogling him before someone notices! I directed that as much at myself as at her, and I wrenched my eyes from the grizzled alpha, turning them instead on the wolf by my side.

Kade lowered his front end in a bow to the alpha, and I followed suit. All around us, the pack threw back their heads and howled, each voice layering over the over until the whole forest rang with an etheric harmony that seemed to flow through my very veins.

It was the sound of coming home.

I threw back my head and joined their chorus, the sound erupting from me in sheer joy. Beside me, I heard Kade's voice ring out, calling to the stars above and the earth below, and the ancestors flowing through our veins.

Devlin turned in a circle and then leaped forward towards the tree line. The wolves parted to make way for him, and his beta and eldest son fell in on his flank as he loped easily through the trees. The rest of the pack fanned out, rushing past us in a stream of fur, pounding paws, and excited yips.

Kade turned his toothy grin to me, and then leaped forward, leading us into the heart of the hunt.

Run. Chase. Hunt.

The words ran through my wolf's mind in time with the beat of our paws on the dry earth, and for the moment, she was utterly content.

It didn't last.

She realized at the same time I did: running in the heart of the pack and surrounded by this many wolves, there was no way we would see even a hair on the hide of our prey.

Run at head of the pack. Best prey ahead.

She made to push for the front of the pack and I checked her stride, making us stumble. I felt Kade's concerned gaze flick to me but I ignored him. There was no way the pack would tolerate us running at its head. My wolf thrummed her irritation at me, but nothing could steal her joy of the hunt. Her eyes scanned the mass of bodies.

Right flank. Next best chance for prey.

She instinctively understood the way the pack and prey moved in relation to each other far better than I ever would. I allowed her to drift towards our right.

Kade turned his shoulder inward, trying to force us back onto our original trajectory. Rage flashed through my wolf and she snapped her teeth at his face. He jerked back and panic flooded me...what the hell had she just done? My heart hammered, but the look in Kade's eyes was...amused?

He wheeled to his right, letting us have our way, and I loped past, driving us onto the pack's right flank.

A few wolves turned to stare at me as I pushed through and emerged on the flank, but then they saw Kade, and none of them moved to stop me. I saw the looks they sent his way as we passed. Respect. He wasn't the alpha, or the alpha heir, but he was respected by these wolves. Liked, perhaps, if the reaction of the few pack members we'd met this morning were anything to go by.

My wolf flattened our ears, irritated by my thoughts distracting her, and I allowed her attention to return to the hunt, to the pounding of paws that filled the air around us, to the rich scent of earth released by our passing.

To the gamey scent of a fleeing prey animal.

Her attention quickened, latching on to the scent at once. We weren't the only ones to catch it; all around us on the right flank I saw noses and ears twitching, and it was all I could do to hold her back from warning them off our prey.

I didn't know what had gotten into her. True, it was rare that we'd been allowed to join hunts in our old pack, but even so, on those occasions she'd been painfully aware of the presence of the higher-ranking wolves, submissive beyond the point of recognition. But now...I barely recognized her behavior.

Impress mate.

Ah. Guess that explained it. But did it, really?

She twisted round and snarled at Kade, and the wolves around us scattered, giving us a wide berth. Shit. Whether she wanted to impress Devlin or not, I needed to rein her in.

Can't impress him if we're dead, you idiot, I thought at her, and I felt her sulky response.

Catch prey. Impress mate.

I snuck another glance at Kade, but he was running on my flank, and making no move to force me to submit in front of the pack. Which was great, because I was pretty sure my wolf wouldn't let us do that right now.

Suddenly, we lurched forward, breaking rank from the rest of the pack. She caught me by surprise and I tried to rein her back in, but she was in control of our legs right now, and she had no intention of handing the controls back over.

Where the hell are you going, wolf? I demanded, but she didn't waste time or energy responding. It wasn't until I caught the single-minded focus of her thoughts that I realized her intentions.

Shit. That was a really bad plan. Like, a *really* bad plan. She had a death wish. She wanted to get us killed. Why else would she be behaving like an absolute idiot? Because I was pretty sure rushing to the front of the pack and claiming the prey was going to get us torn apart by two hundred wolves.

She didn't care. I tried to tune in to her thoughts, but I could catch only snatches. *Mate. Hunt. Deer. Kill. Tree. Scent.*

It was enough. As her legs propelled us through the ranks, our nimble pace easily outstripping the other wolves, shocked eyes turned to stare at us, and at Kade who still followed closely in my wake. Maybe that was why they hadn't turned on us yet.

We've got to stop, I told her. Please. Think about it. We can't do this. It isn't our hunt. It isn't our *pack.*

Mate's pack. Our pack.

Our mate who didn't recognize us. Great. When Jace told me to keep a low profile, I am one hundred percent certain this was the exact opposite of what he'd meant. I grappled with my wolf as we tore through the woods, fighting her for control, and losing. She was incapable of reason right now, and I was a passenger in my own body on its deadly flight.

Ahead, I caught a glimpse of the three wolves running at the head of the pack, and a thrill ran through me. I couldn't help but see the prowess of my intended mate; the elegance in his sleek muscles, the intensity of his stare, the sheer power of his every movement. Every inch of him was the perfect hunting machine, and my eyes followed the direction of his even as my heart pounded at the sight and scent of him.

Ahead of us, a stag fled, flashing its fawn hide in the moonlight. A fitting trophy for an alpha, I could see why he had chosen it.

For a moment, I thought my wolf would be content to run in his shadow, admiring his prowess as he cut through the night to claim the kill.

I should have known better.

CHAPTER TWENTY

"How could you have been so stupid, Jess?"

We were back home—by which I mean back in Kade's home—and I was sitting at the kitchen table while he paced up and down.

"I…I don't know. I just lost control."

"It's my fault. I should have stopped you when you snapped at me. I should have reminded you of your place right then." He stopped and glared at me. "I was impressed by you, by your wolf's ferocity. I just didn't realize idiocy was part of the package."

I hung my head. It wasn't like I could disagree—my wolf *had* been an idiot, and I'd told her that plenty once I'd taken back control of her. Which, unfortunately, hadn't happened until *after* she'd taken a snap at the alpha in some suicidal attempt to warn him off his own hunt.

Who did that? Crazy people, that was who. Shifters who were tired of living. Which wasn't me. Life sucked right now, but that didn't mean I wanted to throw it away. It was only by the mercy of the alpha that I hadn't been torn apart right there and then.

I shuddered. The whole pack had come to a halt, falling completely silent as they stared at me, and I could feel the air humming with their collective shock. And I'd thought for sure Devlin would open my throat right then. She'd got his attention, all right.

"I'm glad you see how serious this is, Jess. I'd take the belt to you right now if I thought it'd make the blindest bit of difference, and if—" He broke off and ran his hand through his hair, leaving it in disarray. My own hair was a mess, too, having been dragged back here right after my transgression. I'd been too shocked that I was still alive to offer any sort of resistance. Kade had tossed some clothes at me and ordered me to get dressed, and here I'd sat since, for what felt like an hour, while Kade paced and yelled and paced some more.

Maybe Devlin wanted to make an example of me to the pack. Maybe that was why he hadn't let them kill me right there and then. He wanted to draw it out and make me suffer, so that no wolf would ever dare show such disrespect to him again. Like any other wolf on this planet would have been dumb enough to do what I did.

Because Devlin was coming here. I knew that much. His beta had left orders with Kade. That was the other reason he hadn't beaten the crap out of me. Devlin probably wanted to do it himself.

I shivered and wrapped my arms around myself. I knew I should have found a way to run. And now it was too late.

Kade pulled out a chair and sank into it.

"Beg for mercy when he comes," he said. I stared at him wordlessly across the table. We both knew there was nothing I could say. "Do you understand me, Jess? Get down on your knees and fucking beg him to spare your life."

"I…"

"Dammit, Jess!" He slapped his palm down on the table and I jumped. "I can't lose you, not like this. We are meant to be together. I don't care that we're not fated, and I don't care that you refuse to follow a single order I give, and I don't care that you drive me crazy. I care about you, and I can't lose you. So you fucking beg, do you understand me?"

I opened my mouth and closed it again. My head was spinning, so full of regret and confusion and terror that I didn't think there was room to process this revelation. I met his eye across the table, and saw the desperation there. I forced myself to speak.

"I understand." My voice was robotic, giving no hint to the tumult of emotions swirling inside me.

"Good." He slumped forward and reached out to take my hands. I let him, not even sure I could stop him if I wanted to. They didn't feel like they were my own anymore. Not like it had felt when my wolf had wrested control from me earlier, but like I was disconnected from my own body.

Maybe it was for the best. I had defied an alpha. I had disrespected him in front of his entire pack. I was already dead, I was just waiting for him to carry out the sentence.

Maybe it had always been inevitable, from the moment I had come to Broken Ridge. Maybe it had been destined to end this way. I hoped it didn't hurt. I'd had enough of pain for one lifetime.

"Thank you," I said. He snorted.

"For what? For showing you too much leniency? For not curbing your disrespect when I had the chance?"

"For caring." I averted my eyes and picked at the table. "I wasn't sure there would ever be anyone who cared when I died."

"Why? I don't understand. Why would you think that?" He pushed back his chair and started to pace again. "Nothing about you makes sense."

"I know."

"That's your answer?" He stared at me. "I know?"

"It's the only one I can give you."

"What happened to trusting me?"

"Well, I'm about to be ripped limb from limb by your *father*," I snarled, "so there's that."

"This is all such a mess." He went back to his pacing. Maybe he thought if he paced long enough he'd wear a hole in the floor and escape through it. I snorted. Probably not, since he already had the key to the front door in his pocket.

His head snapped round to me.

"You think this is funny?"

"Oh, I think this is hilarious. I'm going to die for a ten second lapse of control. I'm in fits of laughter."

"There has to be a way. I mean it, Jess, just—"

"Beg. Yeah, you said." I pushed myself up from the chair. "And we both know how that's going to end."

There was a knock at the door. A single tap, but we both heard it. It sounded like a death knell.

"Sit down," Kade said. "And at least try to look like you're sorry."

I slumped back into my seat as he hurried to the door. It didn't pay to keep an alpha waiting. And who else would be calling on us but Devlin, alpha of the Broken Ridge pack, and executioner of idiotic omegas?

The door creaked open—Kade really should oil that—and then two pairs of footsteps approached. I cocked my head. I'd expected him to bring his beta, at least. Maybe half the pack, complete with pitchforks. I hadn't expected him to come alone.

The father and son stepped into the kitchen, and I twisted my head round to look at him. Devlin. His chiseled jawline was taut, his shoulders tense under the linen shirt he wore. His eyes were hard. My wolf surged inside me at the sight of our mate, and I gripped the table, fighting against her instinct to run to him. Like her instincts had brought us anything but trouble tonight.

My nostrils flared as a slight draught carried his scent to me, that same exotic mix of spice and masculinity I remembered from before, and my pulse quickened.

Our mate. Our mate.

I forced my eyes back to the table in front of me, and hoped he couldn't see the agony in my eyes. Our mate, but not ours. Not really. He didn't recognize us, and he hadn't claimed us. And tonight, he was going to kill us. I closed my eyes for the briefest moment, and when I opened them, they found him again.

He didn't look at me. Instead, he turned to his son.

"Leave us."

"But, Father..." Kade looked confused, and I could see him searching for an excuse to stay. But he shouldn't. He'd been kind to me, despite his dominant asshole tendencies, and he didn't need to see whatever was about to happen. My punishment. My...execution. He should be spared that, at least.

"Get out. Now." He didn't raise his voice, but every syllable thrummed with dominance, an alpha wolf commanding his underling. Kade ducked his head, and obeyed.

Good.

Devlin clicked the door shut behind him, and then it was just the two of us. Alone. A shiver ran the length of my spine.

And then he turned to me.

CHAPTER TWENTY-ONE

I stared up at him, drinking in his terrifying, intoxicating presence. His eyes ran over me, appraising me, and his jaw tightened.

Shit. I was supposed to be...

Sniffing him. Licking him. Showing him our belly.

I shook my head, trying to dislodge her thoughts. Trying to dislodge *her.* I was absolutely not going to do any of that. I was supposed to...

Appease our mate.

A flash of anger burned through me. To hell with that. I'd made a mistake. A stupid mistake. I hadn't asked to come here, and I hadn't asked to go on that hunt. And if he thought I was going to beg for my life because of *one* slip up, he could bite me.

I shoved my chair back and stood, turning to glare at him. I was done with this.

"Sit." His hand clamped on my shoulder—how had he crossed the room that fast?—and he shoved me back into my seat. I sat.

Every inch of my flesh tingled from his touch, four fingers and a thumb of fire on my shoulder, and I wanted to reach up and touch where he'd touched. I wanted to touch him. I wanted to rise from my seat and rip his shirt open and crush my body against his until there was nothing left in the world but us.

But I sat.

He towered over me, and I could feel the intensity of his stare boring down into the back of my neck.

"I'm sorry," I said, giddy with his proximity. "I shouldn't have snapped at you, I lost control of my wolf and I didn't mean to challenge you, I swear, I—"

I clamped my jaws shut, cutting off my apology mid-word. So much for refusing to beg. My resolve had lasted seconds. I glared at my hands splayed across the table. No more begging.

He said nothing.

"Please, it will never happen again, I promise. Just give me another chance. Don't kill me. Don't send me away. Please."

Shit. What was it about this man that made my resolve crumble without even a word?

Mate.

Gee, thanks wolf. Helpful.

It took me a moment to realize he'd turned to stone behind me; not so much as the rustle of clothing reached my ears. I twisted round and the hunger on his face stole the breath from my lungs.

I gasped, the air rushing furiously back into me and I slid from my chair and staggered back. He knew. He fucking *knew*. He saw me.

And he wanted me.

Go to mate. Touch mate. Kiss mate.

I lurched towards him, crashing into his solid, muscular body. His arms reached out to steady me but I was already reaching my hands up behind his head, pulling his face down towards me. He sucked in a breath at my touch, then leaned into me, crushing his lips against mine. Every fiber of my being hummed with joy. He was touching me. Kissing me. His taste was exquisite on my lips and I couldn't even begin to fathom how I'd survived my whole life without him. He was perfection, and he saw me, and he was *mine*.

One hand cupped the back of my head, tangling in my hair, and the other found the small of my back, drawing me closer still, and I went willingly, until every inch of me was pressing against his firm, muscular body. His whole presence dominated me, and I yielded to him willingly.

There was nothing I wouldn't give this man—my body, my heart, my soul.

Then, abruptly, he broke off the kiss. His hands grabbed my shoulders and moved me firmly a step away from him.

"What...?" I searched his face, trying to ignore the hammering of my heart and the twisting of my stomach. "Why...?"

"That can never happen again," he said, turning on his heel and marching two steps away, deepening the gap between us.

"Why not? I don't understand. I *know* you felt that. I know it wasn't just me."

"It doesn't matter what we felt, either of us."

"But..." I stared after him, trying to process his words. He knew. He knew what we were, and... "We're fated mates. Don't you care?"

I didn't manage to keep the hurt from my voice, and his shoulders tensed before he turned to face me. His face hardened.

"I'm not interested in being your mate."

"Really?" I snapped, my voice shaking with pain or anger, I couldn't tell one from the other anymore. "Because that's not what it felt like when you were kissing me."

"Sit down," he commanded. "We're here to discuss what you did, not what may or may not be between us." His voice dropped an octave, sending a shiver of fear and desire through me. "And if you try that again, there will be consequences."

"Try what?" I demanded, ignoring his command. "Taking a snap at you, or kissing you?"

"Both," he ground out, stalking back across the floor. He gripped my shoulders and steered me to a chair, pressing down until I relented and sat.

"You kissed me back," I said, following him with my eyes as he moved to the opposite side of the table, as though putting a physical barrier between us changed things.

"Are you trying to force my hand? Do you want me to mete out the harshest punishment pack law accords?"

"Can you?" I challenged, arching a brow. "Can you do that to your mate?"

"I can do what I damned well please. And in your case, not only can I, but I will take great pleasure in it, insolent pup."

"And could you…kill me?"

His jaw clenched, and he worked it loose again.

"If you leave me no choice."

Sense caught up with me, and I stopped trying to give him an excuse to do just that. Because, contrary to how I was acting, I actually didn't want to die. I bowed my head and lowered my gaze to my hands twisted together in my lap.

"I don't want to leave you with no choice, Alpha Devlin," I admitted in a small voice. I peeked up through my lashes in time to see him raise an eyebrow in surprise.

"Ah, so she can show propriety. Interesting."

I ground my teeth together. Propriety, my ass. I kept the thought to myself—part of my masterful not-dying plan.

"Pack law demands the harshest punishment for those who would challenge their alpha."

"But I wasn't chal—"

He held up a hand and I clamped my mouth shut.

"But I accept it was not your intention to challenge me," he continued, pinning me in place with his stare, so that I could do nothing but nod my head numbly and try to ignore the heat welling in my stomach, and below. His stare smoldered, and I burned from the inside.

"A lapse in control is not the same as willful defiance. You ought learn how to exert some control over your beast."

If only he knew. It was taking every ounce of self-control to stop my beast from leaping over the table at him. And since I presently wasn't licking his entire freaking body, I'd say I had the whole control thing down.

"I will spare your life. This time."

"Thank you, Alpha Devlin."

I liked the way his name tasted in my mouth, the way it lingered on my tongue as my lips formed the sound.

"There will not be a second time. Do I make myself clear?"

I didn't know if he was talking about the snap or the kiss, and I didn't care. There was nothing I could refuse this man.

"Yes, Alpha Devlin."

His brow knitted in frustration, and a groan slipped through his powerful, seductive lips. I played back my words in my mind and heard the lovesick sigh in them.

"Dammit, Jessica, look at me."

He rose halfway to his feet and his hand shot out to grip my chin across the table, forcing my gaze from his lips to his eyes: two hard gray pools I could drown in and die happy. I leaned into his rough touch without meaning to, but I couldn't bring myself to stop. Even the thought of pulling away from him, of breaking contact with his delicious flesh, sent a lance of pain through me.

He shook me roughly—it would leave a mark, I was sure—and I tried to compose myself.

"This cannot happen. Do you understand me? We cannot be mates."

"But we are." My dreamy voice was distorted slightly by his grip and he released me as though my touch burned him, but not in the way his touch burned me. Not in the delicious way he set my soul alight. He released me like I tainted him.

He towered over me, and I could do nothing but look up at him and try to control the hurt and confusion on my face. His expression clouded over.

"You are not good enough for me. I reject you."

CHAPTER TWENTY-TWO

My soul shattered into a thousand pieces.

"You…you don't want me?"

He turned and strode to the door.

Go to mate. Prove ourselves worthy.

Shut up, stupid wolf, I snapped at her. Weren't you paying attention? He doesn't want us. He rejected us. He doesn't think we're good enough for him.

And he was right. How could I argue with what he said, knowing that I was just a lowly omega, a halfbreed?

Devlin paused at the door, with one hand on the knob, but he didn't turn back to me as he spoke.

"You'll tell anyone who asks that I beat you."

"Yes, Alpha Devlin," I whispered hoarsely, taking no joy from the feel of his name on my lips.

He turned back to me then, and I angrily dashed the tears from my eyes with one hand.

"It's better this way," he said. "Trust me."

"Yes, Alpha Devlin," I whispered again, blinking hard. He was right. It was better—better for him, better for the pack. He shouldn't be tainted by an association with me. It would make him look weak in the eyes of his pack, and in the eyes of the neighboring packs. There was nothing weak about Devlin.

His eyes searched my face a moment longer, then he yanked open the door and stepped through, disappearing from my sight, and perhaps, my life.

No. Not disappearing from my life—he would be required to formally accept or reject me from the pack a few days from now. That would be worse. Seeing him again, and knowing that I would never be good enough for an alpha, no matter what my heart told me, and what my soul yearned for.

Should have caught the stag.

One side of my lip lifted up in half a smile, and I scrubbed at my eyes. Yeah. Maybe that would have done it, apart from the bit where the pack would have killed me for trying. Probably would have hurt less than this, anyway. The smile fell from my lips and I slumped forward over the table, fighting the sobs that wanted to burst from me.

I wasn't sure how long I sat there, but it felt like a long time before I heard movement outside. When the alpha ordered you to leave, you left, even if he was your father, and you didn't take chances he would accuse you of eavesdropping. Not if you wanted to keep your ears, anyway. Perhaps it was for the best Devlin didn't want me around. I'd had enough of danger for one lifetime.

…No. I couldn't bring myself to believe that. I would rather live one single, danger-wrought day than spend a lifetime without him. How could one person contain this much pain? How much more would it take for my heart to burst?

"Jess?" I heard Kade calling me from the hallway, but I couldn't find the will to answer. I sniffed, dragging my arm across my eyes.

The kitchen door flew inwards and he stood outlined, horror etched into his face as he searched my face and then the rest of me.

"What happened?" he demanded. "What did he do to you?"

Ripped out my soul, I wanted to answer, but I couldn't. He might have rejected me, but Devlin was still my mate, and exposing his connection to me felt like a betrayal. I couldn't betray him. I deserved to be rejected, but he didn't deserve to be betrayed. He'd already been screwed over by fate once, assigning him such a weak, pathetic mate. I couldn't add to his burden.

I shook my head wordlessly, and Kade hurried to my side.

"Sshh," he said, running his hand over my shoulder, and it was all I could do not to turn round and take a snap at him. How dare he touch the same flesh Devlin had laid his hand on? I swallowed, and did nothing. "Sshh, it's okay. It's over. You're alive. That's all that matters."

No, it wasn't. Being alive mattered least out of all the things I could consider. Being alive meant the agony would go on.

Kade withdrew his hand.

"You're alive, and you're here," he said, as though it was a blessing and not a curse. When I didn't respond, he said, "Come on, let's get you to bed. You'll be better after some rest."

Better? I barked with laughter. How could he think things would ever be better? Sleep couldn't fix this. Nothing could fix this.

"Jess?" He eyed me with open concern. Maybe he thought I was losing it. Maybe I was.

Perhaps this whole thing was a figment of my imagination. That would be nice. Maybe I was really back in my home in Winter Moon territory.

I shivered. No. That was no consolation. I had lived there for eighteen years, but it had never been my home. My home was here. With my mate. And if none of this was real, then he wasn't real, either, and I couldn't bear the thought of that.

This was real. I was here, in Broken Ridge, and my mate had rejected me. The fates really had taken a disliking to me. Perhaps it was because my father slept with a human. Maybe he offended something on a cosmic scale, and I was paying the price for it. The sins of the father...

"Here. Drink this."

I blinked Kade back into focus as he set a glass of water in front of me. Oh. My throat was raw from crying. When had I cried?

I picked up the glass in trembling hands, and saw my splotchy red face reflected back at me in the water's surface. I scowled at it. No wonder Devlin hadn't even thought twice about rejecting me. I was a mess. Weak. Why would he risk everything for someone like that?

I set the glass back down without drinking. Where was the point? I should just curl up and wait for it all to be over.

No.

No, that wasn't good enough. I frowned down at the table. It wasn't good enough to just roll over and give up. He'd rejected me. It sucked. And sure, it hurt right now, but I could survive this. I would survive this. I didn't know how, but I would find a way. I hadn't survived eighteen years to just roll over now. I lifted my head.

"Tomorrow will be better," I said numbly, and from the corner of my eye, I saw Kade nod his encouragement, a flash of relief passing over his face.

Somehow, tomorrow would be better.

CHAPTER TWENTY-THREE

When I woke late the following morning, my resolve had firmed. I was not ready to roll over and give up. I hadn't given up after all the hell I'd been through at Winter Moon, and I hadn't given up after being sold to a stranger in another pack.

This would not be the thing that broke me.

Even so, I took my time getting out of bed. I needed to work out what I was going to do. I needed to work out what I wanted. No, wait, that wasn't right. I knew what I wanted. *Who* I wanted. What I needed was to work out what I was willing to accept.

Was I willing to accept life in this pack without my true mate?

I could hear Kade moving around downstairs—shifter hearing—and though he was hardly the hearts and flowers type, he'd been good to me, for the most part. Better than I'd expected. Sure, he didn't trust me, but I hadn't given him reason to. Maybe that could change, with time, if I opened up to him. I could build a life with him, if I wanted.

Want mate.

Of course, my wolf pretty much hated him for not being Devlin, so there was that. I flopped back on the bed with a sigh.

I could go to Devlin, and try to prove myself worthy. I couldn't risk exposing our bond to the pack, so I'd have to be careful. And he'd already made it clear that he didn't think I was good enough for him— and that was before he found out I was an omega. There was a good chance that pursuing Devlin ended up with me dead.

There was a third option. I sat up and stared out of the window. I could bide my time here, and then run. I might not get away. And if I did, I had nowhere to go. But I would at least have a say in my own destiny, for the first time in my life. That wasn't without appeal.

A hand rapped on my door, startling me from my thoughts.

"Jess?" Kade called through the thick wood. I hadn't heard him approaching. Having shifter hearing only helped if you weren't too wrapped up in your own thoughts to pay attention to it.

"Yes?"

"Can I come in?"

I glanced down at my flimsy nightdress—if I was going for option one or two, I was going to need a shopping trip to supplement my wardrobe—and wrapped the blankets around me.

"Okay."

The door swung inwards and he stood outlined in its frame for a moment, running his eyes over me with an interest that was more than friendly. My wolf snarled, and I ignored her.

"I thought maybe we could go out for breakfast."

"I'm not hungry." My stomach chose that moment to rumble loudly, and I flushed red and ducked my head, but not before I saw Kade raise an eyebrow and quirk one corner of his mouth.

"Yeah, it sounds like it."

"A gentleman would have pretended not to hear that."

"I've never claimed to be a gentleman."

His eyes roved over the curves beneath the blanket wrapped around me.

"So, are we going out for breakfast," he said, his voice low and husky, "Or would you rather stay in?"

I exhaled in an irritated huff. "Fine. Turn around so I can get changed."

Amusement flittered over his face, but he obligingly turned around. I scurried off the bed and rooted through my bags, still packed, in search of a pair of jeans and a top.

"What's the hurry to go out, anyway?"

His silence filled the room and I canted my head as the realization hit me.

"You want to show everyone I'm still alive."

"Trust me, it's better to get it over with."

He probably had a point. No doubt the whole pack was talking about what happened last night. Better to lay the rumors to rest before they spread. Though how the hell I was going to convince them Devlin had beaten the crap out of me last night was beyond me. I still wasn't fully sure why he hadn't.

"Do I at least have time for a shower?"

"Are you going to try to escape again?"

"I don't fit out of that window."

He chuckled.

"I'll wait for you downstairs. Don't be long...or I'll come and join you."

I stared at his back as he left, and then shook my head. Nothing good was going to come of trying to work Kade out. He hadn't made a lick of sense to me since I'd arrived. Maybe he just woke up horny today.

I rushed through my shower and hurried downstairs. Kade looked disappointed, then gave me a rueful smile and held his hand out to me.

"Shall we go and show the pack the rebel lives?"

"Ugh, please don't remind me of how stupid I was." I thrust my hands into my pockets.

Kade shrugged lightly and grabbed his keys.

"You say stupid, I say reckless."

"Isn't that the same thing?" I eyed his back as he strode down the hallway, but he didn't answer, and after a moment I hurried after him. I was quietly relieved not to see Dean and Ryder waiting for us outside; it seemed like they had a habit of turning up whenever I was in the shit. Maybe this was enough to scare even them away.

But probably not. I wasn't *that* lucky.

Kade reached out and rested his hand lightly on the small of my back, and I battled the urge to shrug him off, because I wasn't so stupid that I didn't know I needed the pack to see he was accepting me. This little trip wasn't just about showing I was alive. It was about showing that no matter what had happened, I was still strong, and I was still by Kade's side.

Maybe that was why Devlin hadn't punished me last night. He knew I'd need to be strong enough to face the pack today. I was just surprised he cared, after everything he'd said.

I put him forcefully from my mind. I couldn't walk along this street with Kade's hand on me while I was thinking of another man. And I couldn't afford the distraction right now.

If I thought I was getting stares yesterday, it was nothing compared to how people were looking at me today.

Most of them seemed surprised I was still walking. Some of them seemed unhappy about it.

"Chin up," Kade muttered in my ear. "The alpha passed his judgement. You're here because he wants you here."

If only he knew the half of it… Instead, I nodded and sucked in a ragged breath. Then I lifted my chin, and stared out defiantly at the shifters drifting around us. I was the future bonded mate of an alpha blood of this pack, second heir to Broken Ridge. I had faced the alpha's wrath, and lived to tell the tale. So let them stare. Let them whisper as they scurried about.

They didn't need to see what last night had cost me. They didn't need to see an omega whose soul had been torn in half. They just needed to see the she-wolf who could survive defying an alpha, one who might one day lead this pack.

Let them stare. Let them see I was back in the alpha's good graces. Let them start to trust me.

That way, they'd never see it coming.

CHAPTER TWENTY-FOUR

The week passed slowly. Every day, Kade made a point of parading me in front of the pack. The whispers had started to die down—or at least take place behind closed doors. Every night, he invited me to join him in his room. And every night, I refused. One day, he would lose patience, and judging by his increasingly erratic mood swings, that day wasn't far away.

That was why I was leaving tonight. That, and Devlin would make his official judgement on whether I would be allowed to remain in Broken Ridge tomorrow. If he sent me away, I'd have no control over where I ended up, and possibly no more hope of stealing back my freedom. Tonight was my last chance. I wouldn't squander it again.

The sun was starting to set when I cleared away the dishes from dinner. I'd cooked—I wasn't a great cook, but I was better than Kade—not that that was setting the bar particularly high. Still, I'd cooked an edible meal, albeit one that mostly involved taking the food out of the packaging and putting it in the oven, and I'd made polite conversation while we ate, and generally done everything I could to make Kade think I was cooperating.

"You don't have to do this, you know."

"Don't be silly," I said, loading the dishes into the sink and turning on the faucet. "It's just the dishes, and someone has to."

"Not that, this." His chair scraped back and he stood, gesturing with his arms. "All of this. Trying to find a way into my good graces, convince me to keep you around."

He planted his hands on my shoulders and turned me to face him.

"I already want you around, Jess. I want you. Like I've never wanted anyone before."

Shit. I swallowed. His eyes searched my face.

"How could you even doubt I'd speak for you tomorrow? I'd do anything to keep you safe."

"Like you would for all your property?"

He looked like I'd slapped him, and his eyes narrowed.

"What the hell is wrong with you?"

Shit, again. I was so terrible at this.

"Sorry." I broke eye contact and turned back to the dishes. "I'm sorry. I'm not used to people...caring for me that much. I guess I just don't know how to handle it."

I was pretty sure he cared for his new car more, but I didn't need to give him an excuse to kick the crap out of me and leave me running on three legs tonight. Or worse, keep me under close watch.

"More of that history of yours?" His voice was taut, and I could picture the tension in his shoulders. "One day you're going to tell me about that."

"One day," I lied. If tonight went well, I'd never see him again. And if it didn't, he'd never want to see me again. I turned to face him again, and found myself almost crushed against his chest, he was so close to me. Hating myself for it, I lifted one hand and placed it on his chest. He sucked in a breath, and I lifted my eyes to meet his. "I'm trying, I promise. And I'm so grateful for your patience. Perhaps...perhaps I'll be able to come to you tonight."

His head snapped down and he crushed his lips against mine, pulling my body against him. My wolf snarled in fury and it took every ounce of willpower not to shove him away, or give in to her rage. Patience, I counseled her. We have to fool him if we're going to run free tonight.

The mention of running took the sting from her fury, and I leaned into the kiss, imagining I was pressed against Devlin and blotting Kade's scent from my mind. His tongue slipped into my mouth and his hands slid down my back to cup my ass and jerk me against him.

I moaned softly and unclenched my fists from my sides and tentatively rested my hands on his back, then slid them down to the pockets on the back of his jeans, covering his taut ass.

After what seemed like a small, painful eternity, he broke off the kiss and stared down at me with wonder in his eyes.

And when he was like this, breaking his heart would break mine, too. But Kade wasn't just a guy with a crush on me. He was an alpha blood, a dominant asshole who saw me as his right and his property, not his girlfriend.

And I would never be his.

"Thank you," he breathed. I flushed and stared down at my feet.

"For what?"

"For still being here," he said softly. "For trying. I know it hasn't been easy on you."

"You've tried to make it easy," I acknowledged, because he had, in his own twisted way.

"You haven't," he said, and his lip quirked up into a teasing smile. I laughed without meaning to. Shit, I was going to miss this. I brushed past him to the table.

"Yeah, well, I've got to restore the cosmic balance somehow, right? It keeps you on your toes."

"Yes, you do." He moved behind me again and wrapped his arms around my waist, eliciting another snarl from my wolf. My heart fluttered and I twisted out of his grip, carrying our glasses to the sink.

He perched on the edge of the table and watched me. "And I wouldn't have it any other way."

"Well, that's just as well, Mr. Dominant Asshole, because I don't plan on changing, for you or anyone else."

"Who said anything about anyone else?" he said, his voice taking on a possessive rumble that I would have sold my soul to hear from Devlin— if the bastard hadn't already destroyed it.

He padded over to me again, and rested his chin on my shoulder in a way that was half affection, half possession.

"Leave the dishes," he rumbled, and I felt the vibrations travel up my spine. His hands wrapped round in front of my waist and started moving south. I slapped his fingers away.

"And that, Kade, is how you got a reputation with the rest of the pack for being a slob."

"Hey! I do not have a reputation...for that."

I coughed and raised an eyebrow.

"Well, okay, maybe a little. But who can think of dishes at a time like this?"

"Me."

Because if I gave him what he wanted—what half of me wanted, too—then I'd never run tonight. And maybe tomorrow night I'd still be here, or maybe I'd be on my way to another pack, banished from Broken Ridge and traded to whoever wanted me. I was done being passed around.

I ducked my chin.

"Why don't you head upstairs and make yourself comfortable," I said, trying to keep the tremble from my voice. "I'll come and join you soon."

Something that definitely wasn't his hand pressed into me from behind.

"You will?" His voice was husky and ignited a fire in my treacherous belly.

"Yes," I whispered, my gut twisting painfully like it wanted to crush the life from the spreading warmth. I swallowed, and forced some levity into my voice, smacking at his arm again. "But take a shower first. You stink."

"It's my manly odor."

"It's grim."

He chuckled, and ducked his head to plant a kiss on my cheek.

"See you soon," he murmured against my flesh…and then he was gone.

I could do it. I could finish the dishes and go upstairs and be with him…and forget all about Devlin and what might happen tomorrow. I could make a life with him.

Yeah, sure. And then the sun would rise, and someone could snatch it away again. Or Kade would be back to treating me like a prize race car.

I tried to hold on to that animosity as I quickly dried my hands, cocking one ear to the shower to make sure the water was running before I crept towards the door.

Run? My wolf asked hopefully. Yes, I told her. Soon.

To mate?

I didn't bother answering that. The only thing I wanted from Devlin was his damned head on a stake. He'd broken me when he told me I wasn't good enough for him. I'd known it all along, of course, but hearing it from his mouth…that was something else. Something I didn't think I had it in me to get over. And no matter how my wolf craved him, no matter how my body craved his, I would *never* go willingly to him. And after tonight, he'd be out of my life forever.

Just a few short hours.

I couldn't risk taking anything with me, not even my pile of cash. I had to leave with just the clothes on my back, while Kade was distracted and thinking happy thoughts. I wished I could leave a note for him, but every second I delayed could cost me, and the price was too high to pay. I had to go, and I had to go now.

My hand closed around the small silver key in my pocket. I'd helped myself to it while he'd been busy kissing and groping at the sink. With trembling hands, I slid it into the lock, and twisted. There was a muffled click as the lock disengaged, and I eased the handle down.

The scent of night air rushed in to meet me, and I slipped out into the darkness.

CHAPTER TWENTY-FIVE

I clicked the door softly shut behind me and sucked in a deep breath of the night air. So, this was what freedom tasted like.

But it wasn't mine yet. I needed to get across town and into the woods, and I needed to do it without anyone suspecting a thing. And without anyone seeing me go, if I could pull it off.

Broken Ridge almost certainly had trackers—every large pack did. Trained specifically to track trespassers and runaways, they were usually fast, powerful, and brutally efficient. I would need every second of my head start if I wanted to stay in front of them. So it made no sense that part of me wanted to stand staring up at the large house, the first place that, even if only for a few days, I was able to call home.

I shook myself out, and shook off my idiocy while I was at it. That wasn't my home. That was Kade's home, and I existed inside it only as his property, in the same way his television set and his games console did. And the fact that he'd spoken nicely to me a couple of times didn't change that. He wasn't my mate, and I didn't belong here.

Mate?

Dammit, I should never even have thought the word. I could feel the wolf stirring in me, could feel the direction of her thoughts drifting to an old mansion with an old shifter inside. One who was perfect for us.

One who doesn't want us, wolf. Let's not lose sight of that, I grumbled to her. One who hadn't hesitated to break our hearts, and she might be ready to forgive him for that, but I wasn't, and I never would be. And so what? I didn't need a mate to survive. I didn't need a pack. I was better off on my own than with a bunch of strangers who thought it was acceptable to trade people, and who'd shun me or worse for being half human.

My wolf whined, and I clamped my jaws shut before the sound could escape and bring Kade's wrath down on me. It was time to go, before she gave the game away.

I crept quietly round to the back of the house. It was a slightly longer route, but at least this way if Kade looked out of his window, he wouldn't see me escaping straight across the front lawn.

The rear garden was vast—not acres, but large enough that by the time I reached the far wall, my heart was hammering in my chest so hard I was starting to worry it would do permanent damage.

I pressed myself up against the stonework, taking a moment to catch my breath and try to compose myself. I wouldn't need to go through the center of the town to get to the woods, but I'd still have to go down a few streets, and if I was cringing away from the light and breathing like I'd just run a marathon, I was going to draw attention. I could shift and go through people's backyards—I could be in and out before anyone noticed in that form—but that meant I'd be stuck carrying my clothes or forced to go naked once I was out of town. Neither of those options was a good one. If I was getting out of here, it was going to be on two legs.

I clambered over the wall and landed neatly on the far side. I didn't allow myself another look back at the house because my feelings were all kinds of mixed up as it was. Instead, I ducked my head and started cutting through the trail of back alleys I knew would lead me to the woods.

With each passing step, my wolf became more and more restless. We were moving farther away from Devlin, and she didn't like it. But she was just going to have to get used to it, because no way in hell was I going back to that arrogant bastard. What sort of man told his mate she wasn't good enough for him? And worse, he'd *known* we were mates since we first met, that much was obvious. He'd known we were mates when he'd ordered Kade to beat me that first time. That wasn't what mates did.

GIFTED TO THE WOLF

So screw Devlin. Or more precisely, I wasn't going to screw Devlin. I was getting the hell out of dodge, and it was only minutes before the woods came into sight. I sucked in a breath. Through there, and out the other side, and then I would disappear into the night, never to be heard of again.

I'd leave Jess Whitlock behind in those woods, and become a whole new person, one who didn't have to answer to anyone.

I ducked into the cover of the trees, and sucked in my first proper breath since I'd left the house. I was so close now I could practically taste my freedom.

No freedom! Go back to mate!

My wolf raged so hard inside me that I doubled over, gasping in pain and clutching at my stomach. It was like she was trying to claw her way out from the inside. I collapsed to the floor on all fours, wheezing in the night air and gritting my teeth, trying to lock the wolf down before she could burst from my skin.

Go. To. Mate. She snarled the words at me, fighting every bit as hard as I was, and we were so evenly matched that I didn't know which of us would win.

Dammit, he doesn't want us! I snapped at her, and the words rebounded at me from inside my own skull. I was so badly damaged that my own mate didn't want me—and that was without knowing I was an omega. He didn't want me because *I* was a disappointment to him.

The realization was like a lance through my heart, and in my split second of agony and distraction, I felt it. My wolf took over, throwing herself into the change, and I was powerless to resist. My clothes burst at their seams, falling to the ground around me in tattered strips of useless fabric as black fur erupted all over my body, my shoulders broadened, and my hands changed into claws. A tail burst from my tailbone, and my face transformed into a muzzle, leaving me fully lupine.

Shit.

I was being torn in two—my wolf desperate to drag me back to Devlin, and me desperate to run as far and fast as I could the other way. I felt my legs start to pivot and my head snapped round, back the way we'd come. I gritted my teeth and forced my eyes back onto the track in the forest, and my wolf threw back our head. I caught her intentions and clamped our jaws shut before the howl could escape from our chest.

Call to mate.

I ducked my head and forced my paws to move. It was like walking into a strong wind. Each step was a terrible effort, and my wolf's intentions buffeted against me. She tried to leap to the surface again, and our legs gave out beneath us, sending us crashing into the earth, twitching and panting on the damp ground as we fought a battle against ourselves.

A battle I could not afford to lose.

My wolf was made of strength and instinct, and all the primal parts of me. But I'd survived eighteen years in a pack that hated me, and I had a different kind of strength. Eventually, that resilience won out, and I clambered to our feet, trembling.

The effort of fighting me had weakened my wolf, but she wouldn't stay quiet forever. Being in this form gave her an edge I couldn't afford. I sucked in a deep breath, and shifted back into my human form. My very naked, very cold, human form.

A flash of movement caught in my periphery, and I spun around, gasping as I stumbled back. My eyes fixed on a tall, muscular body, and the cold gray eyes watching me.

"Jessica."

CHAPTER TWENTY-SIX

"Alpha Devlin."

Shit.

Shit, shit, shit.

Fuck.

His eyes roamed over my body and I abruptly realized I was standing there, stark naked. I slapped my arm across my breasts and flung my other down to cover between my legs. One side of Devlin's mouth curled up in cruel amusement...and something else.

"Going somewhere?"

"Um..." I flushed furiously, glancing down to check as much as me was covered as possible. I so did *not* want to have a conversation standing absolutely naked in the woods with Devlin, of all people. There was a predatory hunger on his face as he eyed my exposed flesh.

Abruptly, I was furious. What gave him the right to look at me like that after he'd told me he didn't want me? That I wasn't good enough for him? I scowled up at him.

"Yeah, I am," I snapped. "I'm getting the hell out of this damned town. So help me, or get out of my way."

Hot rage flashed over his face but was gone in an instant, replaced with a stoic mask.

"Is that so?" His tone was low and dangerous.

"You don't want me here. I don't want to be here. So let me go. Please."

He shook his head once.

"No."

"Why? Why do you—" I jabbed a finger at him, then remembered my lack of clothing and slapped my arm back across my breasts. "Are you seriously going to make me have this conversation naked?"

"You have only yourself to blame for that."

My mouth popped open and I snapped it shut again. Screw him. I didn't owe him anything.

Submit to mate. Appease mate.

Yeah, I sure as hell wasn't going to do that. I glared at him, and he simply raised an eyebrow, unfazed by my fury. Bastard.

Lick him.

What the hell, wolf?! I absolutely did not want to lift up his shirt and lick his abs, or trail my tongue south and— I screwed my eyes shut and shook my head, trying to clear the image from my mind.

"See something you like?" he asked, his voice a low rumble.

"You wish."

"Hardly. But I can smell your arousal, little wolf."

Shit. He could do that? Of course he could do that. We all had heightened senses, and alphas, they had the best senses of all. My blush returned with a vengeance.

"A mistake," I said coolly. "But don't worry, it won't happen again. I'm done here."

I made it a single step along the trail before he stepped and blocked my path, his body inches from mine.

"You're done when I say you're done."

"Please, Alpha Devlin," I said, hating the whine in my voice. "Just let me leave."

"You are property of the Broken Ridge pack. You belong here."

I barked a laugh.

"Are you joking? I don't belong here. I've never belonged anywhere less in my entire life." That might have been a stretch, but I was beyond caring.

"You belong where I say. You belong to me."

My heart skipped a beat, but he didn't mean it that way. Which was *good*, I reminded myself, because I hated him. What he meant was I was his property, to do with as he pleased.

"I don't want to belong to you!"

"You insult me," he growled.

"Fine. Then beat me or kill me or whatever you're going to do." I met his eye and held it. "Because I will *never* stay here willingly."

"You will stay if I command it, willing or not."

"Then don't command it, please. I—"

I cut off as footsteps pounded towards us. Just what I needed. An audience. I spun round to search for their source, running along the same trail I'd followed. A half second later, Kade burst into sight.

His eyes fixed on me, and his lips curled back in a snarl.

"You fucking bitch!"

His gaze flicked behind me to Devlin, then back to me in an instant. I backed away a step, almost crashing into the alpha standing right behind me.

"Don't you dare try to run again," Kade snarled, stalking across the dirt track separating us until he was half a dozen paces away and I could see the rage etched into every plane of his face. "You played me!"

"I'm sorry."

"Oh, you will be." His face promised violence and my heart rate doubled. "You're coming home with me, right now, and I'm going to beat you so hard it'll hurt next time you even *think* about running."

He took another step towards me, and a hand slapped down on my shoulder from behind, yanking me back, and then Devlin was standing between me and Kade.

"You will not touch her," he said.

I peered round Devlin's shoulder in time to see the confusion flicker in Kade's eyes. It quickly changed to anger.

"You gave her to me, Father," he said, working his jaw as he fought to keep his voice level. "She is mine to punish and bring to heel."

"She will not be coming to your heel," Devlin replied.

Hope flared in my chest. He was going to let me go. Devlin was going to release me. I didn't know what had changed his mind, and I didn't plan on sticking around to ask. I took another step back. Devlin reached behind him without taking his eyes from his son, and clamped his hand around my wrist, checking my escape.

"She will not be going anywhere with you. She is no longer yours."

"You can't do that!" Kade's voice was a mix of indignation and fury, and for a moment I thought he was going to take a swipe at the powerful alpha.

Devlin, in response, all but pulsed with cold alpha dominance.

"I can, and I have." His eyes never left his son's face, as though daring him to throw a punch. I stayed very still, watching the scene unfold, and trying to work out what the hell was going on. Kade wasn't dumb, I'd seen enough of him to know that, but for a moment I thought he would follow through on the challenge. Instead, he straightened, and calmly met his father's eye.

"With respect, Alpha Devlin, you don't have the right."

"I have every right," Devlin said. "She's my mate, and she's coming home with me."

CHAPTER TWENTY-SEVEN

"Uh, I'm doing what now?"

My head swam with shock, but inside my wolf was practically doing backflips in her jubilation.

Mate. Mate. Mate. Mate!

I tuned her out. I couldn't handle her sheer, unadulterated joy right now, because this was the bastard who'd told me he didn't want me, told me I wasn't good enough for him, and dammit, for a moment there I'd really thought he was going to let me go.

I was such an idiot.

As if an alphahole like Devlin would *ever* give up something he thought of as his property. Even now he was only claiming me to stop Kade from having me.

It was almost painful as the hope in my chest withered and died. I was trapped here. With a man who hated me. A man who wanted me just because I was his by right.

"Your mate?" Kade said, his eyes flicking from Devlin to me and back again. Uncertainty raced over his features, and his face creased into a frown. "I don't understand."

"What's not to understand?" Devlin snarled. "The woman is mine."

Every muscle in his broad shoulders tensed, and Kade took a step back from the dominance that even I could feel radiating from the alpha.

Devlin advanced.

"You will not take her from me."

Kade blanched at his father's word and dropped to one knee, ducking his chin.

"No, Alpha. Jess is yours. I would never challenge you, nor dispute a mate bond." He flicked a glance up at Devlin, then went back to staring at the floor between his feet.

My heart sank, watching him crouched in submission at his father's feet, not even bothering to dispute the fact he wanted to take me away.

I hated Kade. He was my jailor, and a dominant asshole besides. It would be stupid to feel betrayed.

Which didn't stop me feeling it.

Devlin grunted in approval.

"Rise, son."

Kade searched his father's face quickly before rising to his feet. He held out his hand.

"I'm glad you've found your mate, Father. Truly."

Devlin reached out and they clasped hands. Like they were sealing the deal on a car sale. It was as bad as being traded by my father all over again. Except this time...this time my heart didn't know what to feel.

Empty. I felt empty.

Without another word, without even so much as a glance at me, Kade turned on his heel and walked away. Within moments, he'd vanished from sight, no doubt well on his way back to his home.

Devlin pulled off his shirt and I gasped, backing up a pace.

Mate, my wolf all but purred in approval, but my heart hammered and I shook my head wordlessly. I didn't want to consummate our mate bond. Not out here in these woods. Not now. Not ever. Not with him.

He thrust the shirt in my direction, barely even looking at me.

"Put this on."

I stared at it, making no move to take it from him. I could smell his scent saturating the fabric, and there was no way I wanted that wrapped around me. It was one step away from pissing on me to mark me as his property.

"Take it," he grunted. "It won't bite."

Right. Unlike him. I kept my hands wrapped around myself.

"Unless you'd rather I led you back through the whole of town naked," he said, glancing at the tattered remains of my clothing scattered around the floor. "I would prefer the whole pack did not see my mate exposed, but perhaps you feel differently?"

He raised an eyebrow and I glanced down at my very naked body and scowled, then snatched the shirt from him and tugged it over my head. Enough people had seen me naked for one day. Devlin gave me a curt nod.

"You don't have to do this," I said. "You can still let me leave. I know you don't want me."

"Do not presume to tell me what I do and do not want."

His eyes roved over my barely covered body in a way that sent shivers along my spine and left my mouth dry and other parts wet.

Devlin's nostrils flared and he closed the gap between us. My body molded itself against his and I could feel his solid chest and the hardness between his legs.

"I smell you, little wolf."

I smelled him, too. His heady, exotic, masculine scent crowded my nostrils and made my legs weak.

His hands found my shoulders...and moved me firmly back a step. I shook my head, gasping in a breath of clean air. I narrowed my eyes.

"So you don't want me, then."

"My wolf wants yours," he said, staring at the space over my shoulder. "It's enough."

"Not for me, it's not."

He frowned, like my opinion on the matter hadn't even occurred to him.

I planted one hand on my hip. "I'm not coming back with you."

"I don't recall offering you a choice. You are a member of the Broken Ridge pack. My word is your law, and you *will* obey."

Alpha power laced his every word and I battled the instinctive compulsion to drop into a crouch and bow my head, because I was not some sycophantic pack member who worshiped the ground this asshole walked on.

Abruptly, I found myself in a crouch. I narrowed my eyes at him—or I tried, but I didn't seem able to raise my eyes higher than his waistline, and I wasn't quite sure if it was some sort of alpha compulsion that drew my eye to that specific area, or my own desires. I flushed red, my embarrassment burning in my cheeks. Don't think about his cock. Do *not* think about his cock.

Mate is well endowed.

Shit. I flushed even brighter.

"You will obey," Devlin repeated. He strode past me and I regained control over my legs. As I pushed myself from the ground, still wearing his shirt and wrapped in his scent, he paused and glanced back over his shoulder.

"Follow."

I opened my mouth to ask why the hell he thought I would do that, and the sheer smoldering intensity in his eyes set a new fire in my stomach, robbing me of my voice. When he spoke, his voice was low and husky.

"Or do I need to throw you over my shoulder and carry you back?"

I shook my head mutely.

"Then follow."

He pivoted his head forward and started walking. I stared after his back for a long moment, then twisted round to look at the woods—and the road to freedom—over my shoulder.

"I'm faster than you, little wolf," he said, without breaking his stride or looking back at me. "I'd catch you before you made it five steps."

Dammit. I exhaled heavily, and stalked along behind him. I wasn't escaping tonight.

CHAPTER TWENTY-EIGHT

The moon was high in the sky by the time we made it back to Devlin's mansion: it had to be getting on for midnight. In a handful of hours, he would make his announcement to the pack about whether I would be permitted to remain amongst them, or be traded off to another pack. I snorted to myself. I guess that decision had been well and truly made.

If Devlin heard my snort, he made no comment on it. He hadn't said a single word to me the entire walk back here. He hadn't even checked over his shoulder to make sure I was following. But he knew. The bastard knew.

Or maybe it just didn't occur to him that I might disobey his command. Perhaps he was just so arrogant and self-assured that he assumed the moment a command left his lips, it would be followed by all who heard it. And if that was the case, then escaping here was going to be easier than I thought, because I would just bide my time for a few weeks, and he'd never see it coming.

The gates swung inward at our approach, and it wasn't until I stepped through that I saw the two men who had opened them. They shut the gates behind us and resumed their guard posts. Okay, so that made it trickier—the pair of them looked a whole lot more trained and motivated than Dean and Ryder. No matter. I *would* find a way. But now wasn't the time to think about it. I kept my eyes low and tried to appear meek. I could scope the place out after the sun rose.

If the guards were surprised to see Devlin returning shirtless, with those frankly ridiculous abs on display, and with some female following behind him wearing *just* a shirt, they didn't show it. Rather, they bowed their heads in a display of respect that Devlin returned with a curt nod, and looked completely at ease with the whole situation. Maybe Devlin

125

brought half-naked women back to his mansion every day of the week. Maybe he'd get bored of me soon and let me leave.

I dismissed the thought as soon as it passed through my head. Whether Devlin tired of me or not, he'd never let me go. Not willingly. A man didn't get to own a house like this, and become alpha of a pack like Broken Ridge, without jealously guarding everything he considered to be his. A shiver worked its way up my spine. That included me now—and some part of me wasn't unhappy about it.

Fortunately, the rest of me hadn't taken leave of its senses yet. Mate bond or no, this was the man who had rejected me, and made it clear the only reason he wanted me was because he thought it was his right.

He opened the door, and turned to me for the first time since we left the woods. He gestured me inside and I crossed the threshold, wrapping my arms around me as I looked about. The floor beneath my bare feet was laminate and had been polished until it gleamed. The walls were covered in dark wood paneling that looked expensive, and the ceiling was so high above my head I was pretty sure I couldn't have touched it even if I jumped. Several oil paintings adorned the walls, mostly of hunting wolves, and a thick rug ran the length of the entrance hall. I wanted to find the whole thing ostentatious, but it all fit together perfectly. The effect was tasteful. Stunning, even. And it irked me.

The heavy door clicked shut behind me, and I listened for the sound of a key turning in the lock, but none came. Instead, there was an odd, electronic whirring. I spun round, glaring at the door suspiciously, and saw the keypad beside it.

"For security," Devlin said simply, following the direction of my gaze.

There would be no stealing a key from his pocket to bust out, that much was clear. I shrugged like it was no big deal, and turned my scowl to Devlin.

"Are you sure you wouldn't just rather chain me to the bed?" I demanded.

"Don't tempt me, little wolf," he said, and my heart fluttered in my throat. He closed the gap between us, so that I had to tilt my head back to look at him, and I could feel the heat pouring off his body. "You will find that this house is harder to escape from than my son's. And that I am less forgiving if you try."

He turned on his heel and strode away, reaching the door at the far end of the entrance hall before he called out;

"Follow."

I was seriously going to have to set this asshole straight about the fact I wasn't his pet dog before long.

"You can't just keep ordering me around," I said, hurrying after him.

"And yet, I am."

He led us through yet another door, and this one led to a lounge of some kind, with more of the same wooden paneling decorating the walls, though a large television was set into one wall, and several couches lined the rest of the room.

He strode over to an oak cabinet and opened it, taking out a glass and a heavy crystal decanter, filled with a dark amber liquid. As he plucked the stopper out, the scent of alcohol hit my nostrils. He sloshed some of the liquid into his glass, then stoppered the decanter and closed up the cabinet, ignoring me completely, which rubbed me wrong for some reason I couldn't put my finger on.

"You've made yourself a bad deal," I told his back. "I can't cook, I'm a terrible cleaner, and I couldn't sew if my life depended on it."

"Fortunately for you, it does not." He strode over to one of the couches and settled himself on it, leaning back and taking a sip of his drink. "Nor do I need a cook, or a cleaner." He lowered the glass, and his voice dropped an octave. "Though if I did, I assure you, little wolf, you would learn. And fast."

I folded my arms over my chest. "Fine. So what *do* you want from me, then?"

"Right now, I'd settle for your silence."

Wait. Did he just tell me to shut up? Asshole. His eyes roved over my legs, and I realized my crossed arms had hiked the shirt halfway up my thighs. I quickly dropped them back to my sides, and tugged the shirt down.

"If you don't want to hear from me, you should just let me leave town. Because I talk. A lot."

"Not going to happen."

I huffed, even though I'd already known what his answer would be.

"Fine. Then can I at least go back to Kade's house and get my stuff?"

"No."

"What do you mean, no?" I glared at him. "I'm not going to spend the rest of my life wearing your shirt."

"You are my mate. I will provide you with whatever you need."

"Well, what I need is my stuff."

"Possessions are replaceable."

I wondered if he'd still think that if I started shredding his oil paintings and smashing up his glassware. I thought about asking him, but instead I wrapped my arms around myself again. I was too tired to argue, and my heart was a heavy lump in my chest.

"They're my only reminders of home," I whispered.

His posture lost some of its rigidity and the stern lines set into his forehead softened.

"This will become a home to you, in time," he promised. "But I will send someone to gather your belongings in the morning."

"I'd rather go myself."

At once, his face closed off again. "That's not on the table. You will not leave these walls."

"So I'm your prisoner?" I snapped, my ire building again.

"You're my mate."

"I don't think that means what you think it means. Your wolf wants my wolf?" My voice tightened with mockery as I spat the words at him. "That's bullshit, and you know it."

"Oh?" He raised an eyebrow, setting his glass on a small wooden table beside his couch, and rose to his feet in an action that was all languid muscle and barely restrained power. "And your wolf does not desire mine?"

My wolf threw her head back and howled deep inside me, clawing her way to the surface. I gritted my teeth and shoved her back down. She'd ruined enough clothes for one day.

"I'm more than just a wolf."

His eyes ran over my body again, pausing at all my curves.

"Don't I know it," he said, but his deep rumble seemed more resigned than anything else. "Come. I'll show you where you can sleep tonight."

There he went again, ordering me to follow him around like a puppy dog. He paused in the doorway, turning back to me when he realized I wasn't following this time.

"You're trying my patience."

"And you're trying mine," I said. "I'm not your damned pet!"

He exhaled heavily, and a flicker of irritation shadowed his face.

"You're not my pet. You're not my prisoner. You're my mate, and a giant pain in the ass beside."

I folded my arms over my chest, remembered the effect that had on the shirt, and dropped them to my sides again, pouting the whole while.

"If I'm such a pain, why do you even care about 'showing me where I can sleep'?"

"I'm hoping you'll be less of a brat when you're not tired."

My mouth popped open in shock.

"You can't—"

"I can, and I did. Now move your ass before I throw you over my shoulder and carry you upstairs, and trust me, you're not going to like where that ends."

I snapped my mouth shut, and followed him from the room, muttering under my breath.

"Fucking caveman."

CHAPTER TWENTY-NINE

When the sun rose, it found me in an elegantly decorated room, with walls that were painted a soft shade of beige, and a carpet so plush my feet would have sunk an inch if I'd cared to stand on it.

I didn't. I was sprawled in a double bed, on the softest mattress I'd ever slept on, with a warm duvet wrapped around me, and a plush pillow under my head. It was sheer luxury. I suspected that was the reason that, despite everything, I'd managed to get a few hours' sleep last night. *After* trying the window and discovering it was locked. I was pretty sure it was made of some sort of hammerglass, too. Smashing it was out—which wouldn't stop me trying as soon as Devlin made himself scarce.

I stretched and shoved the duvet aside, reluctantly prying myself from the luxurious mattress. I scanned the room and groaned as I laid eyes on the alpha's shirt, lying where I'd discarded it over the back of a chair. With poor grace, I snatched it up and tugged it on. No way was I walking around that bastard's house naked.

I ran my fingers quickly through my hair, combing out the worst of the tangles as I headed for the door. I sucked in a deep breath, grabbed the handle, and yanked it. And yanked it. Then I gave it a rattle. It didn't budge. Shit. The bastard had locked me in!

"Hey!" I shouted, lifting my hand and hammering on the door. "Hey, Devlin!"

What the hell was he playing at? He couldn't go round locking people in their rooms. What if I needed to pee? Oh, God. I pounded the door harder.

"Let me out! Devlin!"

I drew my hand back to slam it against the door again, but before I could make contact, the door swung open. A face I didn't recognize stood there, staring in at me. I quickly took a step back.

"Uh, who are you?"

"Beta Caleb," the man said. "Alpha Devlin has several matters to attend to this morning. Is there something you need?"

Yeah, how about my freedom? But instead, I nodded and said, "A shower. And some clothes."

"This way, then. Alpha Devlin has sent someone to retrieve your belongings."

I followed him along a hallway carpeted with a plush burgundy carpet that probably cost more than my father's house, and if Beta Caleb cared that I was traipsing through it with feet still grubby from my near-naked jaunt home from the woods last night, he kept his opinion to himself.

I had about a billion questions I wanted to pepper him with, but since I was still in my near-naked, grubby state, wearing just his alpha's shirt, I kept them to myself, and tried to battle the urge to continuously tug the shirt down to cover more of my thigh as I walked.

He didn't turn round, sparing the worst of my blushes, and we made the trip in silence.

"Just through here," he said, coming to a stop outside a solid oak door that looked like every other solid oak door we'd passed on this floor. "Alpha Devlin says you may join him in the dining hall when you're done here."

"Oh, may I?" I arched a brow and shook my head, then pulled open the door without waiting for the beta to respond. I may join him, my ass. What the hell made that chauvinist pig think I wanted to spend a single minute with him?

He's our mate.

Don't you start that crap, too, wolf. Like being my mate was enough to excuse his whole multitude of sins, of which locking me up here like a prisoner was certainly not the least.

I looked around the room and a low whistle slipped from my lips. Like the rest of the house, the whole room screamed luxury. I trailed my fingers along a gleaming rail, loaded with plush white towels that looked good enough to curl up in—if my entire body hadn't been dirt-encrusted from last night. My eyes came to rest on the biggest bathtub I'd ever seen, and all thoughts of showering immediately fled, because there was nothing on this earth that was going to keep me from having a nice, long soak while I tried to organize my thoughts. After the events of the last twenty-four hours, I was pretty sure I'd earned it.

I wasn't sure how much later it was when I finally climbed out of the bath and wrapped myself in one of the plush towels, and frankly, I didn't care. Devlin was waiting for me downstairs? Fine. Let him wait. He'd made it clear enough last night that he didn't want anything to do with me, and the feeling was more than mutual. I didn't want a single thing to do with him, or his broad shoulders, or the solid muscle of his abs, or—

I shook my head and cleared the all-too-alluring image. Just because he was hot, didn't mean I was going to jump him the moment I set eyes on him. My wolf huffed, and I ignored her. It seemed like we'd done nothing but bicker since we'd come to this place. I wished she could just see sense over this. No matter what the fates said, there was no way in this universe we could possibly be meant for each other. And there was no way I was about to let my overactive libido make my decisions for me.

When I shoved my head out of the bathroom door, I was relieved to find a familiar bag sitting just outside. I dragged it inside and rooted through, turning up my toothbrush, hairdryer, and some clean clothes. Good. I couldn't get rid of that awful shirt soon enough. I did *not* need that man's scent all over my skin.

I took my time getting dried and dressed, and wondered whether it would irritate him if I headed back to the room I'd slept in last night for some one to one time with a decent book—because I would feel a *lot* better knowing I wasn't the only one getting pissed off. In the end, though, two things made my decision for me: I wasn't certain I could find my way back to that room, and my stomach was starting to rumble.

Dammit. No wonder he'd said the dining hall. He was a shifter, he knew I'd be hungry after last night.

On the other hand, he was in the dining hall…and I was pretty sure with a bit of hunting around, I could find the kitchen. And I could make a halfway decent breakfast, then slink back upstairs without so much as laying eyes on him.

Pleased with my plan, I spent the next few minutes wandering around until I found a staircase, which I was pretty sure was the same one we'd come up last night—I recognized the painting of a gray wolf under a full moon hanging on the wall there. I wondered if it was Devlin in his younger days—he seemed the sort to have his own portrait on the wall—and found myself scrutinizing it for telltale signs before I remembered I didn't care, and hurried down the staircase.

I padded barefoot along the wooden floors, pausing to open each closed door a crack and check inside in the hopes of stumbling across what I was looking for. This place was massive, and the first five doors I opened led to other random rooms. My route carried me past the entrance hall, and after a quick glance around to check I was alone, I crossed to the front door and rattled the handle, but it didn't open. No surprise.

It had a keypad next to it, and I stared at it for a long moment. There was some sort of scanner next to the keypad, and I had a horrible feeling it was a fingerprint scanner. Devlin really took security to the next level. Paranoid, much?

I peered at the pad, thinking about his beta moving around the house, and his eldest son who I'd seen on the day I arrived. If other people had access to the house, then maybe the scanner and the keypad were an either/or option? Nothing to lose by trying, right?

I hovered my finger over the pad, wondering which numbers to attempt first. The voice came from behind me.

"Ah, Jessica. Why am I not surprised to find you here?"

CHAPTER THIRTY

"Alpha Devlin!" I jumped back from the keypad like it had burned me. "I was just—"

"Trying to escape?" He raised a brow, and I opened my mouth to deny it, because I hadn't been, not really, but he raised a hand to cut me off. "I would expect nothing less."

"Uh…" I wasn't quite sure what to say to that.

"You're in a strange place, with a man you don't know. A man who recently rejected you."

Well, yeah, there was that. My cheeks burned bright. The rejection still stung, because he'd made it clear enough last night that he didn't have an interest in me, and the only reason he'd dragged me back here was because I was his mate and he didn't like the idea of anyone else having me.

"It's… Well, it's complicated." He exhaled heavily. "Come. Let's get some breakfast."

My stomach loudly rumbled its approval of that particular plan, and since my original plan of grabbing some food and vanishing off to eat it in a quiet corner without attracting Devlin's notice was clearly out the window now, I was out of options. But I didn't feel like making small talk over breakfast. I folded my arms across my chest.

"I'm not hungry."

"I would prefer you do not lie to me."

"And I'd prefer not to be your prisoner, so I guess we're both screwed."

His face hardened.

"Eat. Don't eat. It doesn't matter to me. Don't try to leave again."

And with that, he turned and stalked away. I stared after his back for a long moment until my wolf stirred inside me.

Hungry.

Yeah, yeah, I know. We burned a lot of calories fighting ourselves last night. We probably should avoid doing that again.

"He's not such a bad guy, you know. Once you get to know him."

I yelped and spun around to find Caleb watching me. How the hell did he creep around so quietly? Or maybe Devlin just distracted me so much that I didn't notice anything else when he was around. I glared at the beta.

"Yeah, well, you would say that, wouldn't you? He's your alpha."

"He's yours, too."

"Not yet," I hedged. "He hasn't formally accepted me into the pack."

Caleb snorted. "Ah, yes, of course. I'm sure he'll reject his mate from the pack."

The word 'reject' burned through my mind, bouncing around inside my skull and sending spikes of pain through my chest. Because he *had* rejected me, and no amount of offering to take me to breakfast was going to change that.

I shrugged, and picked at non-existent dirt under my fingernails.

"He doesn't want me for a mate," I said, staring at my hands. "He doesn't want me here at all."

"Well, that's clearly not true, is it? Because otherwise he wouldn't have brought you here."

"Yeah, right." I snorted. "He just doesn't want to share his toys with anyone else."

I caught Caleb's frown from the corner of my eye, and lifted my head fully to look at him.

"You might want to hold off on the judgement," Caleb said. "You don't know him—you've only just met him."

"Exactly. I'm nothing to him. And here I am, locked up inside his ridiculously stylish house."

Because, even in my ire, I couldn't bring myself to insult the house. Even the light fittings were tasteful.

Caleb snorted with laughter, and then his face grew serious.

"You're not nothing to him."

"I know," I said, before he could go any further. "I'm the pain in the ass mate he didn't want. Well, you know what? The feeling's mutual. I didn't ask to come here, and I didn't ask to be Devlin's mate. I didn't ask to be paired off with Kade, either, but it seems like no-one gives a shit what I want—so why should I care what they want?"

"Good questions. But maybe you're asking the wrong person." He glanced meaningfully in the direction Devlin had gone, and I shook my head.

"You've got to be kidding me. He is the *last* person on this earth I want to speak to."

"Well, I hate to be the bearer of bad news, but you're going to be here for a very long time. You're going to have to speak to him sooner or later."

Not if I escape, I thought to myself, and ignored the rumble of discontent from my wolf.

"And I imagine he'll want you by his side when he makes his announcement to the pack this evening."

"Again with the other people wanting," I muttered.

"Yes," Caleb said. "It's almost like a pack revolves around cooperation…"

"Hilarious."

"There's one thing I don't understand," the beta said, leaning back against the wall and running his eyes over me. "You're young, you're clearly fiery, probably ambitious…why *wouldn't* you want to be mated to the alpha of a powerful pack—even if he is a few years older than you?"

A few years. Right. Try a few decades. But that wasn't the issue here. Not his age, and sure as hell not his body, which for some damned reason I couldn't stop thinking about.

"There's a whole lot more than one thing you don't understand," I said, dodging his question—because there was no way I could answer that. Not if I wanted to keep breathing past the end of the day.

"I dare say that's true," he agreed, cocking his head to one side. Then, he pushed himself off the wall. "I've got some pack business to take care of for Devlin. He asked me to clear his schedule because he wanted to spend some time with you today—not that you want to hear that, right? It probably doesn't fit with your image of him as the big bad wolf."

I looked at him quickly and then away again. Okay, so that didn't sound like something a *total* dick would do, but still...

"You want me to show you where the kitchen is before I leave?" he offered.

I shook my head. "Thanks. I'm sure I'll manage."

"I'm sure you will," he said with a shake of his head. "But just in case you don't feel like blundering around helplessly, you might want to take a right at the end of that corridor, and then the second door on the left."

Seriously. What sort of freaking house was so big you needed actual, bona fide directions to the kitchen?

"Uh...thanks."

"Any time. And just talk to him, okay?"

He turned and left before I could tell him I had zero intentions of doing that. I might be stuck here as Devlin's new pet, but that didn't mean I had to make things easy for him.

War with outsiders. Not with mate.

I rolled my eyes.

"He *is* the outsider, stupid," I muttered to my wolf as I started along the corridor.

He is mate.

Yeah, yeah, I agreed, too exhausted to keep arguing with her. Besides, it was true—he was our mate. And a week ago, when I first laid eyes on him, that had seemed like the most magical thing in the world. Until reality kicked in. Because an omega *couldn't* be an alpha's mate. I was on borrowed time. What sort of dumb universe would match us up together, anyway? Hell, even if I wasn't an omega, I'd still hate the guy. He was arrogant, and conceited, and chauvinistic, and so fucking hot. I groaned and rolled my head back. Being hot was not a personality trait, and the fact was, we were a total clash.

And yet, when we'd kissed, our bodies had felt so compatible.

Dammit, Jess, get it together. There's more to life than sex. Not that I'd know, obviously, what with the whole not-sleeping-with-my-packmates thing I'd had going on back in Winter Moon—which just made it all the more ridiculous that I couldn't think of anything else.

No matter. I just needed to keep reminding myself what an utter arsehole he was until my body got over its infatuation. Easy.

...And maybe, just maybe, Caleb had been right. I should get to know him before I cast judgement. And *then* I could condemn him for being a total prick. And I might as well not be starving when that happened.

I turned right at the end of the corridor, and carried on until I reached the second door on the left.

When I swung the kitchen door open, I wasn't completely surprised to find Devlin inside, seated at the table.

I sucked in a deep breath, and nodded.

"Okay. Let's talk."

CHAPTER THIRTY-ONE

"I'm glad to see you've given up trying to escape."

"If you think I've given up, then you don't know me." Shit, did I just say that? To the freaking alpha? Shit.

Devlin's face darkened, and tension ran along his shoulders. I flashed back to Kade's kitchen, where I'd been bent over the table and had a belt taken to my ass while Devlin watched.

"Oh, I intend to get to know you very well, Jessica. Like it or not, you're going to be here for a very long time."

"Yeah, yeah," I said, pulling open the fridge door and rooting around inside. "Your wingman already gave me that speech."

"Sit."

"Can I at least get some food before you begin the lecture?"

"Sit," he repeated.

Sighing, I closed the fridge door and pulled out a chair, slumping into it with poor grace. Devlin rose to his feet and opened the fridge. My jaw popped open. Was the bastard seriously going to make me watch him stuffing his face while he lectured me? Because my wolf had already taken a snap at him once over food, and I was starting to think she was onto something.

"How do you like your eggs?" he said.

"I...what?" All I could think was that ridiculous joke, *'How do you like your eggs in the morning? 'Fertilized.'* My face burned hot and I felt the crimson flush across my cheeks.

"Eggs. Fried, scrambled, poached...?"

"You're...you're cooking for me?"

"You made it pretty clear last night that you can't cook, and I prefer my kitchen remain unscathed." He shot me a look of amusement, but I couldn't quite decide if it was at my expense. This was a bad idea. I opened my mouth, and he cut me off with a raised eyebrow.

"Don't bother telling me you're not hungry again."

"Starving," I said, as he cracked a few eggs into a pan—but I'd be lying if I said it was the food that had me practically salivating. He moved around the kitchen with an animalistic grace, or maybe prowled would have been a better word…the sheer intensity of every movement sent shivers down my spine, until I had to wrench my eyes away and force them to stare at the tabletop instead.

"So," Devlin said, using a spatula to flick some hot oil over the eggs, "what did you use to do for fun, before you came here?"

"Before you bought me, you mean?" I said, frustration lacing each word.

"Marriage bonds have been used to strengthen pack alliances for hundreds of years," he said, and I didn't think I was imagining the irritation in his tone. This was a sore subject for him? Good. It was for me, too.

"Well, maybe shifters need to move with the times," I countered.

"Maybe your father should have raised you to have more respect."

"If you'd actually met me before you bought me for your son, maybe you'd have known the first thing about me. Don't you think I had the right to have some sort of say in the man I spent my life with?"

I was on my feet, my hands bunched into fists at my sides, and I was trembling head to toe. Devlin's jaw clenched as he tossed the spatula on the worktop and turned to me.

"You've clearly been left to run feral for the last eighteen years," he said, pinning me in place with his glare. "That changes, right now. Like it or not, you are my mate—"

"I'd have to go with not," I muttered under my breath.

"—and you are honor bound by the alliance between our packs to stay in this territory. But since honor seems to be a foreign concept to you, let me warn you: you'll find this house much harder to break out of than my son's, and you'll find me far less forgiving if you attempt it."

"You can't keep me prisoner here!" I snapped, meeting his glare with my own.

"I can do what the hell I like," he snapped back, stalking towards me. "I am the alpha of this pack."

He glared down at me. I glared up at him. I saw the resolve firm in his eyes and my breath caught in my throat, and then his lips were crushing mine, hot and firm. His tongue probed me, and my lips parted for him, welcoming him inside. I moaned into his mouth and his hand slid behind my back, pulling me close to his hard body. My arms wrapped round his taut torso and my hands bunched in the shirt on his back, holding him back, holding him close, I couldn't tell the difference anymore. Holding me in one piece as his slick tongue ruined me from the inside until he was all I could think about, until I was ready to rip off his clothes and explore every inch of his body on the kitchen table.

Then I came to my senses.

I released his shirt and slammed my hands into his chest, shoving him away from me. The kiss broke and he stared at me. Shock replaced the hunger on his face, and I spoke before he could.

"No." I wheeled away, shaking my head, then pivoted back to him. "No, you don't get to do that. You don't get to tell me I'm not good enough for you, and then kiss me like that."

"Jessica…"

"Jess!" I all but shouted. "It's Jess. Can't you at least get that right?"

"Jess. It's complicated."

143

"No, it's not. It's about as fucking simple as it gets, Devlin. You don't think I'm good enough for you, and I think you're an asshole. This," I swiped my hands through the air, "is never going to work."

He folded his arms over his chest and stared at me impassively.

"Are you done with your tantrum?"

"My tantrum? Are you kidding me? Don't you think I have the right to be just a little pissed off right now?"

"I think," he said calmly, "that you're so caught up in what you think you're entitled to that you can't see what's in front of your fucking eyes. You're alive right now *because* you're my mate. And if I didn't want you, I'd have done the right thing and killed you the night of the hunt."

I blinked at him, not quite sure what to make of that.

"Yeah, well," I said, my voice a little husky despite my best intentions, "we don't always get what we want."

He closed the gap between us again, within touching distance but not touching.

"And what is it you want, Jessica?" he said, his voice a rough purr that made my breathing hitch and sent heat swimming between my legs—and dammit, I refused to feel that way about the man who had rejected me, and then locked me away inside his stupid mansion. And no amount of abs and animal presence was going to change that.

I stepped back, and folded my arms over my chest.

"My freedom."

He shook his head.

"You don't want that."

"How the hell would you know? You've barely had a single conversation with me."

"I know what trying to walk away from our mate bond did to my wolf. You don't want that."

My heart thudded painfully, and my wolf squirmed inside me. She agreed with him—no surprise. But I was in no mood for this sympathy for the devil crap.

"But you did walk away. You walked away, and you left me there with a man who wasn't my mate, and you let me think it was forever."

"What's done is done."

Not so much as an apology. I couldn't say I was surprised. He'd probably never apologized a single time in his life.

"You know what's done, Devlin?" I demanded. "Us. We're done. You can keep me here, and there's not a damned thing I can do about it. But I will never like you. I will never touch you. And you better make sure you lock your door at night, because I will end this the first chance I get."

CHAPTER THIRTY-TWO

He turned round calmly and pulled the pan of eggs off the heat. I'd just threatened to kill him—probably not my smartest move ever—and he was more concerned about burning the damned eggs.

"Didn't you hear me?" I demanded.

"I heard you," he said, pulling a plate from the cupboard and setting it on the side.

"Don't you care?"

"You're not the first person to threaten to kill me." He eased the spatula under an egg and slid it onto the plate. "You probably won't be the last, either."

"You're not even going to punish me?" I froze. That was a dumb thing to say.

"Do you want me to?"

He set the plate on the table, piled high with half a dozen eggs, and turned his attention to me. I blushed.

"No. Obviously."

"It's not looking so obvious from where I'm standing."

He ran his gaze over me, his eyes heavy with lust, and I felt the pull to move closer to him. I shook it off.

"Maybe you'd be able to see more clearly if you pulled your head out of your own ass for five minutes."

"Are you sure you want to talk about punishments and asses in the same breath, little wolf?" His eyes exuded menace, and it was hot as hell. I swallowed.

"Um…no?"

I ducked my head, but not before I caught his smirk. He moved in close…then reached out behind me and pulled out my chair.

"Well, if I'm not going to spank that ass, you should probably sit on it."

A blink later, I was in the chair, with no clue whether he'd put me there or I'd gone of my own volition. I blinked again. I seemed completely incapable of coherent thought around this man...and that was going to be a problem.

He moved away and returned a moment later with a couple of slices of toast, which he set beside the eggs. I was about to ask him how hungry he thought I really was, when my stomach rumbled and answered that question for me.

I picked up the cutlery and made a start on the eggs, pausing only long enough for him to add some bacon to my meal. The food was good. Really good.

"You're better than Kade," I conceded, with something akin to relief. At least death by food poisoning wasn't an imminent threat anymore.

"In every way imaginable," he rumbled in response.

Yeah, I wasn't about to even try to unpack *that*, so I swiped some bacon through an egg yolk, and devoured it.

"Why are you such a good cook?"

He quirked an eyebrow. "Why shouldn't I be?"

"Gee, I don't know, maybe because you're an alpha and have an entire pack running around after you?"

He pulled out a chair on the opposite side of the table and sat.

"This house is big, but not quite big enough for the entire pack to run around inside tending my whims."

My lips twitched in amusement before I remembered I hated him, and flattened them into a scowl.

"My first mate taught me," he said more seriously, and I froze, my fork halfway to my mouth.

"Your first mate?"

147

"You didn't think Kade and Jackson were born out of thin air?"

Truth be told, I hadn't really thought about it at all.

"What happened to her?" I asked.

Devlin rose to his feet. "You should finish eating. I'll be presenting you to the pack shortly."

He walked from the room, and I watched him go, then set my fork back on the edge of my plate, still laden with food. His first mate? Seemed like he really cared about her. Maybe he wasn't a total asshole after all. He was just in love with another woman.

Great. Just my luck.

My appetite long gone, I scraped my plate and washed it up along with the pans, because apparently, though Devlin could cook, he hadn't gotten the hang of cleaning up afterwards. I wasn't quite sure why it bothered me that he'd had another mate before me—it was obvious Kade and Jackson had come from somewhere, and even if he didn't have kids, Devlin had been around a lot longer than me. It wasn't like I expected him to have been celibate his whole life.

And it wasn't like I had any feelings for him other than abject hatred—and maybe a slight appreciation of his culinary skill—so who cared if he was in love with some woman from his past? Hell, she could stroll right back in here and take him, for all I cared. She'd be doing me a favor.

Maybe she felt the same way. Maybe that's why she wasn't here, and I was.

Her loss. He's our mate.

Longing pulsed through me, for his scent, his voice, his hard…chest. Longing that I was pretty sure came from my wolf. She had it bad for him. I refused to entertain the idea that I might feel the same way. I'd had, like, four conversations with him, and he'd spent one of those rejecting me, and another telling me to shut up. And like I'd said to Kade, I didn't make friends with dominant assholes.

Kade. A pang of sadness shot through me.

Not our mate.

No, he wasn't our mate, and he hadn't hesitated to step aside for Devlin. And he'd been about to whoop my ass. So screw him.

Only...there'd been moments when what we had, it had felt like the beginnings of something. The beginnings of a friendship. A partnership. And sure, it rankled that he hadn't even tried to argue with Devlin, but what choice did he have, really? The alpha commands, and the pack obeys.

But not me. I had no intention of obeying Devlin. He wanted to parade me around like a good little pet, a trophy mate? He was going to be in for a shock.

...Which would be great, if I had even the first idea how I was going to do that.

I slipped out of the kitchen, and started wandering around the house. I knew the front door was out, but this place was vast. He couldn't have secured every window. I just needed to find one weak spot, and then come back tonight.

My wolf slammed into me so hard from the inside that I staggered. I threw one hand up and caught myself against the wall. She kept pushing and I gritted my teeth, trying to force her back. Not this again. We were going to run out of clothes if she kept pulling this stunt.

Not. Leaving. Mate.

Tremors wracked my body as she fought against my tenuous control.

"Jessica!"

My head whipped round to find Devlin hurrying towards me, his brow knitted with what I would have sworn was concern, if I thought he

149

was capable of such a thing. I sucked in a breath. I so did not need him to see me like this.

"Are you okay?" He placed one hand on my shoulder and searched my face. At his touch, my wolf immediately settled, almost purring with contentment. I straightened, shrugging him off.

"I'm fine," I said irritably, sweeping my hair out of my face. I needed to come to some sort of arrangement with my wolf, because that could not keep happening. And I didn't like that the only thing that calmed her was Devlin's touch, because I would be quite happy if he never touched me again.

Devlin's face hardened and his hand dropped back to his side.

"Good," he said gruffly. "Then get yourself together. We're leaving."

"Already?"

"Is that a problem?" he challenged me.

I shook my head. I could carry on searching the place later. Devlin shadowed me as I backtracked my way to the entrance hall.

"Wait," I said, stopping just before we reached it. "There is one problem."

"Oh?"

"My shoes, last night. That was the only pair I had."

And thanks to my wolf, they were in tatters out in the woods. Devlin worked his jaw—I guess I was being a pain in his ass again—and then he reached past me and shoved the door open to the entrance hall.

"That's not a problem."

I cocked a hip and planted my hand on it. "I'm pretty sure it is, unless you want the whole pack to see me traipsing around barefoot."

Though, given that he'd threatened to make me walk through the whole town naked last night, maybe that wasn't such an issue for him as I thought.

He exhaled heavily—I was definitely trying his patience—then planted his hands on my shoulders, and, before I could tell him to get off me, spun me around and steered me into the entrance hall.

I blinked.

"Oh."

"You're welcome."

There were half a dozen pairs of shoes, including four different types of sneaker, all similar to the ones I'd shredded last night.

"Which ones are mine?" I asked.

"All of them. I had Caleb pick them up this morning."

"All of them?" I took a step forward, frowning, and getting a better look at the sneakers. Although they were similar to mine, there was one major difference. These were all brand new, with expensive labels. I picked a pair out and turned them over in my hands.

"Figures the girl likes shoes," he murmured behind me, and I could hear the amusement in his voice.

"Yeah. I'll be sure to thank *Caleb* next time I see him," I said. I saw the hurt flash over his face so quickly it was gone in a heartbeat, and felt the answering guilt echo in my own chest. Shit. That was a low blow. He'd been trying to do something nice, and I was grateful, really. It was just, well, I wasn't all that used to people doing nice things for me. I didn't really know how to react.

I opened my mouth to apologize, but Devlin stalked past me, his face hard, and yanked open the front door.

"Let's go."

He held it open for me while I tugged the sneakers on, then followed me out as I left.

An awkward silence fell over us as we walked, me feeling like a total bitch and not sure how to make it up, and him trying hard not to rip my head from my shoulders, if the look on his face was anything to go by.

I still hadn't found a way to dispel it by the time we reached the center of the town—a paved plaza set round a large water fountain with a wolf statue in its middle.

At least one good thing could come of today, I mused as the pack started to gather, each member taking a long moment to stare at me. After Devlin formally welcomed me to the pack and told them all I was his mate, they would finally stop staring at me with suspicion and watching my every move. After all, who would expect an alpha's mate to try to run? And as soon as they stopped watching, that was exactly what I'd do.

Devlin cleared his throat, and an instant silence fell over the pack. I looked out at the sea of faces from Devlin's side, watching as they all bowed their heads to him. I scanned the gathered masses. No, wait, not all of them had their heads bowed. One person didn't. Kade. And he looked pissed as all hell.

Devlin glanced his way, and Kade quickly dipped his chin, the picture of respect. But I knew what I'd seen.

"Thank you for joining me today," Devlin said, and his baritone voice carried easily through the absolute silence. The pack raised their heads and fixed their eyes on the alpha, enraptured by his every word.

"I would like to formally introduce you to Jessica Whitlock, formerly of the Winter Moon pack. She is on probation within our pack." He paused, and locked eyes with me. "Should any of you see her attempting to leave, you are ordered to apprehend her, and return her to me for judgement."

Fuck.

CHAPTER THIRTY-THREE

Devlin left me to my own devices when we got back to his house, for which I was grateful. I holed up in my room, the same one I'd spent last night in, and made no effort to leave as afternoon became evening, and evening became night.

I moped and seethed and moped again, pacing the small, barren room. I didn't know what Devlin had done with the rest of my stuff when Caleb had brought it back this morning, but it hadn't made it up here, and I wasn't about to ask.

Probation. What the hell did that even mean? We both knew he wasn't going to throw me out. He'd never make it that easy for me. No, this was some scheme to make sure the whole pack watched me everywhere I went. Not that I was even allowed outside of the house, anyway. But then, that wasn't what he'd meant, and that wasn't why he'd given the order. I suppose I should have been flattered that he thought I would somehow overcome the high-tech security and the sealed hammerglass. Instead, I was pissed that he'd managed to turn the entire pack into prison guards. Getting out of the house wasn't going to be enough.

The moon was high in the sky and the clock on the wall told me it was a little after midnight when I opened my door a crack. If Devlin was a gentleman, he'd have left some food outside my door, but of course he wasn't, and he hadn't, and the last thing I'd eaten was half my breakfast this morning. And I was starving.

I sucked in a deep breath and slipped out into the corridor, then crept along it and down the stairs, pausing to cock my head for any sound of movement along the way. Silence. Good. I wasn't sure I trusted myself not to do something dumb if I bumped into Devlin, like bite his head off.

Or kiss him again.

Ugh. I shook my head, and made for the kitchen. At least, unlike Kade, he could cook, which meant the kitchen was bound to have a decent amount of food in it.

Kade. The look he'd given Devlin earlier had been outright hostile. I hoped he didn't do anything stupid.

Mate will defeat him. My wolf, as ever, sounded completely assured in Devlin's prowess. And this time, I suspected she was right. There was no way Kade could stand against his father…and I felt torn about that.

I swung open the kitchen door and reached up to switch on the light. It flickered and then burst to life, illuminating a shadowy shape looming over the table. I jumped back with a yelp, heart hammering, and then my eyes adjusted to the light and narrowed into a scowl.

"What are you doing here?"

"I live here," Devlin replied, without getting up from his seat.

"Yeah. And it's totally normal to be sitting in the kitchen in the pitch black at midnight." My scowl deepened at the slight tremble in my voice, and I skirted round the alpha, making for the fridge.

"I figured you'd get bored of sulking sooner or later."

"I wasn't sulking! I was…thinking." I yanked open the fridge door and scanned the contents. Milk, eggs, cheese, several types of meat, vegetables…it was groaning with food, and I barely had any idea what to do with most of it. But I knew how to make a sandwich. That'd have to do. My scowl deepened. I'd planned to cook something more substantial, but I didn't much fancy humiliating myself in front of Devlin, so I yanked out the block of cheese and some ham, and tossed them on the worktop, and then went hunting for the bread.

"She doesn't eat all day, and then she just wants a sandwich?" Devlin quirked an eyebrow on his stupid perfect face. "What sort of shifter are you?"

"One who can't cook," I grumbled.

"Ah, yes. Of course." He frowned. "What did your pack actually teach you?"

"How to stay alive," I grumbled, assembling my poor excuse for a sandwich.

"You could have fooled me."

I chucked the sandwich on a plate and slunk round to the far side of the table to claim a seat. "I'm still alive, aren't I?"

"You shouldn't be, after the stunt you pulled during the hunt."

"That wasn't my fault," I groused, prodding at my food. "My stupid wolf was trying to impress you."

He snorted in what might have been amusement, if I was feeling generous.

"It's not my fault I can't fully control her," I mumbled. I took a bite of the sandwich and studiously ignored him as I waited for the flush of embarrassment from my admission to fade from my cheeks.

"Sometimes," he said, his voice barely audible, "I forget how young you are."

"I'm not a child," I snapped, raising my eyes to glare at him. The hunger on his face stole my breath—and I was pretty sure it wasn't my sandwich he was looking at.

"No," he said, without breaking eye contact, his voice a throaty rumble. "You certainly aren't."

I was the first to look away. I'd been ignored my whole life, other than when I was being told what a disgrace I was, and now I'd had two guys within a week looking at me the way Devlin was right now. Like I was desirable. I wasn't sure what to do with that. My wolf, of course, had some suggestions.

Lick him.

Oh, my God. Seriously, it was like living with a teenaged boy inside my head. We are *not* going to lick him, wolf. She huffed in response to my thoughts, but for the most part, she seemed content just to be near him—which made exactly one of us.

I took another bite of my sandwich and tried not to choke on it, which was hard because my mouth was suddenly very dry. It formed a lump in my throat and I forced it down, then traced a pattern in the crumbs left on my plate.

"I…uh…Thank you." I felt a flush spreading over my cheeks again, and kept staring at the crumbs. "For the sneakers."

His thumb brushed my chin, tilting my head up to look at him.

"I will always provide for you."

I stood abruptly, picking up my plate and carrying it to the sink.

"Uh, yeah. About that. Where's the rest of my stuff?"

"In your room."

"Um, no it's not." I heard his grunt of annoyance—that man really didn't like people contradicting him—and pressed on quickly. "I mean, I just came from there, and it's definitely not there."

"That's not your room."

I almost dropped the plate into the sink, just barely managing to catch it and set it down carefully. "What do you mean?"

I sensed movement and turned around quickly to find Devlin towering over me.

"Did you really think I would give you that cramped little room?"

I swallowed and pressed my lips together tightly, because Devlin's shirt was peeking open at the top, giving me a glimpse of his pecs, and my wolf's suggestion to lick him was seeming more reasonable by the second. Everything about Devlin was intoxicating, and his proximity washed over me like a drug.

"You are my mate. You will have a room fit for an alpha's mate."

156

His hand raised to my face, tracing the shape of my cheek from an inch away, like I was some fragile doll he couldn't even touch…but the look on his face said he longed to touch me, and not in a delicate way.

The memory of my first kiss—with Kade—flooded my mind and I ducked aside, scurrying away from Devlin.

"Do you intend to make me chase you, little wolf?" Devlin all but purred. "Because I am a hunter. If you run, I will catch you."

My breathing hitched all over again, because in that moment, I wanted him to catch me, to throw me over his shoulder and carrying me to his room, then toss me onto the bed and—I blinked. None of that stuff. That was what my wolf wanted. Not me. Not with him.

"Lay one finger on me and you'll find you're not the only predator around here," I snarled at him.

I felt my wolf's shock resounding through my chest. Shit. I just threatened the alpha. Again.

Time to make my escape before my mouth could land me in trouble. I made a dash for the door, but he was faster than me. He caught my wrist in one hand, checking my flight and yanking me back towards him.

He slammed me back into the wall, pinning both my wrists above my head, and glared at me. His other hand was planted flat on the wall beside my head, blocking my escape, and he leaned over me, invading my space so that only an inch of electrified air separated us.

His eyes held mine, trapping me with the promise of lust and violence, and I felt my hunger for him surge to the surface, inescapable, irrepressible. Irresistible.

I stretched up and touched my lips to his.

CHAPTER THIRTY-FOUR

Pleasure burned through me where our lips joined, even as danger screamed along my senses. Because this man *was* dangerous, deadly…and there was nothing I wanted more. His lips moved against mine, tasting my defiance, and I locked eyes with him as we kissed.

My lips yielded to his, parting to invite him inside, and he plundered my mouth mercilessly, passionately, deliciously. I squirmed in his grip until I thought my shoulders would burst with holding me back from him, and still his grip didn't relent. He deepened the kiss and I moaned into his mouth. I needed to touch him, to feel him, to explore every inch of his perfect damned body with my hands. And his wicked eyes told me he knew it.

His body crushed against mine, enveloping me with his heat and his scent, and my legs weakened to his touch. He kept my arms pinned high above my head, and his other hand slipped down from the wall, trailing along my face, my shoulder, the flesh of my side through the thin fabric of my material. A shiver of sheer ecstasy rolled over me, and heat pooled between my legs. I moaned again, thrusting against him, and his hand slipped between my body and the wall to cup my ass and hold me against him.

I moaned again into the kiss, desperate with my need, and then his lips broke contact with mine. I keened with need but already he was kissing a trail of fire along my neck, working his way down with agonizing deliberation so that I thought I would die from the sheer need of him.

I twisted my head to nip at his earlobe, leaning into him as much as my arms pinned above my head would allow. He returned the nip to my throat, and the delicious heat between my legs spread until my entire soul was alive with it, burning with the exquisite torture of his touch.

"Say my name," he growled against the hollow of my throat. I pressed my lips together stubbornly and crushed my body against his, feeling every hard ridge through clothes that suddenly chaffed with every touch.

"Say my name," he demanded again, his voice low and husky. Demanding my submission. I shook my head and he nipped at me, then lapped the flesh with his tongue. He drew back, a few ions of electrified air separating his lips from my flesh, and I whined in desperation, but he didn't relent. I broke first.

"Devlin," I moaned in a breathy whisper.

His lips touched me again, blazing a trail of blistering kisses across the hollow of my neck. He paused at my shirt, and nipped at a button, easily separating it from its thread. I parted my lips to protest but he squeezed my ass in his powerful fingers and all that came out was a ragged gasp. To hell with my clothes. Who cared? All I needed was this man, this powerful, dominant bastard, touching and kissing and possessing me.

He kissed his way to the exposed V between my breasts, then paused again, his lips moving against my tingling flesh as he rumbled his words.

"What am I to you?"

"Al...alpha," I panted between ragged breaths, throwing my head back in the delight of his touch, and the torturous need of more. He planted one kiss, then spoke again.

"What am I to you?" he demanded again, his husky voice sending spirals of heat through my soul. I knew what he wanted, and my wolf keened with the need to give it to him, but I fought them both.

His teeth made short work of another button, and his tongue darted across the underside of my breast. A moan burst from me, loud and wanton, and I felt his dark chuckle dance across my sensitive flesh.

"What am I to you?"

"M…Mate," I gasped, and I felt his satisfaction thrumming through me. He took my nipple into his mouth and suckled, and I thrust myself at him, craving more, needing more, always *more.*

His hand slipped down from my wrists to find the small of my back and press me tighter to him, taking more of my breast into his mouth with the insatiable appetite of a starving man.

"Devlin," I groaned again, and he growled in response to his name, his hands roving my body possessively. I lowered my arms from the wall and my hands found the chiseled ridges of his shoulders, then moved lower to explore the rugged planes of his back. My fingers traced an old scar and he growled again, every fiber of his body roaring with power. I found two more scars on his back, each one a medal of honor—a battle he'd won, a rival he'd defeated. And here he stood, this powerful beast of a man, and I was his world.

My fingers found the waistline of his jeans and a sharp pang of desire lanced through my stomach. I tugged at the button, battling to open it between our touching bodies, to free the hardness trapped there and take it into me. I needed him like I needed the air in my lungs, only more, because without the air I would die, but without him I didn't want to live.

I slipped my hand into his pants, and around his throbbing cock. My fingers marveled at the velvet smoothness of his flesh and I pulled him free of his constraints.

"Fuck me," I groaned.

His hands left my back and my ass, and his mouth came away from my breast, leaving it cold in the night air. He stepped back, slipping from my grasp, and shock wrote itself on my features as he went.

A shudder ran the length of his body, and he shoved himself back in his pants. The shock on my face became hurt, and it traveled through every cell in my body. I swallowed a sob.

160

"What? What did I do wrong?" The pain made my voice raspy, and Devlin clenched his jaw and shook his head.

"Nothing. You did nothing. But you don't want this."

"I need you."

He shook his head again. "No. You think you do, but you'll feel differently in the morning. I'm still a dominant bastard, and you still want your freedom more than anything else."

He turned and strode from the room, and I slid slowly to the floor.

Fuck.

CHAPTER THIRTY-FIVE

I wasn't sure how long I sat there alone in the semi-darkness trying to get my head round the fact my mate had rejected me for a second time, and in the worst way I could imagine, but eventually I staggered back up to my room, shoved the door shut, and collapsed on my bed. Then I finished what Devlin had started, because I may have never slept with anyone before, but I still had needs.

It was some time after that, my post-orgasm bliss stunted under the weight of my wolf's grief, that I finally managed to get some sleep. My dreams were full of *him*—tormenting me, rejecting me, using me and casting me aside.

I awoke as the sun rose, drenched in a cold sweat, with one thought front and center of my mind.

I was done.

I'd planned to bide my time, but I couldn't cope with this. I couldn't handle being rejected by my one true mate over and over again. Because yes, I hated the bastard, but on some level, I didn't, and that made it a thousand times worse. Because just for a moment last night, when our bodies had touched and our hands had explored each other, I'd thought there might have been something between us. I'd seen a glimpse of a future. And then he'd snatched it away.

He was right about one thing, though: I *didn't* want this, and there was *nothing* I wanted more than my freedom.

I washed, dressed in my single remaining shirt—my other one being a casualty of last night—and made my way downstairs to the kitchen. I expected to find him there, skulking about waiting for a chance to tell me what a poor excuse of a mate I was, but when I got there, it was Beta Caleb I found sitting at the table. He rose as I entered.

"Jessica. Good morning."

"No, it's not," I grumbled. "And how many freaking times? It's Jess."

A smile flickered across his face. "Jess. Right. I'll remember that."

"Where's Devlin?"

"He had some pack business to take care of."

Kade's face flashed through my mind, full of anger and defiance as it had been yesterday, and my lips pressed into a frown as anxiety stirred in my stomach.

"What kind of pack business?"

"Nothing to worry about," Caleb said cheerfully. "He'll be back later today. In the meantime, he left me to take care of you."

"Guard me, you mean?" I snapped.

"Well, I think he meant cook for you and stuff," Caleb answered with an easy shrug. "I gather it's not a skill of yours."

"Oh." I perked up a little at that. First, because if Caleb was right, I wouldn't have to deal with the utter humiliation of seeing Devlin until later today. Second, I was starving. I was pretty sure I hadn't had a single decent meal since coming to Broken Ridge.

I slid into a seat at the table as Caleb crossed to the fridge.

"So, what can I get you?" he asked.

"Do you know how to make pancakes?" I asked.

"Sure. Coming right up."

He rifled through the contents of the fridge and plucked out a bunch of ingredients he apparently intended to turn into food. My wolf pricked her ears in approval. She wasn't particularly a fan of our accidental starvation, either.

But I had other things on my mind besides food. If Devlin wasn't around all day, then maybe I didn't have to see him again at all. Maybe I could give Caleb the slip somehow. Immediately, I felt guilty for having the thought. Not at the thought of leaving Devlin, of course, but at the thought of leaving Caleb to shoulder the blame. I couldn't imagine

Devlin would be particularly forgiving of Caleb if I escaped on his watch. But that didn't change the fact it might be my best opportunity.

Assuming I could find an excuse to get out from under the beta's all-too-watchful eye.

"Tell me more about Devlin," I said, as the beta set a stack of pancakes in front of me. He raised an eyebrow in surprise, and I shrugged.

"What? You told me yesterday I don't know him. And you're right. But he's kinda hard to get to open up."

"You noticed that, huh?" He gave me what I took for a friendly smile, and sat down across the table from me—taking care, I noticed, not to get too close. Either Devlin had been telling people that I bite, or he really was possessive of his property. Not that I intended to be that for much longer. I just had to convince Caleb I was coming round to the idea of his alpha as my mate first.

"Um, well, we kinda had a conversation, but we got…distracted." I blushed, and shoveled a bite of the pancakes in my mouth. Caleb gave a low chuckle.

"Yeah, I can imagine. It's like that, you know, when you find your mate. Hard to keep your hands off each other."

I shot him a glare. "Yeah, that's enough talk about my sex life, thanks." Or my non-existent sex life, more precisely.

He chuckled again, and nodded.

"What do you want to know?"

"Like, anything. Help me make a connection with him based on more than hormones."

He frowned across the table at me. "You know there's more to mate bonds than hormones, right? You're perfect matches for each other, and not just biologically. You're spirited."

"I'm not a damned horse," I complained.

"Fine. Feisty, then, if you prefer. Stubborn. Determined. You're a survivor. He's all of those things, too."

That made sense, I supposed. He'd hardly have been able to hold his position as alpha if he'd been a pushover. And then there were those scars on his back... I yanked my mind out of that particular rabbit hole before I could get distracted all over again.

"Okay, yeah, we're Cathy and Heathcliff. I get it."

"Who?" He caught my look and pressed on. "He's led this pack for over forty years, and I've been his beta for all of that time."

"And he inherited it from his father?"

"In a way. There was a rebellion not long after Devlin came of age. A wolf by the name of Blaine led an uprising. Do you know much about alpha challenges, Jess?"

I swallowed a bite of pancakes and shook my head, rapt.

"No, I suppose not," Caleb mused. "They're rare. But for a challenge to be lawful, it must be made in a certain way. Any member of the pack can challenge the pack's alpha for control, and the alpha cannot refuse. They must duel, one on one, in their shifted forms, under the next full moon within the pack's territory, with witnesses."

"I'm guessing Blaine didn't do that?"

"No. He came for Samuel in the dead of the night, with five other wolves at his back. All lower ranking members of the pack, looking to snatch power for themselves. They killed him and his mate cold in their bed, while Devlin slept on the far side of the house."

"Hence all the security." Shit.

Caleb nodded. "Hence all the security. He never got over his parents being murdered that way—but don't tell him I said that."

And how could he have? How could anyone get over a trauma like that, even with forty years to sort through it? Here I was, thinking he'd turned this place into a fortress to imprison whichever helpless female he dragged back here, but I'd been wrong. He wasn't trying to keep people in. He was keeping the world out.

"They came for Devlin next, but they made the mistake of only sending two wolves to take him out." He pressed his lips together in a grim smile. "He killed them both, and challenged Blaine for the pack—a courtesy he didn't deserve. And under a full moon in the heart of Broken Ridge territory—or Daybreak Ridge as it was then—he faced Blaine in single combat, and killed him."

"He renamed the territory?"

"He did. A part of this pack became broken on that night, one that could never mend."

"Devlin," I whispered. "Devlin broke."

"Some might say that," Caleb said. "But I would disagree. Devlin is a strong alpha, a powerful and just leader. That night made him the man he is today."

"And the scars?"

"Ah, you saw those, did you?" His eyes danced, then his amusement turned sour. "Evidently, Blaine knew he would never win in a fair fight. So he tipped his claws in silver powder."

I gasped. Even the word repulsed me, and the thought of the metal burning and blistering through skin and boiling the blood beneath made me cringe. No wonder the scars were still so prominent, even after all this time. He was lucky to be alive.

None of which changed a single thing. I picked up my plate and took it to the sink. I already cared about Devlin more than I wanted. It was easier to think of him as a dominant, self-serving bastard, because at least that way, I could hate part of him. And that made the rejection sting less. Understanding him, that made it worse. Because I *wanted* to be the one to heal those wounds, I *wanted* to be the one to stand by his side no matter who rose against him—even Kade, dammit—and it was all too clear he didn't see me that way.

Caleb was wrong. Devlin *had* been broken, and it was beyond even my power to fix.

CHAPTER THIRTY-SIX

I rattled around the house for the next few hours, fighting the urge to pace like a caged animal, because Caleb made a point of sticking close and I didn't want him to think I was doing anything other than mulling over how lucky I was to be locked in Devlin's house. He'd been beta of this pack for twice as long as I'd been alive, and I didn't doubt he'd be quick to become suspicious. So instead, I let him give me the tour, watched a little TV, and flicked through the twenty fashion magazines that had spontaneously appeared in the house, possibly as a result of me being impressed with the sneakers yesterday.

Mate provides.

They were the first words my wolf had spoken since Devlin had run out on us last night, leaving her a whimpering, grieving wreck, so I let her have it. Yes, Devlin was going to lengths to provide for us, and he seemed very determined, even if a little out of his depth. It was endearing—and I didn't need her to be any more endeared than she already was. This was going to be hard enough already.

I tossed the magazine aside, and glanced over at Caleb.

"Do you have any decent shops here in Broken Ridge?"

He glanced at the magazine and raised an eyebrow.

"Found a little inspiration?"

"Devlin might have done a number on my best shirt yesterday." I blushed at the memory, and distracted myself by gesturing to the one I was wearing. "This is my last one."

"I'm sure Alpha Devlin will buy you some new clothes when he returns."

"Yeah, I'm sure. And I'm sure his taste is excellent, as evidenced by the fact he sent *you* to buy those sneakers—thanks, by the way—but I think it would be safer if I did my own shopping."

"Sorry. I don't have orders to take you out of the house."

"You're going to make me say it, aren't you?" I pouted, and crossed my arms over my chest. "Fine. I want to look nice for him when he comes back. But if you tell anyone, I swear I'll deny it."

He chuckled and glanced at his watch. "I suppose we could go to one store."

I grinned and leaped to my feet. "My hero. Let's go shopping."

That had gone better than I'd dared to hope.

It turned out Broken Ridge had three clothes stores—who presumably did good business because an unplanned shift immediately meant you needed to replace your outfit. I chose the most expensive looking one. Don't get me wrong, it wasn't that I was on some sort of mission to spend as much of Devlin's money as possible. I didn't plan on sticking around long enough to actually pay for anything.

I spent a while browsing the racks while Caleb loitered, looking distinctly uncomfortable and completely out of place. I felt another lance of guilt for what I was about to do, but Devlin would forgive him eventually. Whereas he'd never set me free. This was the only way.

I plucked a small armful of garments from the various rails and made my way to the fitting rooms at the back of the store, with Caleb trailing in my wake. I reached the fitting rooms, and a well-dressed woman stepped forward, blocking his path.

"Beta Caleb," she said, inclining her head in a show of respect—because of course she recognized her pack's beta. My breath caught in my throat, but she continued, "I'm afraid you cannot come in here. I'm sure you understand?"

Her eyes flickered across his face hopefully, and for a moment I thought he would object, but then he nodded and stepped back. I scurried forward to the row of fitting rooms, walking past the first few with barely a glance inside, before I found what I wanted. I slipped into

169

the small compartment and glanced up at the window set into the wall with a smile.

I didn't have long—despite the large pile of clothing I was ostensibly trying on, Caleb wouldn't be patient forever, and I'd already used up my quota of luck by finding a secluded bay of fitting rooms and a window to the street. Sure, I'd helped luck along by choosing the most luxurious looking store in Broken Ridge, but that didn't mean I wanted to push it.

Moving as quietly as I could, I reached up and gave the window a little shove. It budged, and no alarm sounded, proving the fates hadn't deserted me just yet. There was no time to waste. I grabbed the ledge and hauled myself up. The window wasn't large, but with a bit of wiggling, I hauled myself through. One sharp shove later, and I was tumbling to the ground. Head first. Crap.

I thrust out a hand and pain shot through it as I landed. I rolled with a hiss, coming up in a crouch with my arm cradled to my chest. A sprain, probably. But it didn't matter. I was outside, and I had lost my chaperone. It was time to get the hell out of this place before someone caught on—and caught me.

I rose quickly, checking left and right along the street, but the small, paved section to the store's rear was deserted. Good. I ducked my head and hurried across the deserted side road, then remembered myself and moved more slowly, still with a sense of purpose in my stride, but not like I was running away from something. I couldn't afford to draw any attention to myself, not while I was still in Broken Ridge territory, and not with Devlin's apprehend order hanging over me.

I sucked in a deep breath, raised my head a notch, and strode along the streets, making my way ever closer to the woods, and my best chance of getting out of here, once and for all.

As the tree line came into sight, I exhaled slowly and allowed my lips to move into a tentative smile. A weight lifted from my shoulders as I moved into the shadows. Even my wolf was silent; as sure sign that, despite all of her hopes, she knew our time with Devlin was done. There was nothing left in Broken Ridge for us.

I set my foot to the trail, and didn't look back over my shoulder.

That, perhaps, was my mistake.

CHAPTER THIRTY-SEVEN

I moved through the woods at a steady lope for hours, shifter stamina meaning it was a long time before I needed to slow for a break. My wolf was silent as I ran, though as I slowed to a walk, I felt her ears prick. I waited for her to argue, or try to wrest control from me again and force me to shift so she could run back to Devlin, but instead she just remained a wary passenger, urging me to keep one eye on the shadows as the afternoon edged towards evening.

She was right. Caleb would know I was gone by now, and no doubt had organized patrols to search for me, with trackers running at their head. Would he have contacted Devlin, too, or was he hoping to catch me without having to admit his blunder to the alpha?

It didn't matter. Whether a tracker caught me, or Devlin himself, the result would be the same.

I ducked my head and slipped into a jog again. I'd lingered too long. I needed to get far, far from Broken Ridge territory. Far from the territory of any wolf. I could hide amongst the humans until Devlin forgot all about me, and I could build a life on my own terms.

The sound of the twig snapping came from off to my left.

I sucked in a gasp and made to twist round, but my beast rumbled a warning that kept my eyes focused ahead and my pace steady.

Don't let him know you've heard him.

Him?

A male. Stalking us from the tree line.

Alone?

Perhaps.

She fell silent a moment, and I did, too, allowing her the space to listen and think. My wolf wasn't just some lovesick pup. She was an apex predator, born to hunt prey through woods just like these.

We're the prey now.

A shudder ran the length of my spine, and my mind formed a single word. Run?

No. If we run, we appear weak. They will attack.

They? I swallowed, and continued at my steady jog. Not alone, then. Wait, attack? Devlin wouldn't hurt me. At least, not in that way.

Not our mate.

Dammit. One of his patrols, then. Or Caleb's patrols. They probably didn't even know what I was to Devlin—just some wolf he'd ordered them to prevent leaving the territory. And if no-one had ordered them not to hurt me, they could easily decide I'd be less trouble to transport if I was injured.

Which was fine, because I had no intention of being caught. How many? I asked her.

Three.

You're certain?

As I can be.

That was good enough for me. Her instincts had never let us down yet—except when it came to Devlin, of course. She growled in response to my thought, and I let it drop. There'd be plenty of time to argue about that when we were far away from Broken Ridge.

We're not in Broken Ridge anymore.

What? I caught myself just as I was about to look around, because honestly, these woods all looked alike to me. But we'd been traveling for hours—I could already feel the temperature dropping, preceding evening's arrival—and though Devlin's territory was vast, it didn't go on forever. I probably shouldn't have been surprised. How long ago? I wondered.

Perhaps a mile.

A spike of anxiety ran through me and I sucked in a deep breath. We were running through an unknown pack's territory, and it was natural that the resident wolves were taking an interest. Unfortunate, but natural. I guess I'd finally used up my quota of luck. We were breaching some serious etiquette, entering a territory without permission of the alpha. Perhaps I should stop and speak to them, and try to explain our situation.

Perhaps not.

Wow, bossy, much?

They could be mate's allies.

Yeah, that was a good point. He'd be doubly pissed if a neighboring pack had to drag me back. It would make him look weak, like he couldn't keep his own house in order. Not that I cared, of course—what did it matter to me what other packs thought of him?

But it would matter if they delivered me right back to him.

Stopping was out, then.

…But carrying on blindly wasn't a great plan, either. I had no way of knowing how vast this new pack's territory was, and no way of knowing if the wolves shadowing me would be content to see me to their border. Worse, if I ran through the heart of their lands, I could find myself confronted by the entire pack. And as a trespasser, that was about the worse plan imaginable. Wolves had been sentenced to death for less.

My stride faltered, feet stumbling over the uneven ground. I swallowed hard and regained my balance, and as I raised my head again, a young man moved onto the trail in front of me.

I skidded to a stop, taking him in. His hair was close cropped and dark, and he wore a day's stubble across his lower jaw. He was my age or maybe a little older, and there was a cockiness about him that immediately made me wary. The heavy muscle across his shoulders made me feel the same way.

I heard two more shifters step from the shadows of the trees on either side of the track, flanking me, but I didn't turn to them. The guy with the stubble was their ringleader. He was the one who would make the decisions.

"You are trespassing."

I bowed my head, but didn't take my eyes from him. He glared at me, his lips pressed into an unfriendly line. My wolf didn't urge me to submit: he likely wasn't an alpha blood. She knew these things.

"Forgive me," I said, directing my answer to his knees. "I'm traveling, and I mean no disrespect."

"You come into our lands uninvited, and you dare speak to me of disrespect. Did you hear that, lads? The little intruder means no disrespect."

He laughed a cruel laugh, and the wolves flanking me echoed the sound. A shiver ran through me, and I knew it was too much to hope the three shifters hadn't seen it. They were predators, and right now, I was their prey.

"We'll teach you the meaning of respect," he said, his lips curving up into an evil smile, and one of the guys flanking me cackled again. The sound echoed back at me through the trees, and I knew I was alone with them. And I was at their mercy.

Should I run? I asked my wolf, searching deep inside for her wisdom.

No.

Shift, then?

No.

Why not?

If we shift, they will, and we cannot take them all.

What, then?

Endure.

Shit. That was the last thing I wanted to hear. Fear welled in my belly as the stubbled shifter stepped towards me, and the pair flanking me closed in on me from either side. My wolf was right. I couldn't run. I couldn't fight. All I could to was survive.

"Take me to your alpha," I blurted.

"Our alpha?" He shared a grin with the other two. "No, I don't think so. You see..." He stepped closer again. "He leaves us to patrol the borders, and he lets us punish intruders as we see fit." His eyes roved the length of my body, down and up again, pausing at each of my curves, leaving no doubt what was in his mind.

"Please..."

I backed away, and hands seized my arms on either side. I struggled, but the shifters were stronger than me, and their fingers bit into my arms.

"Struggle all you want," their leader said, swaggering up to me. He slid one finger into my shirt and shredded it like paper. His voice dropped to a conspiratorial whisper. "I like it when they struggle."

I swallowed my revulsion and stared daggers at him, which only made him laugh again. He reached for my face, and I threw my head back and screamed, long and loud.

"Scream all you want. No-one's coming, trespasser."

He reached out for my exposed flesh, and no matter how I struggled, I couldn't evade his touch. His eyes glistened cruelly in the falling darkness.

"I'm going to enjoy this."

CHAPTER THIRTY-EIGHT

I lifted my legs and slammed them into his chest with both feet. He staggered back, and I felt a stab of grim satisfaction. Then he straightened and his face contorted into a snarl.

"You little bitch."

I tried to wrench my arms free as he came back towards me, but the men holding me gripped tighter. He drew his arm back and smashed the back of his hand into my face. The force of the blow twisted my head to the side, and I felt my lip split open. A gasp of pain slipped from between my lips before I could stop it, and I felt the satisfaction radiating from him.

"You don't like it quite so much when I'm the one dealing out the pain do you, little bitch? Well you better get used to it, because me and my buddies have a whole lot of pain in store for you. But who knows? You might even start to like it."

His hands dropped down to cup his crotch, just in case there was anyway on earth I could possibly have missed his meaning. I didn't quite manage to suppress the shudder that ran through me, and I knew the guys on either side of me felt it. Bastards.

I drew my head back and spat at their ringleader, landing a glob of saliva directly on his cheek. He reached up and touched his fingertips to the stubble there. They came away wet and his face contorted in disgust.

"You're going to pay for that."

He drew his hand back again, this time curled into a fist, and I screwed my eyes shut and waited for the blow to land and the pain to see across my face.

And waited.

I heard the thud of flesh striking flesh…but not my flesh. My eyes flew open. It took me a moment to process what I was seeing, and even longer to believe it.

Devlin had the stubbled shifter by his throat, dangling three feet off the ground and gasping in his grip. His right wrist—the hand he'd been about to punch me with—was hanging at a strange angle, and I could guess what Devlin had done. And I felt nothing but satisfaction.

Devlin tossed him and he flew through the air before smashing into a tree with a strangled cry of pain, and bouncing onto the floor. He rolled up onto his feet, damaged hand held protectively against his chest, but his other hand in a loose brawler's stance. He was tough, I had to give him that. But Devlin was tougher.

He closed the gap between them in a flash, smashing his fist into the stubbled guy's jaw. The force threw him from his feet, and he hit the ground hard again.

"Get off me," I snarled at the guys frozen on either side of me with their fingers still digging into my flesh. They were both transfixed by the sudden violence unfolding in front of them, and one of them had partially shifted, probably without meaning to, and his claws were cutting into the soft flesh of my arms. I couldn't pull loose without shredding myself in the process. And what was I going to do, anyway? It wasn't like Devlin needed my help…but I wasn't going to run and leave him alone here, either.

Stubble Guy scuttled back through the dirt and Devlin stalked towards him, his every movement laced with the promise of vengeance. The other shifter thudded back into a tree, and Devlin's face contorted into something too disturbing to be called a smile.

The shifter came to his feet, back still pressed tight to the tree, and the blood drained from his face, along with the last of his bravado. Devlin was more powerful than him, and I could smell the dominance rolling off the alpha in waves. He was bigger, he was stronger, and he was a better fighter. He could kill that rat as soon as lift a finger, and I saw the exact moment my would-be rapist realized it.

He opened his mouth to say something—to beg, if he had a single brain cell inside his thick skull—but Devlin didn't give him the chance. He clamped one powerful hand around the man's throat, and squeezed. His face turned red and his eyes started to bulge. He clawed at Devlin's arm in a frenzy, but it didn't budge. Devlin was going to kill him, and for a moment, I wanted him to. He deserved it, for me and for every other victim that had crossed his path.

But not like this.

"Devlin," I called, my voice carrying easily across the utter stillness around us. I shook off the hands holding me, and they released me like I'd burned them, and quickly backed up. Devlin's head whipped round to me, his attention captured by my voice or the sudden movement, and we locked gazes for a moment. And then I saw the madness fade from his eyes.

He pulled his hand away from the shifter, and the man slid to the floor, his own hands around his throat as he gasped in ragged breaths.

Devlin ignored him, fixing his eyes on the shifters still flanking me, and they backed up a few more hurried steps as he advanced on them, then shared a glance and dropped into submissive crouches, placing themselves at Devlin's mercy. I wasn't sure that was such a smart place to be right now, but blood was still leaking from my arm, and I didn't much care.

"Get the fuck out of here before I kill you," Devlin spat.

"You've got no right to be here," Stubble Guy wheezed, clutching at his throat. "You're trespassing."

"I know I am," Devlin growled, pivoting to him. "But that is my fucking *mate* and I will gladly go to war for her. So unless you want to tell

179

your alpha that your attempted rape of Alpha Devlin's mate is the reason he's at war with the Broken Ridge pack, I suggest you get the fuck away from her." He stalked back towards the other shifter. "And if you so much as look in her direction again, I will personally make sure you're not around long enough to deliver that message."

Stubble Guy's eyes had been growing steadily wider with each word Devlin spat, and he shot a shocked stare at me, then somehow his eyes went even wider as he realized his mistake and jerked his gaze to the ground.

"I understand, Alpha Devlin. We're sorry. We didn't know she was your mate. We thought she was a rogue."

"And that made it okay to rape her?" Devlin's voice was dangerously low.

"Yes—No! I mean no, Alpha Devlin. Please, we meant no offense."

"Well, bad news for you then, because even your damned face offends me, pup."

"We're sorry! I swear, we didn't realize who you were, or who she was."

I got it then. Why the two shifters had panicked and released me when I called Devlin's name. I guess he didn't have much to do with this pack. Running this way had been the right decision…aside from the fact that it was the dumbest thing I'd ever done.

"Return to your alpha," Devlin commanded. "Tell him what happened here today. Every damned word. Do you understand?"

"Ye-Yes, Alpha Devlin." Stubble Guy flicked a glance to Devlin's face then back down to his feet so quickly he could have given himself whiplash.

"What are you waiting for? Get out of my sight."

And with that, he turned his eyes on me, running them over my body, my undoubtedly pale face, my torn shirt, and then paused on the blood leaking from my arm, and the four neat puncture marks that were starting to heal.

"Stop."

The three shifters froze at his icy command. He looked from my right arm to the shifter backing away to my right, and I felt his fury…and the shifter's answering terror. He gave a small squeak as Devlin took a step towards him.

"You damaged my mate."

"S—Sorry, Alpha Devlin."

"Sorry?" Devlin's face darkened. "You drew blood from my mate, and you're *sorry?* You don't know the meaning of the word, you filthy cur."

Devlin moved so fast it took my brain a moment to catch up. One second he was in front of me, rage flooding every inch of his body, and the next he was behind me, barreling into the cowering shifter. I heard bones break as Devlin drove a fist into his ribs and the shifter staggered back. And this time, I knew he was going to kill him.

"Devlin, no!" I shouted. "I'm okay. Please."

He ignored me and pummeled the man again. Neither of his friends came to his rescue, cowards that they were. They were going to stand back and watch Devlin beat him to death.

"He didn't mean it," I blurted. "It was an accident."

Devlin's face whipped round to me, his fist poised midair, and his other hand pinning the shifter in the dirt.

"You're defending him?"

The ice in his voice sent a shiver the length of my spine, and I shook my head, wrapping my arms around myself.

"Please," I said in a small voice, "I just want to go home."

Devlin's arm dropped and he rose to his feet without another glance at the man in the dirt. As he stepped away, his two packmates closed in, hauling him to his feet and dragging him quickly into the tree line before Devlin could change his mind.

As they vanished, the big alpha came towards me. One look at his face told me exactly how much trouble I was in for running. But I didn't care. He was here, and I was safe.

CHAPTER THIRTY-NINE

Devlin reached for me, and a whimper slipped from my throat. He gave no sign of having heard it, and then his arms wrapped around me and crushed me against his body, surrounding me in his scent. The scent of safety.

He exhaled a breath into my hair.

"It's okay," he murmured. "It's over. You're safe."

He was...he was hugging me. There was nothing sexual about it, nor threatening, nor any of the usual tension between us. I felt protected. Cared for.

I choked back a sob and buried my face in his chest.

"It's okay," he repeated, rubbing his hand on my back.

And maybe...maybe it would be. I inhaled a deep lungful of his scent, and my wolf buzzed contentedly inside my head.

Mate. Safe. Protected.

I knew I should break the embrace. Nothing had changed, not really. He'd come to reclaim his property, that was all. But it didn't *feel* like that was all. It felt...it felt like home.

Mate fought for us. Mate is strong. Mate is worthy.

Except that had never been the issue. He'd always been strong. He'd always been a fighter—usually fighting me. It wasn't that I didn't want him. It had never been that, no matter what I told myself. It was that he didn't want me.

Mate is here.

Yeah, protecting his toy from falling into someone else's hands. But I didn't have the strength to argue with her. Because I wanted her words to be true. I wanted him to want me—even though, against every warning he'd given me, I'd run. Again.

"How much trouble am I in?" I asked in a small voice against his chest. I felt his answering dark chuckle rumble through my whole body.

"Heaps," he said, and the promise sent a shiver through me. It wasn't entirely a shiver of fear, either. But I was too tired to analyze my warped mind right now.

"Home?" I asked hopefully, lifting my head a fraction to peer up at him through my lashes. His chin dipped in response, and as I made to pull away, his grip loosened, letting me go.

His eyes burned hot as he took in my body, but he covered it quickly. He shrugged out of his shirt and held it out to me in one bloodied fist. I stared at it in silence for a long moment.

"To keep you warm," he said. "It's a long way back to our territory."

Our territory. Our home. I accepted his shirt wordlessly, and slipped it on top of the shredded remains of mine before buttoning it, and cocooning myself in his spicy, welcoming scent.

He wrapped one arm around my shoulders, and I couldn't tell if he was holding me up, or just holding onto me, and I didn't care. I leaned against him, letting his warmth wash over me as we moved through the alien territory.

And with each step closer to our packlands, I felt myself growing more and more certain of what I knew. Maybe I'd always known it. Maybe I'd known it before I was even born. Because fate didn't make mistakes.

"I don't think you've ever been quiet for this long before," Devlin murmured in my ear as we walked. "Not even in your sleep."

My mouth popped open.

"I do *not* talk in my sleep," I protested.

"No, I suppose it would be hard to find time to talk with all the snoring."

"Snoring? I don't snore." Heat flushed my face. Did I? And wait, why did I care if Devlin thought I snored? "Anyway, I'm surprised you can hear anything above the sound of your own orders being barked all over the place."

He chuckled.

"That wasn't meant to be funny," I pouted. His hand rubbed my upper arm in a gentle caress, and I exhaled a breath that seemed to come from the pit of my stomach. I stared at the floor as we walked, avoiding his eye. "Sorry I ran."

He pulled us to a stop and my heart stuttered. He placed both hands on my shoulders and turned me to face him.

"Jessica—Jess. What you did today was reckless. Dangerous. You betrayed Caleb's trust, and mine."

"He's not in trouble, is he?"

"You're not good at being quiet, are you?" Dark amusement flashed through his eyes. "No, he's not in trouble. And that wasn't my point."

"What's—" I clamped my lips together, and Devlin suppressed a smile.

"What's my point?" He exhaled heavily and stared off over my shoulder for a long moment, until I wanted to point out that the reason I talked so much was because if I didn't, our conversations would never go anywhere. After a long moment, he met my eye.

"It's my fault you ran," he said. "I know that. I didn't—couldn't— give you what you needed. What you did today was reckless, but this isn't on your shoulders. It's on mine."

My throat squeezed tightly, so that I couldn't get a word out. *Couldn't.* That was what he had said. He *couldn't* give me what I needed. He couldn't give me him. And what had happened back in the clearing, that didn't change anything. How could it? No matter what I wanted, no

185

matter what he wanted, no matter what our wolves wanted, he couldn't give himself to me. That was what he had said.

His hands fell away from my shoulders, and his eyes left mine.

"I understand," he said. "It's too much to ask you to forgive."

"Forgive?" The word forced its way from my lips, and my brow furrowed in confusion. What was to forgive? And then I knew. "You don't want me. I understand."

"What? Where the hell did you get that idea from?"

"I—" I blinked, searching his face as he searched mine.

"Dammit, Jess, I've never wanted anyone more than I want you."

"Then..." I shook my head. "Then I don't understand. You just said you couldn't give me what I needed."

"And you somehow think that means I don't want you?"

"Are we speaking the same language here, Devlin? Yes, that's what I think. Of course that's what I think. What the hell else am I supposed to think when the guy who occupies my every thought says something like that?"

"Your every thought?" His eyebrow quirked and a smirk tugged at his lips, making him look hotter than ever, then abruptly it was gone, and the smoldering intensity was back. "I want you. You're *all* I want. And when I saw them, what they were about to do to you... I would have killed them all. Without hesitation."

His eyes broke contact with mine again and he distanced himself from me by a step before turning back to me.

"I failed to protect you. I drove you away, and I put you in danger. I'm not good for you. Not safe for you. I have one job—to keep you safe—and I failed."

My heart thudded in my chest, but before I could find the words, before I could even work out what I felt in response to that, he continued.

"You deserve better than me. Not someone who's incapable of looking after you. I told you before you weren't good enough for me. I thought that might scare you away, I thought somehow I could spare us both this agony, but I was wrong. And..." He took a slow breath. "And I'm sorry."

I barked a harsh laugh, and pain raced across his face. I shook my head.

"You think I want your apologies? I don't need someone to look after me, Devlin." He raised an eyebrow, and I quickly amended, "Present situation excluded, obviously. And I'm not saying I couldn't have handled myself if you came along."

He snorted in amusement.

"Hey, I had them right where I wanted."

"Yes. Of course."

"I was going to unleash a whole can of whoop-ass at any moment. I was just—"

"Luring them into a false sense of security?" he suggested. I nodded.

"Yeah. That."

"Well, it worked. They were looking very secure."

"Rude." I gestured with my hands. "It was part of my cunning plan."

He caught my right hand out of the air and wrapped his around it, then stroked one finger softly over my arm, where the wound was hidden beneath the sleeve of my borrowed shirt. The muscle twitched at his touch.

"How is your arm?"

"Healing. It'll be fine."

"And you?"

I shrugged and ducked eye contact. That was a question I didn't think I'd be ready to answer for a while. I started walking down the track again, and Devlin came with me, my hand still snug in his.

187

"There's one thing I don't understand," I said.

"Only one thing?"

I rolled my eyes, but pressed on with my change of subject.

"If Caleb's not in trouble, why did you come alone? And where are the rest of your trackers?"

"It was too dangerous for them to cross into Setting Sun territory."

"But not for you?"

I twisted round to look at him, and the heat in his eyes made my heart stutter, and an answering heat welled in my core.

"I thought you were worth the risk."

"Even though I'm a pain in your ass?"

"Especially because of that." Abruptly, he looked away from me and dropped my hand, and rejection stabbed painfully through my chest.

"But you still don't want me, or can't have me for whatever stupid reason is bouncing around inside your head?"

"Jessica, I—"

"No," I cut across him. "This is bullshit, Devlin. You don't get to keep telling me shit like that, and then hiding behind some dumb excuse. You're a coward, Devlin. You're a fucking coward."

"You want to know the truth?" There was an anger in his voice as he challenged me, and I matched it with my own anger, one hand planted on my hip.

"Yes, I want the damned truth."

"You want the truth." He nodded, and my breath caught in my throat as I searched the tension in his shoulders. He turned to me, and his eyes slid off to one side. His voice was quiet, barely a whisper in the night air.

"I killed my mate."

CHAPTER FORTY

I staggered back a step like I'd been hit.

"You—"

My lips couldn't form the words, and I felt my face twisting to show every bit of horror that was bouncing around inside my head. Devlin *killed* his last mate?

Devlin saw my reaction, and nodded.

"I loved her, and I killed her. I'm bad for you, Jessica. I kill everything I touch. My mate, my parents. It's only a matter of time before I'd destroy you, too."

I took another shaky step back as his words rattled around my head. His mate, his parents… No, wait. That wasn't right.

"Caleb said…" I swallowed acid and searched his face. "Caleb said there was an uprising."

"Yes. Blaine had them murdered in their beds, while I slept and didn't raise a finger to protect them. I killed them as surely as if I'd slit their throats myself."

"But you didn't. You didn't do that."

"I did nothing to stop it."

"Devlin, you were younger than Kade and Jackson are now. You couldn't have stopped it. If someone killed you, would you hold them responsible?"

The hostility on Kade's face the day Devlin announced my probation flashed through my mind, but I shoved the image aside.

"That's different," he said eventually.

"No, it's not." I caught his hand in mine, tightening my grip a fraction when he made to pull away. "You're not to blame for what happened to your parents. For any of it. It's not your responsibility to keep everyone safe."

He did pull his hand away then, and I let him go.

"Yes, it is. I'm alpha, and that's my first responsibility. My duty to the pack. And I failed."

"You weren't alpha then," I said softly. "You were just a scared kid. One who's blaming himself for other people's crimes. You're not a killer."

He barked a laugh that was all bitterness and anguish.

"My other crimes aren't so easily excused."

"No?" I raised an eyebrow, glaring at him. "You killed your last mate, then—with your own hands?"

"I may as well have."

"That's a no."

He shook his head and stared out into the tree line. "Trust me. That one's all my fault. It happened because of me. Because someone used her to get to me."

He sank down onto a fallen log, his back turned to me.

"I was away a lot," he said to the foliage. "We had a young son— Jackson—and I'd been alpha of Broken Ridge for enough years to have made some enemies. I was negotiating alliances with surrounding packs. I thought that more power would make us safer. I couldn't have been more wrong."

He paused and sucked in a breath, and I moved to stand behind him, not touching him. He kept staring out at the trees, but I didn't think he saw them.

"Lily was eight months pregnant with Kade when she told me about the affair. She didn't want any lies between us, she said. She wanted his birth to be our fresh start. So she told me about the other shifter she'd been sleeping with."

His hands shifted into claws and dug into the log, splintering the dried bark. His arms trembled, and I heard his teeth grinding together, and then his claws became hands again.

"I tracked him down. I knew him, of course. I'd shut down his smuggling ring the year before, and stripped him of his rank. He never forgave me. But he didn't come after me, not directly. He went after Lily. He seduced her to get to me, and he was quick enough to throw it in my face when I caught up with him. The things he said about her..." He shook his head. "I'm glad she never heard them. I warned him off. I told him to leave and never come back."

He twisted round to look up at me.

"That was my mistake. I should have known better."

"What happened?" Because I knew the story didn't end there. The raw agony in Devlin's eyes told me that much.

"There was a fight in the packlands two weeks after Kade was born. I went out to deal with it. I should have known it was a trap. Four of Niko's friends. They jumped me as soon as I arrived. I fought as hard as I could, but by the time I defeated them..." He shook his head. "I raced home, but I was too late. Niko was standing over Lily's body. He ran as soon as he saw me, but it didn't matter. She was gone. My beautiful Lily was dead."

I blinked back tears and settled my hand on Devlin's shoulder. He started, like he'd forgotten I was there, then placed his hand over mine and twisted round to look at me over his shoulder.

"At first, I didn't understand why she hadn't just run from him. And then I heard a cry. Kade's tiny body was under hers—she died protecting him." He swallowed. "She died doing my job."

I slid my other arm around down over his chest, embracing him from behind, and rested my cheek against his.

191

"That's why things are difficult between you and Kade?" I said. "Because she died saving him?"

"No," Devlin said. "Things are difficult between me and Kade because Kade isn't my son. He's Niko's."

CHAPTER FORTY-ONE

My head reeled from the revelation. Eventually, I regained some control of my jaw.

"Does he know?"

Devlin shook his head, something close to panic flashing through his eyes.

"No. And he must never find out. I made a promise to Lily."

"He won't find out from me," I said, and the panic faded from his face. "So, that's why you're such a good cook, huh? Having to feed two growing pups every day?"

He snorted. "It was the one thing I could get right. Pack business meant I wasn't around enough for them. The pack raised them as much as I did. For a long time, I was caught up in hunting down Blaine and visiting justice on him, so that he could never harm another member of my pack. I should never have let him live the first time, and Lily paid the price. I vowed I would not make the same mistake again."

He glanced over his shoulder, back the way we came, and there were no prizes for guessing what he was thinking. His hand on top of mine curled into a fist.

"Hey," I said softly. "You can't kill everyone who looks at me the wrong way."

"Watch me."

I placed my other hand on top of his, and smoothed his fist out flat, then traced patterns on his palm. He thrummed low in his throat.

"Protect me by staying with me," I whispered.

"Always."

I stepped away, still holding his hand, and tugged him to his feet. I didn't want him thinking about my three attackers.

"Anyway, I'm starving. And we've already established that I can't cook, so I'm counting on you to whip up something that won't give me food poisoning."

He chuckled, then his expression darkened as he cast a look back the way we came. I tugged on his hand until he looked at me.

"Please?" I said. His eyes softened, and he nodded his head.

"You've had a long day. Let's get you home."

"How much further until we cross over into Broken Ridge territory?"

"About half a mile back," he said, shaking his head in dismay at my apparent lack of respect for his realm. He raised a valid point—if I was going to be the luna of this pack, their alpha's mate, then I should at least know where the pack's boundaries lay. Of course, if anyone had actually let me out into the grounds for more than five minutes since I got here, I might have had half a chance of knowing that already. But that was an argument for another day. I didn't want to argue with Devlin right now.

My wolf stirred inside me, and in my shaken state, it took me a long moment to recognize what she wanted. Then I grinned, and tugged Devlin's shirt over my head. He eyed me with something like alarm.

"What are you doing?"

"Shifting," I said, and tugged off the tattered remains of my own shirt. "Now that it's safe."

I kicked the rest of my clothes off, and glanced up to see Devlin in front of me, completely naked. My wolf all but purred in satisfaction as I ran my eyes over his powerful body, catching on his abs and then moving down to the glorious cock hanging between his legs.

"Keep looking at me like that," he growled, "and neither of us is going to get around to shifting."

My breath caught in my throat, and my wolf didn't utter a single sound of protest, despite the fact running was about her favorite thing to do in the world. Or used to be. Apparently, she had a new favorite thing, and it was ogling Devlin. I shook my head to hide my amused grin. She was literally panting inside my head.

"Oh, and why's that?" I teased, watching him from between lowered lashes.

"Because," he growled, and I couldn't help but notice his magnificent cock was hard and jutting towards me as he closed the gap between us, "I'm going to fuck you right against that tree."

I trailed my fingertips across his chest and reveled in his sharp intake of breath at my touch. And then I shoved him back a step.

"Down, boy. If you want me, you're going to have to catch me."

He watched with a languid smile on his lips as I embraced the inner wolf, and the heat of the shift rushed over me, leaving me on four lithe limbs, jet black with a splash of white on my right shoulder.

I darted away into the tree line, one ear flicked back. A second later, I heard four paws pounding through the foliage behind me and risked a glance over my shoulder. Devlin was breathtaking, even in this form.

Especially in this form, my wolf corrected me. Right. It stood to reason she'd be more impressed by the beast than the man. It seemed to me that he was perfect in whatever form he took, but a vision of his naked human body swam up behind my eyes, and I didn't think I'd be forgetting it anytime soon.

My brief glance had become an ogle again, and the moment I realized, I snapped my head forward—and narrowly avoided running straight into a tree. I ducked aside at the last second and heard Devlin chuff with amusement behind me.

I flashed my tail and kicked my pace up a notch so that I was running at near full speed, and the bigger, heavier wolf doubled his speed, keeping up with me effortlessly. I twisted round to look at him as he drew alongside me, and wondered if he was remembering what I was remembering: our first hunt, when I'd taken a snap at him. Then I saw the sparkle of amusement in his eyes. Yeah, he was remembering all right, the bastard.

We ran together, him letting me lead our way by half a head, content just to follow as I took us through the territory, running to everywhere and nowhere in companionable silence. I'd never run with another wolf, not like this, always having preferred my own company to the spoiled alpha brats and even my own brothers back in Winter Moon. It had been easier to be by myself, a lone wolf in the heart of the pack, than to handle being ostracized by the other wolves. It had been easier not to want what I couldn't have. But I hadn't known it could be like this.

I didn't know how long we ran together, but by the time I slowed, darkness had fully fallen. I thought at one stage I saw another wolf, but if I did, they melted away without joining us.

The foliage above our heads had thinned enough to give us a glimpse of the night sky, with the moon hanging amidst the stars in all its glory. I threw my head back and howled, and a split second later, Devlin's baritone joined mine, weaving a harmony through the night air.

I lowered my head and closed the gap between us, and my tongue shot out to lick once at his muzzle. He backed up a step and a whine slipped from my muzzle, the pain of his previous rejection rising to the surface.

He shook out his whole body, then shimmered back into his human form. I hesitated, then shifted, too.

"You've had a long day," he started, and his warm baritone washed over me, luring me to him.

"Yes," I agreed, my voice breathy. "I have."

"We should get you home."

"Yes," I agreed again, "we should."

And then I stepped towards him, tracing my hand across his bicep.

"Jess…"

I twisted up, pressing my lips to his, silencing his protests. He turned to stone under my touch and I pressed my naked body to his, working my mouth against his. All at once he started kissing me back, slipping his tongue into my mouth as one arm wrapped around me, pulling me closer to him.

And then he stopped.

"Wait."

"I don't want to wait," I said, and crushed my lips against his again. He kissed me back fiercely, then groaned and pulled back a second time.

"Listen to me. After everything you've been through today… You don't want this. You don't have to do this."

"No, you listen," I said in that same breathless whisper. "I want you. I want all of you. And it has nothing to do with what happened earlier, and everything to do with us." A bolt of panic shot through me, and I searched his face, trying to stifle my fear. The knowledge that I wasn't good enough for this man. Would never be good enough for this man. "Unless…unless you don't want me?"

A growl bounced around inside his chest.

"Look at me," he said, reaching out and tucking one finger under my chin. He gently lifted my head so that my eyes met his. "I will tell you every night for the rest of your life if I must. I want you. I want you more than I want anything else in this world."

"Then prove it."

He exhaled in a groan, then bent his head to mine.

"You're going to be the death of me, Jessica Whitlock."

CHAPTER FORTY-TWO

His lips crushed down against mine and I moaned into his mouth, pressing my entire body against his. His cock jutted against me and he sucked my bottom lip into his mouth, nibbling it in a way that sent arousal burning through me.

"Devlin," I groaned, grinding myself against his leg.

His lips abandoned mine, planting a trail of whisper-light kisses along my throat, and then down to my breasts. He sucked one of my nipples into his mouth and the breath rushed out of me in a ragged gasp. My legs trembled beneath me, turned to liquid by his fiery kisses and he cupped my ass with his hands, backing me up until I was pressed against one of the broad oak trees.

He sank to his knees in front of me and I whimpered at the loss of his mouth from my body, and then I felt his hot breath between my legs. My breathing hitched, and as his tongue flicked across my clit, I all but lost myself.

"Devlin," I panted, as he drank deeply from me. "I...I need..."

I didn't know what I needed. I needed *him*.

He drew back, and I felt his eyes searching my face.

"Don't stop," I gasped, and he pushed his way back between my legs, licking and sucking greedily.

The pleasure built with each touch until I could think of nothing but the sensation of the man between my legs. My alpha. My mate. Mine. Heat flashed across my whole body and tremors wracked me from head to toe. I came with a loud cry, and Devlin caught me as I lost control of my legs, sliding me down onto the soft leaf litter.

For a moment I lay there panting, basking in the afterglow of the best orgasm of my life. I hadn't known it could be like that...but then, I didn't think it could have been like that with anyone other than Devlin. We were made for each other, compatible in every way. Not two halves of a whole, because I was my own person, a whole on my own, and yet with him I was *more*.

I rolled into Devlin's embrace, then paused as his rock-hard cock pressed against my thigh, anxiety stirring in my gut. I'd never been with a man before. No-one at Winter Moon had looked twice at me, and I'd liked it that way. Even after my eighteenth birthday, none of the guys had shown an interest, and I'd been relieved. But it didn't mean I hadn't heard the other girls talking. I knew what to expect. I just hadn't expected it to be so...big.

"I..." I swallowed, and tried again, my voice a hoarse whisper. "I've never..."

I glanced down at the rod between us, and up again in time to catch Devlin's eyes widen, and then his face softened.

"You don't have to," he said. "If you're not ready, we'll wait."

I shook my head.

"I'm ready. I want you inside me. I just..." I flushed and looked away.

"What?"

"What if I'm not any good?"

He was silent, but I felt his chuckle vibrate against my flesh, and then his lips pressed to my neck.

"You're my mate," he said, in between kisses. "Good is not a strong enough word for what you are. Everything about you is perfect."

"Even my bratty attitude?" I teased through a smile. He nipped at my neck.

"Even that."

My hand slid down between us to encircle him, and the butterflies fluttered in my stomach again. He was huge, and somehow he seemed to

199

grow even larger at my touch. My hand caressed the velvety soft skin, and he sucked in a sharp breath.

"Is that…is that okay?" I asked hesitantly.

"Better than okay," he rasped, as my hand continued to explore. He rolled his head back, then jerked it forward to meet my eye again.

"Are you sure you've never done this before?"

I blushed and a smile played over my lips.

"Yes."

He nipped at my throat.

"That's 'Yes, Alpha' to you," he rumbled. His hands found my hips and tossed me onto my back. I landed with a sound that was a cross between a yelp of surprise and a squeal of…something else, and then he was on me, pinning my hands to the ground above my head.

"Who am I?" he demanded, staring down at me. I bit my lower lip and stifled a chuckle. His empty hand trailed down my side and I squealed again, bucking in his grip.

"My alpha!" I gasped, and no sooner had the word burst from my lips, his mouth closed on top of mine, sucking me into one of those all consuming kisses until I could think of nothing but his tongue plundering my mouth and the taste of my own arousal. I groaned, arching my back into him, and his hand moved from my hip to the flat of my stomach, and then between my legs again. He played me until I whimpered with need, and then his touch vanished.

"Ready?" he asked, his lips moving against mine.

"Yes, Alpha," I panted, and then I felt a hardness nuzzle the entrance between my legs. My breathing hitched with a delicious mix of fear and anticipation, and the desperate desire to have him inside me. He didn't keep me waiting, easing us together so softly that I felt nothing but pleasure as we became one.

He twisted his head to nip at my earlobe and my eyes widened as he eased deeper inside. We moved as one, rocking in the soft leaf litter of nature's bedroom. The heat in me built and built until I was trembling with pleasure and with need.

"Devlin," I gasped, and his mouth came down to claim mine one last time. We reached our climax together, crying out into the night, and then collapsed to the floor, spent.

CHAPTER FORTY-THREE

It was gone noon when I awoke the following day. It had been a long day, and by the time we made it back to Devlin's home—*our* home—everything that happened had caught up with me. I'd been half asleep even before Devlin had carried me over the threshold, and everything beyond that was a blur.

I pushed aside the duvet, noting with some distant part of my mind that I was back in my own room, and hunted around for a clean set of clothes. We'd retrieved ours before coming home last night, but they got messed up long before we made it. And the shirt—I took one look at that, with its jagged tear down the front, and tossed it aside with a shudder. That, I'd rather not see again.

Thanks to my prematurely abandoned shopping trip—hard to believe that was only yesterday, so much had happened since then—I didn't have much left, but I found an old pair of skinny-fit jeans and a tank top, which would do.

I took a quick shower, spending the bare minimum time to get myself cleaned up after our adventures last night, and then hurried down the stairs. I made straight for the kitchen, then when I got there, changed my mind. I wasn't really hungry. Instead, I drifted around the house aimlessly, wandering from one room to the next. I was halfway through my second lap when I realized what was bothering me.

Shit. Was I *missing* Devlin?

Mate? My wolf asked hopefully, perking one ear.

Oh, shut up. I slumped against the nearest wall. Had I really hurried downstairs, expecting to find him waiting for me in the kitchen, and then been *disappointed* when he hadn't been there? Shit. I had. I shook my head and laughed under my breath. And here I'd been blaming my wolf for fangirling over the big bad alpha. We were as bad as each other.

But…well, after last night, I'd expected him to stick around to see me today. Sure, I was up late, but… I shook my head again. What did I even care if he had some stupid pack business to attend to, or whatever? It wasn't like I felt betrayed he wasn't here. That would be stupid.

I pushed off the wall and headed back to the kitchen. Just because the high and mighty Alpha Devlin wasn't here didn't mean I was going to starve myself. I yanked open the fridge and plucked out a few ingredients—it had been too much to hope that I'd find a ready meal here. I put some pasta on to boil and threw half a dozen random vegetables into a pan. I wasn't going to go hungry—out of spite, if nothing else.

How dare he share that incredible experience with me last night, and then just disappear on me? I thought…I choked up a laugh as I slumped at the table. I thought we'd had a connection. God, I was such an idiot. Could I be any more naïve? Clearly, it had meant more to me than it had to him.

That, wolf, I chastised my inner beast, is the last time we give in to our base instincts.

She rumbled her discontent wordlessly at me. Seriously. *Devlin* was the one who'd screwed us over, and she was pissed at *me?* Ugh, there was no reasoning with her. Maybe food would draw her out of her mood.

Hunt?

No, because we're stuck here. Thanks to the mate you're busy fangirling over.

Meat?

Pasta. Can't survive on meat alone.

Can.

Oh, my God, I could hear the pout in her voice, and she didn't even have lips to pout with. I was pretty sure this was what going mad felt like. I slumped my head onto my arms and ran through all the ways Devlin most definitely did *not* deserve my…affection…or whatever the hell this was.

My nose twitched at the smell of his bullshit.

No, wait. That wasn't bullshit. That was something burning. Crap.

I pried myself off the table and glanced over at the hob, where a curl of dark smoke was coming from one of my pans. With a sigh that felt like it came from my toes, I ambled over. Turned out you couldn't make a half-way edible pasta sauce by just chucking ingredients in a pan and turning on the heat. I killed the gas under it and tossed the pan's contents, then threw it in the sink to soak. Ugh. That really did stink. I leaned over the sink and shoved the window open to let some fresh air in.

Then I blinked.

The window.

It opened.

Apparently, he hadn't remembered to lock it like he had every other window in this prison of mine.

Interesting. I eyed it speculatively. It was big enough that I could climb out of it and take a stroll around town without an escort. I guess Mister High-and-Mighty-Alpha thought one night of mind-blowing sex would be enough to make me his devoted pet.

We are devoted.

Oh, shut up. We are not.

The sex was very good.

As if. We don't even have a point for comparison. It might have been terrible sex.

Was not.

Well, yeah, okay, she was probably right about that. Hard to imagine anyone else knowing how to touch my body the way he did last night.

And the way we moved together, as though we were two parts of the same creature. As though I was welcoming him home inside me.

I shook my head to clear the ridiculous thoughts. Because if he felt the same way, he'd be here now, wouldn't he?

Anyway, it wasn't like I was planning to run again. A shudder ran the length of my body. No. There were things out there much worse than anything I'd face in Broken Ridge.

Then stay.

We're not a damned house pet, I all but snarled at my inner beast, and I felt the echo of her indignation. We were a wild, powerful creature—omega or no—and we were born to be free. Born to lead this pack as Devlin's luna, if the fates were right. Not to be a sparrow in a gilded cage.

Because I *was* Devlin's mate.

Mate.

Her tone was dreamy, and I rolled my eyes. Yes, fine. I liked him. Yes, fine, the sex was good. Better than good. But he needed to see that I had my own will. My own needs.

Starting with the need for a decent lunch over at the café. Don't sweat it, wolf, I told her cheerfully as I tugged on my sneakers. We'll probably be back before he is. And we can get a burger in town.

Rare?

Maybe, I hedged. I preferred my meat well done in human form. But in truth, rare would keep her quiet, and I needed some quiet right now to sort through my feelings about Devlin. Because frankly, they were a mess, and I wasn't going to get to grips with them sitting inside his house.

I hopped up on the counter, stepped carefully around the sink, then jumped down into the front garden. As an afterthought, I pushed the window to so that it wouldn't be immediately obvious from the outside, but left it open enough that I could get my fingers between the sill and let myself back in—because I did *not* want to have to sit on the doorstep like a stray cat waiting for Devlin to come home.

I flicked my hair back over my shoulder, and strode across the expansive front garden with as much confidence as I could muster. And then I spotted the guards on the front gate. Crap.

They were looking out onto the street, so I ducked back before they spotted me, and followed the wall round until I was out of their line of sight. I was really going to have to talk to Devlin about his tendency to be a little overprotective. Whenever he actually showed up, that was. Which, hopefully, wouldn't be until *after* I'd had my lunch.

I jumped up, grabbing hold of the top of the wall, and hauled myself over. My wolf stopped sulking long enough to make sure I didn't faceplant on the far side, and I straightened with a grin, then headed for the café.

Though the Broken Ridge territory was vast, the town itself wasn't, so it was less than ten minutes later that I reached the street I wanted, and I could smell the delicious scents of food even before the café came into sight. My stomach rumbled in appreciation and I quickened my pace. Because seriously, if Devlin caught up with me before I got served, I was going to take another snap at him. Although I was starting to think he liked that.

"Jess!"

I spun round at the sound of my name, and then my eyes widened in surprise as I saw the figure hurrying towards me. He crossed the road, grabbed my arm, and towed me into an alleyway.

"Kade! What are you doing?" I tugged my arm loose from his grip, peering past him to the street—seemed like no-one had noticed the alpha's son dragging me into a dirty alleyway. A shadow moved in the alleyway's mouth, and then Dean was blocking my view. Playing lookout for his buddy, I guessed. Great.

"Thank God you're okay."

His eyes flickered frantically across my face, searching for I wasn't sure what.

"I'm fine. I ran into some trouble yesterday, but Devlin took care of it."

He nodded.

"I heard you ran. I was worried for you. I grew up with him, I know what he can be like. I don't blame you for not telling me he was your mate. How could anyone want that for a mate?" He shook his head, and snatched up my hand again. "You just have to hang in there, Jess."

"I…" I frowned, not quite sure what to make of what he was saying, and the weird way he was behaving.

"It's okay," he said. "I'm going to find a way for us to be together."

CHAPTER FORTY-FOUR

"What do you mean?" I asked, plucking my hand from Kade's and staring at him. Inside my chest, my wolf rattled in fury.

"I care about you, Jess. And I know you care about me. We had a connection. You belong with me, not with my father."

"Devlin is my mate," I protested. Kade shook his head.

"I'll find a way to break it, I swear. What we have is stronger than a mate bond."

"Break it?" I blanched, and it was all I could do to keep my wolf from bursting out of my skin. I didn't think it was possible, but just the thought of it, the thought of Devlin being ripped from me, was enough to make me nauseous.

"There has to be a way. I'll find it, and then we can be together."

"Are you crazy?"

"No." He shook his head again. "For the first time in my life, I can see clearly. I want you, Jess. I've always wanted you. And I won't rest until we're together again—even if it means killing my father."

Rapid breaths wheezed painfully in and out of my chest. Kill Devlin? No. I couldn't let anything happen to him. I *wouldn't* let anything happen to him.

Protect mate, my wolf snarled. *Kill the threat.*

I sucked in a deep breath and made an effort to get my terror under control. If Kade and my wolf were both going straight for the killing solution, then I would have to be the voice of reason. I touched my hand lightly to Kade's arm.

"Kade, I'm sorry. I'm with Devlin. I *want* to be with Devlin."

His brow knitted, then he shook his head, and his eyes softened.

"No-one's listening, Jess. You don't have to pretend when you're around me. Shit, what did he do to you to make you so afraid?"

"No, you don't understand, I—"

"Ssh, it's okay, you don't have to say."

I ground my teeth together in frustration. I was trying to spare his feelings, because in his own way, he did care for me. But we were going round in circles here. He cast a glance to the end of the alleyway, where Dean still stood guard, and then turned his eyes back to me again.

"You should go," I told him.

"Show me your neck."

"What?" I took a step back from him.

"Your neck. Show me. Has he claimed you yet?"

My wolf seethed silently inside me. I didn't know a lot about claiming marks, but I'd heard about them, of course. I just never thought for one moment I'd ever have one. It was a small bite, usually, placed at the back of the neck, marking a wolf as mated. Devlin hadn't claimed me, and honestly, I wasn't sure what that meant.

Kade read the answer on my face.

"Don't you see?" he said, his eyes bright with fervor. "This is a good thing, Jess. It means there's still hope. There's still a way out for you."

"He will mark me," I said, and I wasn't sure if I was trying to convince him, or myself. Because Devlin had the chance to mark me last night. He could have sealed the mate bond in the woods, or when we made it back to the house, and he hadn't. And he hadn't been around this morning, either.

Maybe the issue wasn't that I wanted him. Maybe the issue was that, despite everything he'd said, he still didn't want me.

Kade misread my heavy silence.

"Wait, I've got it," he said. "Jess, I know the answer."

His whole face lit up and the words tumbled out of his mouth so quickly they started to run together. He took a breath, but his smile didn't falter.

"Kneel down." He glanced towards the street again. "Quickly."

"What?"

"Kneel down. If I mark you, it means Devlin can't. He won't be able to seal the mate bond."

I took a quick step back. Again, Kade misread my reaction.

"It's okay. It'll only hurt for a moment, I promise. And then we can be together."

"Kade, this is crazy. He'll kill you the second he sees it. And you're not my mate. It would probably heal up in a few days."

"Then at least it will buy us a few days. And that's all I need." He threw another of those crazy glances Dean's way, his eyes wild, and then lowered his voice. "I mean it, Jess. I'll kill him. Take control of Broken Ridge. His time is done."

My wolf roared inside my head, drowning out the last of his words.

Kill the threat to our mate and pack. Kill. Destroy.

I stood frozen as I wrested control back from her before she could do something really dumb—like get *us* killed. Because I didn't know this Kade, and I sure as hell didn't trust him.

He reached for my shoulder and I made to take another step back, but found myself pinned against the wall behind me. I swatted Kade's hand aside, and my wolf glared at him through my eyes.

"Kade, stop."

"Jess, we don't have time."

"Dammit, Kade, there is no we!"

He blinked sharply at my raised voice, and I caught Dean flick a glance in our direction before he went back to playing guard. Hurt flashed over Kade's face. Shit. I didn't mean to hurt him—I didn't *want* to hurt him. But since when had what I wanted actually been a feature of my life?

Since now.

210

She was right. If ever there was a time to stand up for what I wanted, this was it. And what I wanted was Devlin. And I wanted Kade's blessing, too.

My wolf didn't agree on that last point, but I ignored her, and she settled back with a rumble.

"I'm sorry, Kade," I said, searching his face. "I care about you, I do. But as a friend. You were good to me, and you were the first person I ever really had a connection with. And I will never forget that. Ever. But my heart belongs to Devlin."

"Devlin." Kade's voice was flat. Hollow. "You love my father."

I swallowed, and nodded. "I do. But you're important to me, too, Kade."

I reached my hand out to him, and this time, he backed away, and it was my turn to feel a searing pain in my chest.

"Don't touch me," he snapped.

"Kade, don't do this. We'll still be friends."

"I don't want your pity, Jess," he said, his lip curling back into a snarl, "and I don't want your friendship."

I flinched back like he'd slapped me and opened my mouth to say something—anything—to fix this, but no words came out. I could see the lost little boy in his eyes, see his heart breaking, and I wished desperately I could find some way to fix it.

And then his eyes hardened.

"You're going to regret this, Jess. If you won't have me, then you won't have anyone."

CHAPTER FORTY-FIVE

I stared after Kade's back for a long moment, then got the hell out of there and made straight for home. My appetite was long gone, and suddenly, my rebellious little jaunt seemed like a stupid, childish idea.

Idiotic.

For once, my wolf didn't disagree with me. We hurried back across town, senses on high alert. What had Kade's threat meant? And it had been a threat, that much I knew. But would he attack me? Try to ruin me? Worse, attack Devlin? Or find some way to make him hate me?

I pushed the thoughts from my mind long enough to scan the area, but no sooner had my wolf confirmed we were alone, the thoughts shoved their way back in again. Did Kade mean to forcefully claim me?

Will not submit to another.

Yeah, now *that* was something we could agree on. Vehemently. But Kade was stronger than us, and he always had Dean or Ryder in his shadow. They could overpower me, if they wanted.

Mate is stronger.

Which'd be great, if he was watching over us twenty-four seven.

Stay in mate's lair.

Which is what I should have done in the first place. Why the hell had I been so stupid?

Stupid.

Gee, thanks wolf.

Stupid to run from mate. Stupid to disobey.

All right, yes, I get it.

Stupid to resist Alpha Devlin.

You're wrong about that, wolf. It's not me resisting him. I was the one who'd made the first move, and I was the one who'd done all the chasing. He'd rejected me more than once.

He was the one chasing last night. And he didn't reject us then.

I sucked in a deep breath and nodded. It was true. I just wasn't sure how he felt about me today.

I scrambled over the wall and landed with a soft thud on the other side. A weight lifted from my shoulders and my heart rate steadied. And just like that, it seemed my prison had become my sanctuary.

Was always sanctuary. You were just too stubborn to see it.

"All right wolf," I muttered as I straightened. "I think that's enough lectures for one day."

"Oh, I disagree, Jessica."

I jumped back with a yelp, and found myself staring at one very hot, very pissed off alpha.

"Al—Alpha Devlin," I stuttered. "What are you doing here?"

He arched a brow at me.

"Are you questioning me, little wolf?"

I shook my head and clamped my mouth shut.

"Good. Because I would hate to think, after disobeying my very specific order not to leave the house, that *you* would think to question *me.*"

He advanced on me as he spoke, and I shrank away until my back was against the wall.

"You're very determined, I'll give you that," he said, and his gaze drifted to the wall. "Though I have no idea why you're so desperate to escape."

I snorted and his gaze sharpened and snapped back to me. I clamped a hand over my mouth and tried to fake a cough, but apparently he wasn't convinced.

"Am I amusing you?"

I shook my head, sending my dark tresses tumbling around my face. Then a flash of anger rushed through me.

"Actually, yeah, it does make me laugh."

"So I see, little wolf." His voice warned me I was crossing into dangerous territory, but I didn't care.

"I'm supposed to stay here like some meek little house pet on your say-so, just because we screwed last night? When it clearly didn't mean a damn thing to you."

"Is that what you think?"

"That's what I know."

He stretched a hand towards me and I froze in place as he tucked a stray lock of hair behind my ear. His hand lingered on my cheek a moment, and I started to lean into his touch before I caught myself.

"It seems your body knows something different."

"It knows you didn't mark me last night."

He froze, and then quickly pulled his hand away.

"I…can't."

"You mean you won't," I snapped. "Because I was just a quick fuck."

"I didn't hear you objecting last night."

I lashed out, aiming a slap at his face, but he caught my wrist mid-air. I gasped in shock and pain as his hand closed around it and squeezed.

"That will be the last time you raise your hand to me."

"No," I said, glaring at him. "It won't. Not my hand, not my claw, not my tooth. But it will be the last time your cock comes anywhere near me. So don't worry about claiming me. I'm not yours, and I never will be."

I yanked my hand, but his grip didn't loosen.

"You are what I say you are."

"Bite me, Devlin. Oh, wait, you don't want to."

"Dammit, Jessica!" He released my wrist and stalked two paces away, then turned back to me. "Of course I want to. I want the whole damn world to know what you are to me. But you *can't* be that to me."

"Why not? Because I'm an— because I'm not good enough for you?" My heart hammered in my chest. Shit. I'd almost told him I was an omega. I could *never* risk him finding out. He was the most powerful alpha I've ever met, but he was still bound by the law. The one that would demand my death. An omega could not be the mate of an alpha.

Devlin's eyes narrowed for a moment, and then he exhaled heavily and shook his head.

"You are a stubborn wolf with a bratty attitude who talks far too much... but you're more than good enough for me. And I wish I could be what you need. What you deserve."

"You are," I said, and immediately hated the way my voice sounded like a lost little kid. Dammit, I was not a kid anymore...and I hated this bastard. I had since the day he'd first rejected me, and that wasn't about the change just because we'd had a quick roll around in the woods.

After he saved us from being raped and killed. She sounded like she was swooning. Stupid wolf.

Yes, and then dragged us back here to continue being his unloved prisoner. Face it, wolf, he's no better than those guys he beat the crap out of.

Pain shot through me, and I doubled over, teeth clenched as my wolf tried to rip through my skin and force the change.

"Jess?" Devlin closed the gap between us and I could hear the concern in his voice as he reached one hand out to me.

"Stay back," I warned him, and the voice was half mine, half distorted by my beast. I gritted my teeth as I battled her, fighting for control of our body as pain ripped at me from the inside. I forced her back and made myself straighten. Sooner or later I was going to have to do something about that, because being at war like this was killing us both.

"What happened?" Devlin asked.

215

"Nothing." I shook my head and stared into the space over his shoulder. "Can we go back to my jail cell now please?"

His jaw clenched, and I watched him work it loose from the corner of my eye.

"Dammit, Jessica, why can't you see that I'm trying to help you?"

"I don't want your help," I snarled at him. "There's only one thing I want from you: my freedom."

"You keep telling yourself that, little wolf," he rumbled in that delicious voice of his.

Damn the bastard. Damn him to hell. Damn him for being right—because even now, as his dark stare pierced me, I could feel the heat behind my cheeks flowing south, pooling between my legs in a sharp ache of desire. A shiver ran the length of my spine as his nose twitched, and I knew he was scenting my arousal.

I took a step toward him, no longer in control of my own limbs, drawn to him like a moth to the flame, and it was a fitting analogy, because he would destroy me, and I would welcome the destruction.

I trailed my fingers across his bicep and the muscle twitched at my touch.

"You drive me crazy," he groaned, rolling his head back. At least I wasn't going insane alone. But to hell with sanity if it meant depriving myself of the one thing I'd ever truly wanted. Because I hadn't been lying to Kade—my heart, and every inch of flesh that housed it, belonged to Devlin, and there was not one part of me that would ever change it.

My hand kept moving, exploring the planes of his chest, barely concealed behind his plain white tee-shirt. He dipped his chin to watch me, control and lust warring on his face.

"You're going to be the death of me," he growled.

"Yes, but it's better than dying of loneliness," I whispered, and closed my lips over his.

CHAPTER FORTY-SIX

"You confound me," Devlin said to me, tracing the shape of my bare shoulder as we lay side by side in his bed several hours later.

I arched a brow and rolled over to look at him more closely.

"Oh no," I teased. "I must be in trouble if you're busting out the big words."

"Big words?" One corner of his mouth quirked up in amusement. "Confound has only two syllables."

I poked my tongue out at him. "You know what I mean."

He nipped at my lips and I evaded him with a smile, then pressed a kiss to his lips. He deepened it, invading my mouth with his tongue, licking and tasting and dominating me until I was moaning into him, and getting wet all over again. His body rolled to cover mine, his hands planted on either side of my body, supporting his weight so that we were almost touching, and it was all I could do to keep from thrusting my hips at him.

Then he broke away.

"Yes, confound," he said, and I growled in frustration. He chuckled under his breath, and his voice, when he spoke, was a low murmur.

"I told you I didn't understand why you kept trying to escape. But the truth is the opposite. I don't understand why you come back."

I snorted. "You mean other than that you keep dragging me back here like a caveman?"

"I don't recall there being much dragging last night," he said softly. I opened my mouth to give him some attitude, but something stopped me. He met my eye and continued. "I told you my truth last night, Jess. Let me catch a glimpse of yours."

My breath caught in my throat, and the unexpected vulnerability in his expression caught me off guard. Enough that I allowed a small sliver of truth to slip through the cracks in my already battered defenses.

"When you rejected me, it almost destroyed me." Pain flitted across his face, tightening around his eyes, but I didn't let it distract me. "But the more you push me away, the more I crave you."

I sank back onto the bed and stared up at the ceiling and fought back a bitter laugh. God, I was such a fucking mess. What the hell sort of woman wanted a man who repeatedly shoved her away?

Devlin grunted and his weight shifted beside me. "It's a helluva thing, the mate bond, isn't it?"

I rolled onto my side and studied his face as he stared at the ceiling above us.

"Is that all this is?" I asked eventually. "Some sort of compulsion? A genetic quirk?"

Devlin snapped his head round to look at me.

"No. Not for me. Not anymore. The more I get to know you, the more I want you."

And it scares the hell out of me, he didn't have to add. It scared the hell out of me, too. Only one thing had scared me more.

"I didn't think you felt it," I said. "At first. I thought maybe I was broken."

He barked a bitter laugh, and shook his head a fraction.

"Oh, I felt it, little wolf. The moment I set eyes on you, it was all I could do not to rip you from Kade's side and make you mine. To take you right there in that courtyard. It took every ounce of the willpower I've built up in my very many years on this earth. And for a moment, I thought I would do it anyway."

His possessive tone sent a shiver through me, and my words escaped as barely a whisper.

"But you didn't."

"But I didn't. Claiming you felt disloyal. To Kade, to my pack. To Lily."

"You must have loved her very much."

"More than I thought possible. More than I imagined I could ever love again—until I met you. But I was—I am—in love with a ghost. A memory. Claiming you felt disloyal to *you*, too."

His hand traced my neck, sending tingles that danced and shimmered across my flesh with delicious anticipation. His fingers came to stop where my neck met my shoulder. Where the claiming mark belonged.

"I was determined to ignore the mate bond, out of respect for you both. You, certainly, seemed uninterested in mating." His hand moved to trail the length of my rib cage and I shivered with anticipation. Devlin had spent a large part of the last two hours showing me exactly what those hands were capable of. He chuckled. "How the mighty have fallen."

I poked my tongue out at him and he nipped at it. His eyes quickly grew serious again.

"I thought I could spare you being with a man who could give you only half of himself, and none of what you needed. A life with Kade would have been better than that."

His eyes searched mine, perhaps seeking confirmation of his words. If so, he wouldn't find it. Because no matter what friendship I might have with Kade—or might have had, before he tried to force his claim on me in the alleyway—I could never have loved him. From the moment I had first seen Devlin, no matter how much I'd fought against it, he had been the only man for me. I felt my wolf's smugness glowing inside me and mentally rolled my eyes at her. Yeah, okay wolf, you were right. Go gloat in silence.

"No matter how I fought it, you were my every thought. That night I found you trying to escape into the woods—for the first time—" He raised an eyebrow in reprimand and I just smiled innocently. "—I had decided to tell Kade the truth and bring you back here. As my prisoner, if need be. It was too much, the thought of you with another man. Even one who believes himself to be my own flesh and blood. Even one who might have been more suitable for you." His voice had grown serious again and he held my eye, locking me in place. "Do you understand, Jessica? It was and is the most selfish thing I have ever done. I deprived you of your liberty, and your chance of happiness, to sate my own jealous desires. It was an unforgivable act."

"I forgive you," I murmured, still meeting his eye. "Because you are the only one who can sate *my* jealous desires."

I lifted one hand and traced his jawline with the backs of my fingers, running them over the first traces of stubble growing them. He groaned softly and leaned into my touch.

Abruptly, he pulled back and searched my face again.

"Why did you think you were broken?"

"What?"

"When you thought I hadn't recognized the mate bond, why did you think you were broken?"

My heart thudded in my chest and I swallowed painfully, breaking eye contact with him. He caught my chin between thumb and forefinger, turning my face back to him.

"You're still hiding something from me."

It was a statement, not a question, and it filled me with terror. I loved him. He loved me. But our love was forbidden, and it would turn to ash under the burning scrutiny of the law.

"Tell me," he commanded, and I felt a compulsion tugging at the edges of my consciousness. I gasped, my eyes widening. I'd thought alpha compulsion was a myth. But as his command echoed through my head, I knew I'd been wrong. His command would force me to speak the truth, and damn us both.

"Please," I whispered, my throat so dry that the words almost stuck there. "Ask anything of me, but not that."

"Fuck." He released me like I'd burned him, and rolled off the bed onto his feet.

"Devlin?" The single whispered word bounced around us in the silence, and he jerked his head round to look at me. Dark lust rolled over his features, warring with disgust. Hatred.

"Jess, I—" He spun away again and snatched up his pants. "Fuck!"

And without another word, he strode out of the room, slamming the door behind him.

I clutched the blankets to my chest, frozen in place. What the hell was going on?

CHAPTER FORTY-SEVEN

"Seriously?" I arched a brow and cocked a hip at Devlin. "Aren't we a little beyond this now?"

"If I believed you were going to run again, little wolf," he rumbled in my ear, "I would have chained you to the bed."

My breath caught in my throat and my heart thudded furiously. A flush of heat spread between my legs at the mental image, and a flush of red across my face at my treacherous body's reaction. Devlin chuckled darkly.

"But perhaps you would enjoy that a little too much."

I opened my mouth to retort and Devlin covered it with his, his tongue slipping between my lips to claim my defiance. Whatever I'd been about to say fled from my mind—hell, all rational thought fled from my mind—until there was only him, touching me, tasting me, devouring me. His hand tangled in my hair, drawing me closer, and I went willingly, melding every inch of my flesh to every inch of his, and everywhere our skin touched, wicked fire erupted and threatened to burn me with my own desire. His other hand slipped under my shirt to find the small of my back, engulfing me in his embrace. My hands returned the gesture, darting under his shirt to explore the smooth flesh of his back, flesh that my fingertips had already committed to memory.

I moaned into his mouth and my hand roamed further south to grip his ass cheek through the heavy denim of his pants. He gasped and I swallowed the taste of his arousal, a thrill running through me as his cock sought me out from behind its confines.

A cough sounded from one side of the kitchen and I made to pull away, but Devlin finished the kiss before he released me, leaving me flustered and flushed, and more than a little frustrated.

"Sorry, Caleb," I said, my cheeks growing pink again. We weren't used to have company anymore, and despite more than a week having passed since Devlin rescued me in the woods, we were still having more than a little trouble keeping our hands off each other. Not that either of us was trying all that hard, admittedly.

Caleb looked pained, but sighed and forced a shrug. "Mated couples, right? I'm sure the pair of you will get some self-control…in a decade or two."

"Don't count on it," Devlin said, and if the heat in his eyes was anything to go by, he was right. And I didn't mind in the least. Kissing Devlin for a decade was no hardship in my mind.

And then my sanity returned. I rounded on Devlin as my annoyance came crashing back down on me.

"Don't go thinking you can just distract me," I warned him. "I mean it. I don't need a chaperone while I sit around the house all day."

"My word is final." He turned to Caleb, ending the discussion before I could demand some sort of answer. Fuck, he was a bastard.

A hot bastard.

Not helping, wolf, I mentally ground out, but my chance to retaliate was long gone, and we both knew it.

"I expect to be gone for a few hours," Devlin said to his beta. "I would prefer to discover my mate still on the grounds when I return."

He turned back to me with a look that promised we'd finish what we started when he got back.

"And I mean it," he said, closing the gap between us, so that he seemed to steal all the air from the room. "Give Caleb a hard time, and I *will* chain you to the bed."

"Promises, promises," I muttered under my breath.

He lowered his head and planted a kiss on my forehead, then his expression melted to tenderness as he met my eye. "Please behave. I need you to be safe, my love."

My heart stuttered, and I forgot to give him any attitude.

He drew away and started for the door. I frowned.

"Wait, what about you?"

He raised an eyebrow in unspoken question.

"If Caleb's staying with me," I clarified, "Who's going with you?"

"I am moving around the Broken Ridge territory, of which I am the alpha. I dare say I will be safe, little wolf."

I opened my mouth, then snapped it shut again. I hadn't mentioned Kade and his threat because neither of us had left the house since he made it. But if I told Devlin now, not only would he want to know why I hadn't told him sooner, he would almost certainly kill Kade—for something he'd said in anger. I mean, he was just hurting. Kade wouldn't really follow through on it, right?

You deceive yourself. Kade is dangerous, and we should inform our mate. Immediately.

Devlin reached for the door. "I'll see you for the hunt."

The hunt! Of course. My immediate terror faded, replaced by a new one. Because if Kade was going to follow through on his threat—

When.

I fought the urge to roll my eyes. If, when, whichever. Either way, that was when he'd do it. On the full moon hunt. When the whole pack was focused on the prey, and none of them would spot one wolf stalking their leader. My mate.

The door clicked shut, and I tried to swallow my fear. There was plenty of time to prepare before then. And we'd be ready for him. My wolf bared her teeth in agreement.

And in the meantime, since I was stuck here, and Caleb was stuck here, maybe I could satisfy my curiosity. There was something that had been playing on my mind for the last week.

"Hey, Caleb, I've got a question."

"No," he said flatly. "I'm not taking you shopping."

I smothered a smile. "Me and Devlin were in bed the other day—"

"Stop," Caleb said, raising a hand. "I don't want to hear anymore. Bad enough I had to watch you making out."

"Funny." I pulled a face at him. "We were *talking*, and there was something he wanted to know… Something I didn't want to tell him. And he tried to use his alpha compulsion on me—which, you know, I thought was a myth."

Caleb's eyebrows shot up into his hairline. "He compelled you?" He let out a low whistle. "He must have wanted to know the answer to that question really bad."

"So, it is real, then?"

"Very." He leaned back against the counter and rubbed his temple. "And it's something Devlin vowed never to use."

"Why?"

"Really? He has the power to compel any member of his pack to do almost anything, and you ask me why he won't use it? You're mated to the man. Does he seem like the sort of person who would enjoy stripping someone's free will from them?"

I decided not to mention the fact I'd been brought here as a prisoner. "So why didn't it work on me? Or at least, not properly."

"The thing you have to understand, Jess, is that an alpha's power of compulsion comes from his pack, and works only *on* his pack. The bigger the pack, and the more trust they have in their alpha, the stronger the alpha's compulsion. His power is over the pack, because it comes *from* the pack. The only exception is on the alpha's luna, once the bonding ritual is complete."

He meant the claiming bite. The one I still didn't have. That didn't make any sense.

"He seemed angry," I said. "Maybe he meant it to work."

"Did he try again?" Caleb asked. "Has he even brought it up again?"

I shook my head in answer to both questions. He'd done nothing to try to force my secret from me.

"Then I think you have your answer. It wasn't you he was angry with. A wolf like Devlin doesn't break his word easily."

*

The day passed slowly, and each passing hour tested my resolution to keep Kade's threat to myself more strongly, but eventually Devlin returned, and we spent time making up for the hours we'd been separated. As if I could dream of running from this man. I could no more be separated from him than from my own soul. Even when we weren't in bed, his presence was intoxicating.

We were eating dinner when the pounding started at the door. I cut off mid-word, and the pair of us shared a brief frown before Devlin rose to his feet. I got to mine a split second later.

"Jessica…" He raised an eyebrow in warning.

"Don't bother. That sounds urgent."

"Exactly. You should wait here."

He lifted his arm to bar my path, and I ducked under it. I thought I heard him sigh as he hurried after me, and easily overtook me before we reached the door. The benefit of longer legs.

He pressed his thumb to the scanner—he still hadn't programmed it to accept my thumbprint, the bastard—and pulled the door open.

The sight that greeted me drove all thoughts of my irritation straight from my mind.

"Father. Forgive me for disturbing you."

Kade had a black eye and a cut above his brow, but I barely spared him a glance. His hand was wrapped around the forearm of a barely conscious figure slumped at his feet.

"I was running patrol this evening and I came across this intruder."

The figure lifted his head and stared out at me through the one eye that wasn't swollen completely shut. His entire face was bloodied and bruised so badly that it took me a moment to recognize him. And then I did.

I gasped, my hand flying to my mouth.

"Dammit, Kade," Devlin snarled. "You shouldn't have brought him here. Jessica does not need to be exposed to this level of brutality. Jessica, go inside."

"No, it's…it's not that." I forced the words out. "Devlin, I know him. He's my brother."

"Father," Kade said, "I came here so that you could formalize the sentence. This man—likely sent by Jess's father—invaded our territory, and attacked me. Under pack law, he must be sentenced to death."

CHAPTER FORTY-EIGHT

"What?" I gaped at Kade. "No, you can't."

"Jessica…"

I whirled on Devlin.

"No. He's my *brother*. Whatever you think he did, he's innocent. I won't let you kill him."

"Father. If I may? I will help Jess calm her nerves while you escort the prisoner inside. I have already sent Dean to alert Beta Caleb."

I opened my mouth to argue, but something in his eyes gave me pause. I snapped my jaw shut and nodded. Devlin eyed me warily for a moment, then grabbed Jace's arm and dragged him to his feet.

"Don't hurt him!" I cried, but Devlin simply hauled him wordlessly into the house. I made to follow, but Kade caught my arm, snapping me back to my senses. I turned and glared at him as Devlin's footsteps, and the sounds of my brother stumbling along in his merciless grip, receded.

"I don't know what game you're playing, Kade," I snapped, shaking off his grip, "but if anything happens to my brother because of you, I swear I will never forgive you."

"I don't need your forgiveness, Jess," he said, a sneer spreading across his face. He looked me up and down, his lips twisting in disgust. "There's *nothing* I need from you."

"Because I chose my true mate over you? Kade, do you hear yourself?"

"Oh, it's not about that. You see, me and your brother had a little chat after I captured him. Wait, should I say…your half-brother?"

I gasped and staggered back.

"There's nothing I need from you, because you *are* nothing." He spat at the ground in front of my feet. "To think I wasted all that time on a filthy *omega*."

I shook my head in horror. He knew. Kade knew what I was. Devlin was going to kill me. The whole pack was going to tear me apart.

"You're worthless," he said. "You should have been *begging* me to accept you. But what did you do? You tried to escape, again and again, you ungrateful little cur. And then you had the gall to reject me."

"I'm sorry! But you know how strong the mate bond is—"

"Would you shut up about the damn mate bond?" he snarled, then cast a glance through the open doorway behind me and lowered his voice. "Don't worry, *omega*. Your secret is safe with me. For now. But if you want to keep it that way, you're going to start doing what you're told. You answer to me now, is that clear?"

I swallowed, searching his face. He wasn't going to tell. I just had to find a way to make him keep quiet. There had to be a way.

There is. My wolf's snarl sent a chill along my spine. *Kill him.*

He stepped, closing the space between us in a heartbeat until he was staring down into my eyes.

"I said, is that clear?"

Bite. Kill. Destroy the threat.

He laughed darkly, in a sound that was eerily similar to Devlin.

"Oh, I know what you're thinking," he breathed in my ear. He raised one hand to stroke my cheek and it was all I could do to stop my wolf taking over and ripping it off at the shoulder. "But I'm an alpha-son. Killing me is punishable by death. You can't silence me that way." His voice hardened. "So, I'll ask again. Is. That. Clear?"

Hope deserted me, leaving an aching hollow inside my chest. I couldn't fight him. I couldn't stop him. All I could do was give him whatever he wanted.

"Yes," I whispered.

"Yes, what?"

"Yes, Alpha-son."

"Good. Do try to remember who your betters are, *omega.*" He spat the word in disgust, and I hung my head. He was right. I was an omega, and that was all I would ever be. I should never have allowed myself to fall for Devlin. I should never have dreamed of a life by his side. I wasn't worthy of him, of that life, and I never would be.

"Now, I suggest you get your worthless mongrel ass inside and make sure Devlin kills your brother before he can spill your secret to the entire pack."

"What? No, I—"

"You'll be hearing from me, Jess."

And with that, he turned and stalked away into the falling darkness, leaving me shivering and shaking on the doorstep of what, for a moment, had almost been my home.

A sob worked its way up my throat. It was over. Gone. All of it.

No weakness. Only strength. This isn't the time to break down.

I sucked in a sharp breath of the cool evening air. She was right. Whatever was going to happen to me was out of my hands right now. But Jace needed me, and if the last thing I could do was save his life, then I was damned well going to do it—whether he revealed my secret or not.

I hurried inside, shutting the door firmly behind me, then followed the sounds of labored breathing. I was surprised when it led me to the kitchen—but then, I'd been all over this house, and Devlin didn't have a torture dungeon. I guess the kitchen was as good a place to torture an innocent man as any.

I paused in the doorway. Jace was slumped in a chair, and Devlin was leaning over him with his back to me, doing I could only guess what. Jace groaned in pain and I stepped inside.

Devlin straightened and frowned, scanning the empty space behind me.

"Where's Kade?"

230

"He's gone to see what's keeping Caleb," I fabricated quickly—because I could hardly tell him what had really happened. Not if I was going to save Jace before Kade revealed my shameful secret and Devlin handed me over to the pack.

"Good," Devlin nodded, and turned round fully. There was a damp cloth in his hands, and some of the blood had been cleaned from Jace's face. He pressed the cloth to Jace's swollen shut eye, and my brother winced again.

"Wait," I said, stepping forward hesitantly. "What's going on?"

Devlin lowered the cloth.

"He's your brother, Jess. I'm not going to kill him. Not without a lot of evidence that he was breaking the law—and not even then, if I can help it."

"Thank you." I crossed the floor and squeezed his hand, a sob rising up my throat.

"Do you doubt me so easily, my love?" he murmured.

I flushed pink, and then something caught my eye. One of Jace's arms was wrapped in a sling. "What happened?"

"Kade," Devlin said with a grimace. "He has a broken arm, and at least several broken ribs."

"But he'll be okay?"

"His shifter healing will take care of it in time."

Time. The one thing we would only have if we could convince the pack he hadn't committed a crime. I nodded and pulled open the freezer, emptying some ice into a towel and pressing it gently over Jace's ribs. He winced, but nodded his thanks and moved his uninjured arm to pin the bundle in place.

A knocking came from the direction of the front door, and Devlin straightened again.

"That'll be Caleb." He handed the damp cloth to me. "I'll leave you in Jessica's capable hands."

"Thank you, Alpha Devlin," Jace said through swollen lips.

"Don't thank me yet, pup," Devlin grunted, and left the room.

"What's going on, Jess?" Jace hissed as soon as the alpha was out of earshot.

"I was about to ask you the same question! Did you really attack Kade?"

"Of course I didn't. I came here to check on you, to make sure you were okay. As soon as I turned up at Kade's house, he attacked me, and— Look, it doesn't matter. What are you doing here, in the alpha's house?"

"He's my true mate, Jace."

"Your what?" His eyes widened and he gaped at me, then he lowered his voice and carried on in a rush. "Jess, you can't have a true mate. It's too dangerous… And an alpha? Are you crazy?"

"It's not like I had a choice, Jace," I hissed back. "And trust me, I tried to fight it. But it's a mate bond, not a Valentine's card. What was I supposed to do?"

"I know, I know, just… be careful, Jess."

"I will."

"No, you don't understand. When I got to Kade's house, he recognized me right away. Him and his friend jumped me and tied me up. They kept asking about you in between beating me. I should have let them kill me rather than answer. Jess, I'm so sorry. He knows your…" He cast another glance at the door over my shoulder. "Your secret."

"I know." I grimaced. "He took great pleasure in gloating about it. You did the right thing. He would have killed you if you didn't tell him, and I don't care what you say, I'm not worth dying over."

"That's bullshit, Jess. I know you weren't treated right growing up, and I'm sorry I didn't do more to stand up for you. But you're worth it, I promise. I'm your brother, and I should have looked out for you."

"I…" I wasn't quite sure what to say to that. Jace *had* looked out for me growing up, even protecting me from some of the beatings the other kids had thrown my way. No-one else had ever stood up for me that way.

Footsteps behind me spared me from finding an answer, and I straightened to find Devlin and Caleb entering the room.

"This is him?" Caleb said, eyeing Jace. My brother quickly bowed his head and averted his eyes.

"Yes, sir," Jace said.

"He's innocent," I said, my eyes blazing. "He didn't do anything. Kade attacked him. He was just looking for me. So you can't punish him. You can't. He hasn't broken any laws."

"It's not me you've got to convince," Caleb said with an amused smile, holding up his hands in surrender.

"And I'm already committed to your cause," Devlin said. "But Kade will say he attacked first, and Dean will back him up. The pack have no reason to disbelieve them."

"But why would Jace attack anyone? He doesn't have a motive," I said, clutching at the sliver of logic. "My father sent me here to strengthen our alliance, not destroy it."

"If I was Kade," Caleb said, pulling out a chair and dropping into it, "I'd point out that the pact has already been broken. You were promised to an alpha-son."

"And I'm fated to an alpha!" Jace winced and I realized my hand was digging into his shoulder. I released it quickly with an apologetic smile, and stepped away before I made his injuries any worse. "Surely no-one can believe he would possibly object to that?"

"A broken pact is a broken pact," Devlin said grimly.

233

"Fine." I set my jaw. "Then I'll sneak Jace out of here."

Devlin tensed, and Caleb shot a look at him and back to me.

"Even if that wouldn't undermine Alpha Devlin's authority," he said quickly, "Dean is standing guard outside the front door, and your brother is in no fit state to scale the walls."

"During the moon hunt, then. When everyone's busy. I'll stay back here—tell everyone I'm ill or something—then sneak him out while the pack's hunting."

I drew in a deep breath and nodded to myself. It could work. Dean would never miss the hunt to stand guard. And all I needed was an hour, just long enough to get Jace out.

"No." Devlin folded his arms across his chest. "I forbid it."

I ground my teeth together. "I don't care what you forbid. He's my brother!"

"Jess, please," Jace said, his voice low and somber. "Don't disobey your alpha for me."

"You will be at the hunt," Devlin growled, suddenly invading my space and glaring down at me. "You will not defy me in this, little wolf."

"Why? Why does this stupid hunt matter so much?"

It was Caleb who answered.

"If you don't attend the first full moon hunt after you're mated to the alpha, you will be exiled."

CHASE MEADOWS

CHAPTER FORTY-NINE

Exiled.

Separated from Devlin. Forever. My heart squeezed painfully, and my wolf snarled and snapped in fury.

Never. Will not leave mate. Will kill for mate.

Easy, wolf. No-one needs to die. Yet.

Will kill anyone who tries to send us away.

Which *isn't* Caleb, I reminded her firmly. Rein it in, we need to think. And fast. So knock off that snarling and ranting for a minute.

She huffed but fell silent, and I suddenly became aware that the whole room was watching me.

"Um, yeah. Okay. Exiled would be bad."

Devlin exhaled slowly and nodded, touching one hand briefly to my shoulder in the lightest of caresses, and somehow, without moving back a single inch, he was no longer invading my space, he was simply inhabiting it, no more an intrusion that the presence of my own hand. I leaned into his touch. Nothing on this earth would rip me from this man's side.

But that didn't mean I was ready to throw Jace to the wolves. Literally.

"Maybe if we leave him here, and leave the doors unlocked…" I started, but Devlin cut me off with a shake of his head.

"He's in no fit state to travel alone. He wouldn't make it to the border. And I doubt his healing will take care of his injuries before dawn."

I sagged. "When the hunt will be over, and he'll be back under guard. Kade's thought of everything."

"Kade?" Devlin frowned. "He's just honoring his duties to the pack."

I tilted my head back to peer up at him. Could he really be that blind? I suppose neither of us had seen much of Kade since Devlin had brought

235

me here, and I'd kept my mouth shut about what had happened between us in the alley, more fool me. Devlin had no idea about Kade's newfound animosity for me, or his reason for it. And I had to make sure it stayed that way. One word from me, and the whole story would be out. Me and Jace would be dead, and our packs would be at war—because Devlin hadn't been the first to break the pact. My father had sent an omega to be bonded to an alpha's son. Packs had gone to war over less.

"Jessica? What aren't you telling me?"

I could tell him about the alleyway, maybe, and nothing else—just let him know about Kade's jealousy. I hesitated.

A pounding started at the door again, and Devlin swore under his breath.

"It would appear we're out of time," he said. "Caleb?"

Caleb fell in at Devlin's shoulder, and the pair of them set off for the front door.

"Wait, what's going on?" I called after them. "Why are we out of time?"

"That'll be the pack," Jace said, and I whirled back to him. "They've come to see my punishment meted out."

"No, they can't. I'm going to get you out of here, Jace. I'll find a way."

He shook his head sharply, then winced.

"No. You have to let it happen. I'll try to convince them I'm innocent, but you can't let anyone learn your secret. And Jess, mate bond or not, you need to get out of here. Because it's only a matter of time before Kade tells them who you are. What you are. You have to go."

The lance of terror that shot through me was physically painful. Leave Devlin? No. Impossible.

"I'd rather die."

"Jess, don't be stupid! Look, when they come in here, I'll distract them. I'll plead my case. But you need to go while they're focused on me. This is your chance, Jess. You can finally be free." He searched my face urgently. "I'll keep them busy for as long as I can."

"I'm not going to let you buy my freedom with your death!"

"Yes, you are. I should have done right by you when we were growing up. This is my penance."

"Save your breath." I folded my arms over my chest. "You're not dying for me, and I'm not leaving Devlin."

"Jess…"

"Stay here. I'll be back."

I didn't give him chance to answer before I raced down the hall. I heard raised voices before I reached the door.

"The prisoner will have a fair trial. In the morning."

"He should be executed before the hunt begins."

A few voices rose in agreement as I rounded the corner and brought them into sight. Devlin stood outlined in the doorframe, with Caleb at his right shoulder. I moved to take my position on his left.

"I am your alpha!" Devlin said, his loud voice immediately quelling the masses. Several of the gathered shifters cringed back. Half the pack had to be here. What game was Kade playing?

One we won't let him win.

Great. Any plans for how we're going to pull that off?

Silence answered my question, which I took to be a no.

"I am your alpha," Devlin repeated, his voice closer to its normal volume, but still carrying easily through the utter silence. "You have trusted me to guide you this far, and you have trusted me to be your voice. I speak for you now, when I say that it is in the pack's best interest to be thorough in our investigation of this alleged intruder, and his alleged crime."

"But Alpha, there are witnesses!"

I didn't see who said it, but Devlin's gaze locked on to a shifter near the back of the pack.

"There are also extenuating circumstances," Devlin said, his stare boring into the man. "Or would you have me lead us recklessly into war? Perhaps you would rather stand in my place and have the pack follow you? Do you wish to challenge me, Roy?"

The man visibly paled, and he averted his eyes right to the floor. "No, Alpha Devlin. Forgive me."

"Return to your homes," Devlin commanded. "Prepare for the moon hunt. My new mate and I shall see you *all* in the clearing."

He swept his ferocious gaze over them, and the pack quickly started to melt away. I stared after them in shock until Devlin stepped back and shut the door.

"Did you use alpha compulsion on them?"

"There are powers far stronger than that, little wolf. Such as self-preservation."

I blinked a few times as he stalked back to the kitchen.

"He wouldn't have, though, right?" I said to Caleb. "Killed any of them, I mean?"

Caleb shrugged. "Probably not. Unless they'd really provoked him."

"Right. Of course. Obviously. Because that's completely normal." I realized I was babbling and clamped my mouth shut.

"He's an alpha," Caleb reminded me. I snorted. Like I could forget. But he was on my side. At least until he found out the truth.

"Come on," Caleb said, his voice abruptly gentle as he reached for my arm. "You should get some rest before the hunt."

I shrugged him off. "My brother needs me."

And I was starting to think there was only one way I could save his life. A shiver ran through me, but I lifted my chin and retraced my steps to the kitchen. I was vaguely aware of Caleb moving behind me.

Devlin looked up as I came in, but it was Caleb he locked eyes with.

"Put Jace in the secure room. You know the one."

"Alpha Devlin," Jace said, lifting his eyes only as far as the alpha's chin. "I will not try to escape, you have my word. I am ready to face the justice of your pack."

"I'm not worried about you getting out," Devlin said.

I blinked. "You think one of the pack would break in?"

"It doesn't pay to take chances," Caleb answered for him. "I'll do it at once, Alpha."

Jace's eyes widened in panic. "Please, Alpha Devlin. Call your pack back, all of them. I'll make a full confession."

"No," I ground out, meeting my idiotic brother's eye. "You won't. You have nothing to confess."

"They want blood," Jace said. "Better mine than the alternative."

"Take him," Devlin commanded Caleb, and the beta immediately took hold of Jace's arm. He didn't resist, allowing himself to be led from the room.

"Why would he want to confess?" Devlin demanded, as soon as we were alone.

"He thinks I still want to escape." It was close enough to the truth. I sagged back against the counter behind me. "He wants his death to be a distraction for you all." I tasted bile at the back of my throat.

"And you never did tell me why you were so hell-bent on escaping," Devlin said, his voice a low rumble as he closed the gap between us and planted his hands on the counter on either side of me, trapping me there. His body invaded my personal space, his scent invaded my senses, and his sheer presence invaded every fiber of my being. My wolf rose to the surface, feral and aroused by his dominance, and for a moment I almost didn't resist her—resist *him*—but then he lowered his head to my ear, and his voice sent sparks of anticipation and trepidation coursing through me like competing waves of electricity.

"It's time for the truth, Jessica."

I tried to shake my head, unable even to think words, let alone speak them, but he nipped at my ear, and I felt his growl vibrate through the human cage I was trapped inside. One that, just hours ago, had felt like the safest place on earth to be.

"No more stalling. No more lies. I will spare your brother, and in return, you *will* tell me the truth."

He'd save Jace. That was all that mattered. Maybe that was all that had ever mattered. I'd been allowed a few blissful weeks with Devlin; enough to know I would never survive without him. Better to face the price fate demanded of me than to let Kade tear us apart.

"I'm not who you think I am," I whispered. I sucked in a deep breath, and forced the words out. "I'm an omega."

CHAPTER FIFTY

Devlin's eyes widened a fraction, then his face hardened and his expression darkened. His hands dug into the counter on either side of me, his fingers shifting into claws that left deep gouges in the polished wood.

I bit back the sob that threatened to work its way up my throat. Whatever hatred he had for me now, I deserved it. I'd lied to him. I'd tried to cover up my shameful truth, and I had no right to feel sorry for myself.

That didn't stop agony lancing through my chest as his entire body turned rigid and he refused to even look at me.

But why should an alpha look at an omega, except to condemn her to death?

He shoved himself away from the counter and stalked halfway across the kitchen. His movements were stiff and I could make out the taut muscles rippling across his shoulders beneath the thin fabric of his shirt. Muscles I had been running my hands over only hours ago as we made love.

Muscles I'd had no right to touch.

My eyelids slid closed, trapping the unshed tears behind them. I had no right to cry at the thought of losing him. He'd never been mine to begin with. An omega had no right to love an alpha.

"You're an omega," Devlin said, his voice hollow. I nodded without opening my eyes. If I looked at him now, I would beg him to forgive me, beg him to still love me, and as wrong as it had been to lie about what I was in the first place, it would be even worse to embarrass him by asking him to ignore it. I was not a child. I understood that actions had consequences. I had deceived him. I had chosen to stay and I had chosen

241

to stop fighting. I had chosen to let him love me. And now I had to face the consequences.

My death.

"Your father lied," Devlin said, and this time there was a hint of anger in his voice.

"Yes, Alpha Devlin," I whispered hoarsely, eyes still closed and head bowed so that my chin was almost touching my chest. My head seemed too heavy to lift.

"Your father sent you to us, knowing what it would mean!"

There was a loud crash and I flinched. My eyes flew open of their own accord and fixed on the shattered remains of the toaster oven he'd flung across the room. I dared flick a glance in his direction, just long enough to see his heaving shoulders and his thunderous face. War. It would mean war. But I would not be around to see it.

He turned and caught me staring. I tried to wrench my eyes away but they refused to obey.

"You are mistaken," he said abruptly. "You do not understand what the word means. Kade met your parents."

Bitter hope clawed at me, tearing me apart from the inside. Finally, I dropped my gaze.

"No, Alpha Devlin," I said. "He met my father and my stepmother. My father cheated on her with a human, and I was the result. I know what the word means."

His hands curled into fists. "Fuck!"

My father had tricked him—my *pack* had tricked him—and now he was fated to an omega. Every pack in the country would consider him weak, and I couldn't blame him for his fury. If I wasn't so selfish, I'd wish I'd never met him, never put him in this position. But I couldn't bring myself to wish away the last few weeks. They were the only happiness I had ever known. In what world was it fair he should be punished for that?

"Please, Devlin," I said, and my voice trembled. "I have only one request."

"Oh?" There was an edge of bitter amusement to the word, and he stared at me expectantly.

"Kill me now, so the pack don't find out what I am. Don't let my status taint you."

Devlin barreled across the kitchen and I screwed my eyes shut, cringing back against the counter as I waited for the pain to come—a punch, a kick, a bite—some punishment for my impertinence.

A finger brushed lightly against the underside of my chin, lifting my head a fraction. My eyelids cautiously opened to find a world of agony written in Devlin's eyes as he gazed at me. He shook his head wordlessly, and tucked a stray strand of hair behind my ear.

"Jessica, I would never... I *could* never hurt you."

I tore my head away, my heart screaming as I broke contact with him.

"I know the law, Devlin. An omega fated to an alpha must die."

"Fuck the law," he growled, and my mouth popped open in shock. Devlin ducked his head and crushed his lips against mine, kissing me roughly and desperately and demandingly, and with an urgency I could not deny.

I stretched up, kissing him back, letting his tongue into my mouth without hesitation, because there was no part of who I was I would deny this man, even knowing what he must do.

His hands dropped to my waist and lifted me effortlessly, his lips exploring mine the whole time as he sat me on the counter and moved between my open legs to press his body against mine. My legs tangled around him, trapping him in my embrace, trapping him in this one moment that was all we had left.

His hand tangled in my hair, crushing me to him, as though we could become one if only we tried hard enough, and his other hand found the small of my back, reaching under my shirt to caress my soft flesh with calloused fingertips. My nipples hardened against his chest and heat shot to my core. I moaned into his mouth. How could he undo me so thoroughly with just a kiss? And how could something that was this wrong feel so damned right?

His tongue withdrew and the kiss slowed until his lips were just barely touching mine.

"Fuck the law," he said again, so that I could feel his defiance moving against my lips. "They'll take you over my dead body."

I pulled back and stared up at him in horror.

"Devlin, no!"

He wanted me to live. He still cared about me. And the hope that was soaring inside me flared brightly in its dying embers, like a moth finally caught in the flame. Because caring about me would destroy him, and I could not stand that.

A sob tore from my throat and I flung myself against his shoulder, burying my head in the scent that, just for a little while, had been my home. And I prepared to say goodbye.

"You are the best man I've ever known, Devlin," I murmured, and he barked a harsh, bitter laugh in response, but said nothing. "You will never know what it means to me to hear you say those words. Never. But you cannot protect me from this."

"Like hell I can't."

"Then you shouldn't. Just... Just walk away while you still can. And promise me my brother will be safe."

"No Whitlock blood will be spilled in this territory," Devlin said, and then cracked his knuckles. "Unless your father shows up."

I shook my head and peered up at him.

"I know he insulted you—"

"Insulted me? Do you think I care about that? Jessica, he sent you here knowing it could mean your death—and that is the one thing I cannot tolerate." He searched my eyes. "My life is nothing without you in it. Before I met you, I thought I had everything I wanted. But now I see there was only one thing I truly needed, and I will not live without you."

My breath caught in my throat. What did I do to deserve a man who cared for me like that? I could live a thousand lifetimes and never be worthy, and love him for a million years and never tire.

"Now," Devlin said, stepping back. "Enough talk of dying. We have a hunt to lead."

"We can't. Haven't you listened to anything I've said?"

"Jessica, I would listen to you recite the dictionary and still be enthralled. Now listen to me. I don't care that I'm an alpha, or that you're an omega."

"But you *are* an alpha," I said. "And I *am* an omega."

"And in a few hours, you'll be a luna."

"If we do this, every pack in the country will hunt us."

Devlin grinned, and his teeth flashed in the moonlight.

"Let them come."

CHAPTER FIFTY-ONE

The full moon hung above us in the clearing, shining bright and clear in the gaps between the treetops. The whole pack stood gathered in their human form, which just seemed odd. I'd never seen them all together like this, aside from the rabble Kade had raised and sent to kill my brother.

Jace.

I hid a shiver. I hoped he'd be okay.

Alpha has spoken. All wolves are here.

Not that she'd counted, of course. She was just so completely unable to comprehend the idea that someone might disobey the alpha, or that anyone would want to miss the hunt, for any reason.

The alpha commands. The pack obeys.

Usually. I shoved the thought aside and focused on the gathered shifters. This was tradition, apparently, whenever an alpha took a new mate. On the first full moon after the mate bond had been formed, the pack must swear allegiance to their new luna. I'd never seen a ceremony like this before—back in Winter Moon, the alpha and his luna had been a bonded pair since long before I'd been born. Not that I'd ever been close to either of them, of course, aside from the one or two times they'd wanted to torment me.

But this wasn't the time to dwell on that. I glanced over at Devlin by my side and he gave my hand a reassuring squeeze. He knew everything, my darkest secrets, and he was still here. I wasn't sure it was smart, but I didn't have the strength in me to fight what I felt for him. I was too selfish to insist.

He turned to Caleb and nodded. The beta came to stand in front of me, then dropped into a crouch on one knee, with his head bowed.

"Luna Jess," he said, "I, Beta Caleb Meyer, solemnly swear my true allegiance to you on this day, for all days to come. In the face of battle, I will stand beside you, and in the face of danger, I will lay down my life for you. Should I ever raise tooth or claw against you, may the ancient gods cast me aside, and condemn me for all time."

"Reveal your true form to me, Beta Caleb," I said with as much solemnity as I could muster while trying to remember my words. Caleb lifted his head a fraction and shot me a wink and a grin. I pressed my lips together, trying to keep a straight face, and then he burst from his clothes, erupting in fur and teeth as he took the form of his wolf. He shook out once, and his fur settled into place, and then he laid flat on his belly in front of me, twisting his head to the side to offer me his throat.

"Rise, Beta Caleb Meyer. I see you."

With a flick of his tail, he rose to his feet, and trotted round to take his place at Devlin's side.

Jackson, Devlin's eldest son, came forward next, and repeated the same oath and pose of submission and then it was Kade's turn.

For a moment, I thought he would refuse. I could see the simmering fury in his eyes and practically smell him chafing against swearing his allegiance to an omega—one who, as far as he was concerned, was ready to obey his every whim to keep her shameful secret. I met his eye, and saw the taunt in them. Sure, he would swear his allegiance in front of all the pack, but he had no intention of honoring his oath.

He has no honor.

That was something we agreed on. When I commanded him to show his true form, he shifted and laid flat, then met my eye deliberately before revealing his throat, like he was taunting me, daring me to lay a tooth on it.

Challenge accepted.

Wait, what? No it damn well isn't, wolf. This is not the time to attack another member of the pack, even if he is a prick.

"Rise, Alpha-son Kade Mitchell." I narrowed my eyes a fraction and met his. "I see you."

If Devlin noticed that my words were as much a warning as an acknowledgement, he made no comment on it, and Kade sauntered off to take his place in the pack. Smug bastard.

The swearing of the oaths ran on through the night. Every member of the pack physically able to shift pledged their allegiance, and those too young to shift and unable to join the hunt would make their oaths to both me and Devlin when they came of age.

Eventually, the oaths were done, and the whole pack had sworn their oaths, and Devlin shifted. And now everyone was watching me. I sucked in a deep breath, and moved to stand in the center of the gathered circle. How much had changed since last time we stood in this spot, I thought wryly. Then I laid eyes on Kade, and my levity vanished. Not all of it was for the better. I'd be glad when this hunt was over and I could get back to working out how to save Jace—and deal with Kade. The constant threat of death hanging over me wasn't exactly a barrel of laughs, either.

With the pack watching, I called my wolf to the surface, and shifted. My clothes burst off, falling to the ground around me in tatters. I shook myself out and stood proud in the center of my pack. *My pack.* A thrill ran through me at the words. Broken Ridge was my home, and these wolves were my pack.

Devlin threw back his head and howled, long and deep, and I lifted my head to join him, my own softer voice weaving a melody through his baritone. One by one, and then all at once, the rest of the pack joined in, until the haunting sound seemed to fill the entire world around us.

When the chorus died away, Devlin rose to his feet and started for the edge of the clearing. We would run through the woods side by side, as one, as we led the pack. My mouth opened in a wolfish smile, and I turned to join him.

Something crashed into my side and the force threw me through the air. I hit the ground hard, pain shuddering through my entire body. I blinked up in confusion, and saw a heavy-set cream wolf towering over me. Dean. What the hell was going on?

My wolf flung me to my feet before my brain could catch up, and I was already on four paws before I registered the pain in my back left leg. I bit back a whine as I moved, and then something else caught my eye. A flash of pale flesh. Human flesh.

"Alpha Devlin," Kade said, rising to his full height. "I challenge you for the right to lead this pack."

CHAPTER FIFTY-TWO

Devlin barged past Kade, shifting back into his human form mid-stride in a way I'd never seen anyone do before, and made straight for me.

"*Alpha* Devlin," Kade said from behind me, and there was an unmistakable taunt in the way he said his father's rank, "You must acknowledge the challenge, or forfeit."

Devlin didn't so much as spare him a glance. His eyes stayed locked on me as he made to shove through Dean, too. I locked eyes with my mate and growled in reprimand, then jerked my chin at Kade. He could go back to being all over-protective later—*after* he dealt with the challenge to his rank that would probably kill us both.

Devlin scanned my face carefully and nodded. Then he turned his eyes on Dean.

"If one hair on my mate's hide is harmed, I will have your throat, pup."

"Father," Kade called from behind him, and under the moonlight I saw the smug satisfaction on his face. "By law you must acknowledge my challenge and fight me under the first full moon that follows—which is now—before midnight passes—which is in about ten minutes. Or you can step aside and allow me to take my place as alpha of this pack."

Devlin's hands curled into fists.

"Never, you treacherous cur. I'll fight you. Gladly."

"Good. I hope your mate's injury won't prove too much of a distraction. I'm sure the healer is at hand to help her."

Devlin's eyes jerked back to me, and I snarled again. Like hell was I going to be the distraction that undid Devlin. Screw Kade and his cheap tricks.

Kade chuckled, and Devlin turned back to him. "I trust my mate is strong enough to handle your pet. She was certainly strong enough to handle you."

Kade's amusement darkened. "Enough talk, old man. Shift so I can prove to everyone here that your time is done."

Devlin lifted his chin. "Try."

The pair of them shifted and the pack moved restlessly around them, forming a ragged circle with the fighters on the inside. There was only a small gap in the ring, through which I could see them—and they could see me. Dammit. The last thing I needed right now was for my injury to distract Devlin. I'd never seen Kade fight, but I knew without a doubt he couldn't be trusted to fight fair.

Should have killed him in the alleyway.

Yes. But right now all we could do was trust Devlin to handle it.

Mate is strong.

Yes.

Am still worried.

Yeah. Me, too. Terrified, in fact. I could barely catch my breath as the pair squared up to each other, and not just because my flank was throbbing. The pain in my leg seemed to be getting worse. My shifter healing needed to kick in already, so I could be ready to help Devlin if he needed me. Pack law be damned—Kade would be looking for a way to kill Devlin, and I *would* find a way to stop him. On three legs, if need be.

Kade moved first, throwing himself forward and snapping his teeth at Devlin. The grizzled gray alpha dodged easily, taking a short step back so that Kade missed him by inches. He countered with a snap of his own at Kade's shoulder, and the younger wolf skittered back, crouched, and threw himself forward almost in the same movement. Devlin dodged, but not quickly enough, and Kade caught his hindquarters in a glancing blow.

My breath caught in my throat. He was a good fighter.

251

Not as good as mate.

Maybe. But better than any of us thought—Devlin included. He couldn't afford to get complacent. Any mistake, any mistake at all, and Kade was going to punish him for it.

The two fighters circled each other, each moving a little more warily than before. They locked eyes as they moved, and Kade's hackles rose. He peeled his lips back in a snarl. My wolf analyzed his movements dispassionately, head cocked to one side.

His human emotions disadvantage him.

Kade? Interesting. I could see it now, the anger that seemed to thrum through his every movement. His hatred of Devlin clouded his judgement. It made him hasty.

He broke from the circle first, lunging across it, jaws open wide. Devlin dodged back, too slow again, and again Kade's shoulder scored a glancing blow on the alpha's hindquarters, spinning him around. My heart stuttered but Devlin's mouth was already open and clamping down on Kade's hind leg before the younger wolf could react.

My wolf swelled with pride.

Mate fooled him. Kade is no match.

Yeah, yeah, don't get carried away just yet. One bite doesn't make a victory, I warned her. But even I could see that Kade was hurting as he broke away. Devlin made no move to follow up, and it took me a moment to realize he was giving Kade a chance to back down. I rumbled my disapproval. Kade wasn't going to back down. As long as he could fight, he would.

Kade didn't waste any more energy circling. It was clear his back leg was hurting him, even if he tried not to let it show. His movements were a little stiffer, his steps a little choppier. Human eyes would never have been able to tell the difference, but there were no humans here, and we were all aware of the weakness. I took a step forward for a better view, and pain shot along my flank. I whined and twisted round to stare at it in surprise. It shouldn't be hurting that much.

A crash sounded from within the circle and I jerked my head round in time to see Devlin on the floor and Kade pinning him in place with his full weight while he snapped his teeth at Devlin's face. Panic flooded me. Devlin must have been distracted by my whine and now Kade had him trapped. If he—

Devlin coiled his hindquarters before I could finish that thought, and slammed them into Kade's soft underbelly. The air exploded from his lungs in a huff and Devlin kicked again, tossing him across the circle. The younger wolf hit the ground hard, his hind leg kicking out twice before he clawed his way back to his feet and shook himself out.

Mate is injured.

I yanked my gaze back onto Devlin and saw the thin red gash on his face. Kade had bitten him. My shoulders tensed, ready to kill that spoiled alpha brat, but my wolf stayed me.

No. Do not interfere.

Since when are you against diving into a fight? I demanded.

Challenge is sacred.

My hindquarters trembled and I slumped into a sit. Standing was uncomfortable. More uncomfortable than it should have been, come to think of it.

"How are you feeling, mighty luna?" a voice whispered in my ear. I started, and twisted round to find myself staring at Dean in his human form. I snapped my teeth in warning, and turned my attention back to the fight.

"Oh, don't be like that," he said. "I'm just showing concern for my alpha's mate. Of course, when Kade wins, we'll have a new alpha. I wonder where that will leave you?"

A shudder worked its way through my frame and Dean's throaty chuckle resounded in my ear.

"Maybe Kade will let me have you as a plaything. I'd enjoy teaching you your place. After all, he let Ryder have the pleasure of killing your brother."

CHAPTER FIFTY-THREE

I whipped my head round and stared at Dean's gloating face.

"Oh, you didn't notice he left once the fight got started?" he said with a smirk. "I'd say you have five minutes, maybe ten, before he reaches Devlin's house and finishes what me and Kade started."

I lurched to my feet, twisting round to stare at Devlin, and then in the direction of the house, torn between the two. But there was nothing I could do to help Devlin right now, and Jace needed me. I could make it to the house in ten minutes, less at a flat-out sprint.

I lurched to my feet and spun around, almost tripping over my back leg. Dean rose from his crouch, his lips twisting into a smirk.

"Little stiff there, Jess?" he taunted, only the way he said it, it seemed like there was more to it. It didn't matter. I didn't have time to worry about him; I could only trust that Devlin would win his fight, and that when he did, Caleb would watch his back.

I broke into a fast, uncomfortable trot—something was definitely wrong with my back leg, and more than it should have been just from Dean crashing into me. I shook my head and dug deep.

Come on, wolf. We need to go. Little help?

I felt her strength bolstering mine as I kicked up into a sprint, only registering the pain in some distant part of my mind as I tore through the woods until the sounds of the fight quieted and then faded entirely. We were running alone through the night.

I burst from the woods and onto the deserted streets of the town, and still I didn't allow myself to slow. The pain seemed to grow with every passing step, until it was throbbing and burning and pulsing and I knew something was very wrong.

I clamped my jaws shut and pushed myself harder. We were only a minute from the house, and we couldn't be too late, we just couldn't.

Ryder's scent was all along this route: he'd passed here, and not long ago. I just had to get the rest of the way to the house before he could find a way in. For the first time, I was glad Devlin was so paranoid about security. It meant there was still a chance I'd be in time.

I rounded the final corner and the house's high walls came into sight. I raced to the gates, but they were shut, and anyone who knew the code was at the fight. I couldn't scale the gates in this form, or the wall with my injured leg, but as a human I could haul myself over, and shift back inside the house to deal with Ryder.

I'd wasted enough time already. I sucked in a deep breath, and willed myself to return to my human form.

Nothing happened.

Wolf? I probed my mind. Are you fighting me?

It didn't *feel* like she was fighting me, but…

Not…fighting…

I froze. Her voice was barely an echo in my mind. Panic flooded me. What was going on?

"Ah, Jess. So nice of you to join us."

Ryder stepped into view on the far side of the gates, and tossed a figure to the ground at his feet. Jace barely groaned at the rough treatment—not a good sign. He was conscious, but only just, and he looked like he was completely out of it.

But he was alive.

"I suppose you're wondering why you can't shift?"

I lifted a lip and snarled at him, and he chuckled in response.

"Always such a temper. I think Dean's planning to beat that out of you—if you survive tonight, of course. How's the leg?"

A whine slipped from my lips and I backed up a step, before I steeled myself and glared at him.

"Not good, then. It's the silver poisoning, you see."

256

Silver poisoning? I twisted round to stare at my leg in horror, and under the gate's bright lighting, I saw it. The slick wet patch. A wound. Just a small one. I wouldn't even have felt it amidst the impact of Dean crashing into me. If it had been a normal wound, it would have healed before I'd had a chance to notice it. But it wasn't a normal wound. My nostrils twitched, but I couldn't pick up the scent of silver. No...wait... It was there, but it was faint.

"It was my idea, the poisoning. Just a tiny trace amount, so that you wouldn't notice it until we'd lured you out here. It could probably have stayed in your system undetected for days—unless you sped its progress through your bloodstream. By taking a nice run, for instance."

Shit. They'd planned this. They'd planned all of it. They'd wanted me out here, alone and weakened. It was Lily all over again. Except I didn't plan on going down without a fight.

Just as soon as I shifted into my human form and hauled myself over. Ryder must have caught the direction of my gaze.

"Good luck with that. I imagine the silver poisoning has already progressed to the point where you can't shift. It severs your connection to your wolf, or so I've heard. First the wolf dies, and then you." He cocked his head to one side. "I wonder what would happen if she died before you were given the antidote. Perhaps you'd be trapped as a wolf forever. I imagine you'd make a good guard dog."

I flung myself at the gate, snapping and snarling. My wolf's fury was a dull echo inside my skull. I could sense it already. She was fading. We were dying. But if we were going to do one last thing together, it would be to save my brother, and if that meant putting some teeth into Kade's lackey at the same time, so much the better. Too bad it wasn't Kade himself.

Ryder's laughter rang in my ears.

"Save your energy, omega. It won't last you long, and I wouldn't want you to miss this."

He hauled Jace up onto his knees by his hair, exposing his throat. Jace was so out of it he barely even reacted, other than a flicker of a grimace passing over his face. I didn't know if he'd been poisoned or just so badly beaten he was barely conscious, but either way he was in no state to defend himself.

Ryder flashed his teeth at me, and held up his free hand. Under the light of the full moon, his fingers shifted into long, wickedly curved claws with deathly sharp tips that glistened in the night, and then he lowered them to Jace's neck.

"Say goodbye to your brother."

CHAPTER FIFTY-FOUR

Come on, wolf, I urged. Just these last few seconds. One last surge of strength.

So… weak…

We can do this, wolf. You've been my strength since the day I first shifted. Now it's my turn. Just get me over that gate, and I'll take care of the rest.

My wolf made no reply, but I felt her gathering the last of her strength. What I was asking of her might kill her, but I wouldn't be far behind. It had never been our lives that mattered.

I circled round, sank back on my haunches, and holding onto my wolf's strength, threw myself at the gates. My front paws slammed into the vertical iron bars halfway up, and my back paws a split second later, smashing into them just long enough to kick off again, launching me to the top. I scrabbled at the top horizontal bar, and for one horrible moment I thought I would topple backwards to the ground, but then heat spread through me, and powered by determination and terror, I hauled myself up, and threw myself over the other side.

Ryder's eyes widened as I bore down on him, then I smashed into him with the full force of my dive, sending him crashing to the ground, and tearing his grip from my brother.

I twisted round, searching Jace's neck and face for any trace of blood, and then I caught the rise and fall of his chest. Relief coursed through me, making me dizzy. He was alive.

Something moved under me and I snapped my head back to Ryder in time to see his muzzle lengthening, and fur sprouting from his body as it changed shape, shifting from human to wolf.

Crap.

His powerful back legs slammed into my soft belly, tossing me through the air. I hit the ground hard, the air erupting from my lungs in a whoosh and leaving me limp on the cold earth.

Ryder sprang to his feet, shaking his fur out and peeling back his lips, letting me get a good look at every one of his fangs. Fangs that would soon be embedded in my throat if I didn't move.

He snarled as he stalked towards me, slabs of muscle rippling with every step he took, and a shiver ran through me. Move, dammit. Get *up!*

I lurched unsteadily to my feet, but before I could find my balance the bigger wolf lunged at me. I staggered to one side and he flew past, missing me by fractions of an inch. He growled in frustration and pivoted round, advancing on me again. I backed away, my hind leg throbbing with every step I took.

It had been a dumb plan. I was too weak to fight, the poison had spread too far through my system, but even if it hadn't, I'd never be a match for a wolf like Ryder. He was a fighter. A malicious beast who reveled in violence, and he would crush me like a bug. But it didn't matter. My place was here, between him and Jace, and if I could just hang on, just stay here long enough, help would come. I was done, but Jace could survive, if I could just hold out a little longer.

I clenched my jaws and bared my teeth, hackles raised all along my back. A snarl ripped from my throat, warning Ryder back. He huffed a sharp bark of laughter, and stalked forward on languid limbs, his own hackles raised and far more impressive than mine. But I'd been running away from fights my whole life. That stopped. Now.

Movement. Behind me.

I saw Jace bracing his one uninjured hand on the floor, ready to push himself up. Idiot! He was clearly too weak to shift, and he'd last about ten seconds in this fight as a human—if Ryder took his time. His eyes were wide and sweat was pouring from his body. He didn't look capable of killing a fly, never mind a powerful wolf. I redirected my snarl at him, and with a gasp of pain and resignation, he slumped back to the ground. Good. He needed to save his energy for escaping.

…And that meant I needed to buy him some time.

My eyes locked onto the beast in front of me, and I stalked towards him, my whole body vibrating with fury. He hesitated mid-step, his furred forehead dimpled with surprise, and his ears flickered back. Ryder was a bully, and like all bullies, he was a coward. He'd expected me to curl up and die, but if he wanted my blood, he was going to have to take it.

And I saw the moment he realized it.

He canted his head, trying to fathom the change in me, and I didn't waste a moment of his confusion. I crouched, then sprang forward, slamming my body into his. My open jaws latched onto his neck as we thudded into the ground, but his thick fur protected his throat from my fangs. I snarled in frustration and worked at the layers of fur, desperation pulsing through me as I worried at him and tried to find the soft flesh beneath that would end this fight.

Ryder grunted as he got his legs under him, and rose effortlessly to his feet. He shook out, tossing me aside as though I was nothing. I thudded into the dirt, and a sharp pain shot through my shoulder and burst from my throat as a whimper. I tried to struggle to my feet, but the moment I put my weight on my front leg, it gave way and sent me sprawling back into the dirt. Broken. Something was broken.

Pain thrummed through me, draining the last of my strength, until I couldn't even lift my head to watch Ryder advance on me. I hoped Jace had escaped. I hoped Devlin had defeated Kade. But I wouldn't be around long enough to find out.

Devlin.

261

My heart squeezed painfully. I would never see Devlin again, and if I'd been in my human form I would have wept bitter tears at the time I wasted fighting and arguing with him, the time we'd both wasted denying what we'd felt. Why hadn't we cherished every precious second? Why had I ever let my omega status drive a wedge between us? I should have known he'd stand by me, that the mate bond was stronger than anything that would try to destroy it. Fate didn't make mistakes. It had destined me for the one shifter on this earth strong enough to deal with what I was, and real enough not to care, and I hated myself for not seeing it sooner. So much time wasted. And for what? For why? For fear. I'd wasted so much time being afraid.

I wished I could have seen him one last time. But it was almost over now. I could feel the last of my strength bleeding from me.

You there, wolf?

I'm…here…

That was some comfort, at least. I would die a shifter. Die with my wolf. We'd had a good run, for an omega.

Mate…

Devlin. I could almost smell him, could almost hear his voice calling my name. I closed my eyes, and let the fantasy wash over me. His image swam up behind my closed lids, and I reveled in it. My lips twitched.

"Jessica," my fantasy said, his voice hoarse. "Jess, I'm here. It's over. You're safe. Come back to me."

Hands touched my body, and more voices shouted, almost drowning out that beautiful fantasy. A whine slipped from my lips.

"It's okay. I'm here. Come back to me."

I drew in a shuddering breath. Always, my love, I wanted to say, but not so much as a whine left my lupine lips.

I drew in one more shuddering breath in the closing darkness, and then my chest went still.

CHAPTER FIFTY-FIVE

I awoke—which was a surprise in itself—in a soft, warm bed, surrounded by familiar scents. I groaned softly, not quite able to remember how to open my eyelids, and in no hurry to work it out. It was comfortable here in the soft, warm bed. If only my throat weren't so parched, and my head so fuzzy. I couldn't quite remember—

"Devlin, she's awake!"

Ugh, there was no need to shout, my head hurt enough. And I felt so *weak...* Why was I so weak?

The memory came flooding back to me all at once. The poison. Shit. Ryder. Jace. The alpha challenge.

Footsteps hurried through the door, and a delicious scent crowded my nostrils. Something stirred deep in my mind.

Mate.

Wolf! You're still alive?

Mate, mate, mate. Mate!

I could feel her jubilation, and if she'd been in control of our body, our tail would have been wagging like a pup at its first feed.

Open eyes, she demanded. *See mate.*

That seemed like a good idea to me. I concentrated hard and my lids fluttered open as Devlin swept to my side and snatched up my hand in his. The bright light seared my eyes, shrouding him in a halo of dazzling white, and it was all I could do not to snort with laughter. He was no angel.

"Something amusing you, Jessica?"

I sighed with utter contentment. That rugged voice was the sweetest symphony any person had ever heard, and I could spend a lifetime listening to it. Then again, I could think of better uses for those lips.

The urge to kiss him was so strong, so sudden and unexpected, that I was already halfway sitting before the pain caught up with me. I gasped and suddenly Devlin's arm was wrapped around me, lowering me back to the bed with a tenderness I wouldn't have imagined him capable of, once.

"Easy," he chided me gruffly. "You were almost killed."

I grunted. "Must be Tuesday."

"Funny. I suppose I need not tell you how reckless you were?"

"Jace was in trouble—Jace!"

"He's fine," Devlin said, planting a hand on my chest to stop me attempting to sit again. Probably for the best. I really wasn't up to it.

"And Kade?" I pressed. Devlin grimaced.

"Alive, against my better judgement. But banished. You won't have to see him again."

"He lost the challenge, then? Despite trying to cheat?"

A flicker of amusement passed over Devlin's face, and I watched dreamily as the corner of his mouth twitched.

"Did you doubt me?"

"Only for, like, a second or two." My smile fell away. "What happened to Dean, and Ryder?"

"Dean stood trial and was exiled for your poisoning and attempted murder. Ryder…did not survive the attempt."

I started to nod, then frowned.

"Stood trial? How long was I asleep?"

"Two weeks."

"Oh."

"The lengths some people will go to in order to avoid cooking lessons," he said with a smirk.

"You said you didn't want me for my cooking ability," I reminded him, and his eyes fixed on my lips as I spoke. My breath caught in my throat, then he was bending over, and touching his lips to mine. I kissed him back like he was the air I needed to breathe, drawing him into me, tasting, touching, teasing. Our lips moved as one, and I moaned into his mouth. He tasted of hope. Of happiness. Of every good thing that had ever and would ever happen to me. He tasted of home.

Someone cleared their throat, but neither of us broke off the kiss.

"Take a walk, Caleb," Devlin murmured against my lips.

"Shall I walk to the doc's room? I'm sure he was just joking about Jess needing her rest..."

Devlin growled, but broke away from me. I pouted, and he smoothed the hair from my face.

"Caleb is right. You need to rest while you recover. Your healing was severely hampered by the silver." His jaw tightened, and he sucked in a breath and worked it loose. "The doctor says it will take a while to return to its full strength, and until then, you're to do nothing that might hinder its progress." He pressed his lips together, and fixed me with a stern look. "Besides, you've done a good enough job of trying to get yourself killed without my help."

"Yeah, about that..." I chewed my lower lip. "Exactly how much trouble am I in?"

"Oh, more than you could possibly imagine, little wolf," he said, his eyes glistening with promise.

"Am I interrupting?"

I twisted round to see the figure standing outlined in the doorway.

"Jace!"

Devlin's hand caught my uninjured shoulder and pressed me back into the bed before I could move more than an inch. I rumbled my annoyance at him and he did that deep chuckle low in his throat that made me catch my breath.

"Come in," Devlin said. "Perhaps you can do a better job than I of reminding your sister that she is *supposed* to be taking it easy."

"Doubt it," Jace said, approaching my bed with a grin. "Given that my advice to her was to keep her head down when she got here and not make any trouble."

"Shut up," I said, pulling a face at him. I looked him over carefully. He was dressed in new clothes, and he was clean-shaven. There was a slight shadowing under his eyes—probably thanks to me—but his color had returned, and the smile on his face seemed natural and not at all forced. He was carrying a tray in his hands, which didn't shake at all, and he wasn't even wearing a cast. "You're looking well. How long have you been up?"

"A while. My poisoning was only mild, so my shifter healing was able to take care of my other injuries."

"Been keeping busy, I see," I said, nodding to the tray of food in his hands. "When did you learn to cook?"

"Alpha Devlin taught me, when he wasn't watching you."

"He did?" I raised an eyebrow at Devlin, who gave me an amused smirk in return.

"I did," Devlin said. "It's nice to meet a Whitlock who doesn't share your aversion to learning anything remotely useful."

I poked my tongue out at him. "Rude." I turned back to Jace and narrowed my eyes. "Exactly how long have you been up and about for, anyway?"

"Long enough for him to have told me your darkest secrets," Devlin answered for him.

"You already know it," I whispered, looking down at my blankets as I picked at a stray thread.

He caught my hand in his and squeezed it.

"If that is your darkest secret, little wolf—" He raised my hand to his lips and nipped at my knuckles. "—I'm going to be very disappointed."

I raised my eyes to meet his, and the smoldering intensity sparked a heat in my core.

"Well," I murmured, "I would hate to disappoint."

"As if you could, little wolf."

Jace cleared his throat as he set the tray down, and my cheeks flushed pink. I quickly tore my eyes from Devlin before I could do something I regretted, like scare my brother away for life. Wait...

"Not that I'm not pleased to see you or anything, Jace, but how come you're still here?"

"Alpha Devlin kindly offered me a place in the Broken Ridge pack. I've accepted."

"You have? That's great! But... Didn't our father have something to say about that?"

"Your father has gone very silent," Devlin said, and his jaw tightened. "Which is for the best, because there's a thing or two I'd like to say to him, after the way he treated you."

I reached up and stroked a hand along his muscular forearm.

"That's in the past now."

"Yes. It is. And it's time for us to focus on the future. *Our* future."

Our future. I liked the sound of that. And then the dreamy smile slid from my face.

"We can't have a future."

"Says who?" Devlin demanded, and the look on his face threatened violence. I shook my head.

"Says the law. I am what I am, and you are what you are, and the law forbids us from being together."

"If you were an omega, that might be true."

"But I am—"

He mock-glared at me, and I mimed sealing my lips and tossing the key.

"You have been accepted into this pack, and every wolf here has sworn an oath to you. You are mated to the alpha. You ceased to be an omega ranking wolf the moment the first oath was sworn. You are now a luna."

I blinked at him. Could it really be that simple? I found it hard to believe that no-one had ever told me that before...or any of the other omegas who wound up rejected and worse.

Jace leaned in towards me and dropped his voice to a conspiratorial whisper.

"He announced it to the pack while he was still holding Ryder's head, and asked if anyone else dared challenge him over it. Total badass."

Ah. Now that sounded more like the Devlin I knew...and loved. Ryder's head, though?

"That's totally gross."

He deserved it.

Yeah, wolf, he did. And worse besides.

Mate is perfect.

Yeah, yeah. You're preaching to the converted, you know.

"Most of the pack were surprisingly amenable to the idea," Devlin said, his face a mask of innocence.

"You surprise me," I deadpanned, rolling my eyes.

But I didn't care. Jace was safe, Kade was gone, and somehow, despite everything, I got to keep Devlin. Forever. What more could I possibly ask for?

I ran my eyes over him from head to toe.

Well, okay, there was one thing...

EPILOGUE

Two Weeks Later

"Do we really have to go tonight?" I asked, glancing at the full moon through the window as I washed the last dish and set it aside to dry.

"Yes."

"But can't I just—"

"No."

I narrowed my eyes at Devlin. "You don't even know what I was going to say."

"I don't need to know," he said, leaning back against the wall and watching me without a trace of pity on his face. "Because you're going."

"Says you." I rolled my eyes at him. Big mistake.

"Yes, says me," he said, pushing himself off the wall and stalking towards me. "Have you forgotten who I am, little wolf?"

My heart fluttered in my throat and heat shot through my core. I shook my head mutely.

"Because I would hate to think you're planning to disobey your alpha."

He towered over me, invading my space, and my whole body burned with the need to touch him, to taste him, to hold him. Which was exactly what he intended, the bastard.

"Since when are you so reluctant to hunt?" he asked, and I couldn't tear my eyes from his lips as he spoke.

Since last time I went on a hunt a psycho tried to kill me, was what I meant to say. But when I opened my mouth, what came out in a husky whisper was, "Since I found other things I'd rather do."

His lips crushed mine, claiming my mouth without warning. I stretched up into the kiss, moaning with satisfaction as I tasted him, and my body melded against his. One of my hands rose up of its own accord and found Devlin's pec through the thin fabric of his shirt. He chuckled into my mouth, and broke away from the kiss.

"Oh, don't worry about that," he said, his hand catching mine and pinning it in place. "Once the hunt is done, I'm planning on taking my time fucking you senseless."

"Nuh-uh," I said, trying my hardest not to literally drool. "I can't wait that long."

Fire burned in his eyes, and he growled low in his throat.

"You undo me, woman."

"Then come here," I said, sliding one finger into his waistband and tugging him back to me. "And let me put you back together again."

He snatched me up into his arms and I yelped with surprise, then he tossed me effortlessly over his shoulder so that my ass was pointing up in the air, and my eyes were getting a good look at his denim-covered ass. I squealed and kicked my legs, and he slapped a hand down on my ass, making me yelp again.

"Are you going to give me trouble, little wolf?" he rumbled as he carried me up the stairs, caveman style.

"Heaps," I said with a grin, yanking up his shirt from behind—not an easy feat while upside down, but soon I had my hands on the naked flesh of his back. He sucked in a sharp gasp as I trailed my fingernails across him, and then whipped me from his shoulders and tossed me onto our bed. The air exploded from my lungs in a giddy burst, and Devlin towered over me. He flicked a glance to the window, and the moon rising in the sky beyond it, and then back to me, a smirk tugging at the corners of his mouth.

"Plenty of time yet to remind you who's the alpha, little wolf... before we go to the hunt."

I pouted up at him. He stared down at me. I was the first to blink. And then squirm.

He pinned me in place with one hand on the flat of my belly, and ripped my sweatpants away with the other, shredding them as though they were made of paper.

"Hey!" I protested.

"I hate these things," he rumbled, and tossed them aside. "They cover up your legs."

"Yeah, that's kinda the point."

"I *like* your legs."

I eyed the remains of my sweatpants and swallowed a mournful sigh. An idea struck, and I tugged on my lower lip with my teeth as I gazed up at him.

"Let me stay here tonight," I bargained, "and I won't replace them."

"No deal. I quite enjoyed tearing them off."

He reached for my tank top and I batted his hand away.

"Oh no, you don't. This is my favorite tank."

"Remove it," he commanded. "Quickly."

I squirmed out from under his hand and tugged the tank top off, tossing it across the room. He grabbed hold of my hips and dragged me back towards him.

"Bra," he ordered, staring down at my heaving chest like he wanted to devour me. I shook my head and he raised an eyebrow.

"No?" His finger trailed across the top of my panties and a bolt of heat shot through my core.

"No," I gasped. "You first. Shirt."

"You seem to think," he said, slipping his finger inside my panties and stroking the cusp of my folds, "that you're in a position to bargain."

He slipped a finger inside me and I arched my back, a moan working its way up my throat.

"Bra," he repeated.

"Shirt," I moaned.

271

He trailed his free hand from my throat down to my breasts.

"What's in it for me?" he asked, amusement tugging at the corner of his mouth. I untwined my hands from the sheets and caught his hand between them, drawing it up to my mouth. I parted my lips and flicked my tongue over the tip of his thumb.

"Find out," I said, and licked it again, then shoved it away from me. He rolled his head back with a guttural groan, and yanked his shirt over his head, and tossed it on top of the shredded remains of my pants. I reached behind my back and unclipped my bra, discarding it and letting my breasts spill free as my eyes roved across the broad plane of his chest.

"Pants," I said, rolling onto my side and propping myself up on one elbow. He eyed me with amusement, then tugged his pants off.

"Commando this evening?" I raised an eyebrow.

"Your turn."

I grinned and shook my head.

"Going back on your word, little wolf?"

He grabbed my ankles and flipped me over, delivering three quick slaps to my ass. I squealed and then moaned with need as he started to massage me through the thin fabric. I lifted my hips and he peeled them off.

"Much better," he rumbled, and flipped me onto my back again. I gazed up at him, and the lust and possessiveness in his eyes stole the breath from my throat.

"Mine," he growled.

"Yours," I agreed.

He covered me with his body, claiming my mouth with his and then breaking away to plant a trail of kisses moving south, across my neck and between my breasts.

"Devlin," I moaned, pressing myself against him.

He kept working his way down until he reached between my legs, then he paused and looked up at me, a mischievous glint in his eye.

"Why is it you're so desperate to avoid the hunt?" he asked.

As if he could ask at a time like this. I needed him inside me. Now.

His tongue flickered over me and he met my eye again.

"Why don't you want to hunt?"

"The others," I gasped, clenching my hands in the sheets as his tongue flicked over me again. "I haven't seen them since they found out I'm... an omega."

"You're not an omega. You're a luna."

"Semantics," I growled, rolling my head back. "I'm half human."

He lifted his head to look at me clearly. "You've seen Jackson."

"Yes, and nice as it was—and by the way, if you ever even think about...introducing me as....his 'soon-to-be stepmother' ever again, I will cheerfully strangle you—assuming he doesn't beat me to it."

"I trust you have a point?"

"Besides murder?"

He nodded, and I wrenched my mind back on track—no easy thing with him doing his damnedest to distract me—something he was frustratingly good at.

"My point," I said, breaking off to gasp as he lowered his mouth back to my clit, "is that some of them might still...have a problem...with what I...am." I threw my head back and tried to catch my breath.

"And will I let anyone hurt you?"

His words vibrated through me and I couldn't even meet his eye because I was pretty sure I was going to die if he didn't take me right now.

"Will I let anything happen to you?" he pressed.

"No..." I hedged, and he lapped at me again.

"And will I let anyone hurt you?"

"No…"

"So," he nipped at my bud and then lifted his head to meet my eye, "Is there any reason for you to be worried about the hunt?"

"No?"

"That's right," he said. He claimed my mouth with his again, and for a while we forgot about words and hunting and who was alpha and who was omega. He entered me and we moved as one, forgetting about everything that existed outside of this room, outside of this moment, outside of us.

He drove me to the brink of climax, until I was panting and mewling, and out of my mind with need.

"Devlin…"

"What am I to you?" he demanded.

"Mate," I gasped.

"Mate," he repeated, nuzzling at the point my neck met my shoulder. My breath caught in my throat.

"Prove it," I demanded.

"Are you ready?" he murmured in my ear.

"Yes."

His mouth found the spot and teased it with his lips, sending heat spiraling through me.

"Claim me," I said, my voice husky with need.

His lips parted and his teeth grazed my skin. He bit down and a sharp sting burned through me. I came with a loud cry and he collapsed on the bed beside me, lapping at my healing wound. I rolled over and caught his mouth with mine.

"Mate," I murmured against his lips.

"Mate," he repeated, meeting my eye.

He wrapped his arms around me and I went willingly into his embrace. I'd fought against being mated so hard for so long, but I'd had no idea it could be like this. In a few short hours, we would lead the hunt. We would lead *our pack*. Contentment thrummed through me.

It didn't matter that I was an omega, or that he was an alpha. He was my mate, and there was nothing in this world I wanted more.

Printed in Great Britain
by Amazon

40684399R00158